PENGUIN

T0200843

JASON AND TH

APOLLONIUS OF RHODES (third century BCE) was a citizen of Alexandria in the time of the Ptolemies. Though little is known of his life, his fame rests solely on the *Argonautica,* a poem that was from the start unfairly compared with Homer's *Odyssey,* but from which Virgil was not ashamed to borrow. Unlike Callimachus, a fellow Alexandrian poet with whom he had a long and complex history of mutual artistic emulation and innovation, Apollonius developed the classical traditions of the Homeric epic, expanding them to include a flair for romance and realistic psychological insight that was entirely his own. Some ancient sources suggest that Apollonius composed an earlier, less successful version of the poem. These sources posit that the poet retired to Rhodes and possibly there composed a more successful version. On his later return to Alexandria, Apollonius became a tutor to the future Ptolemy III Euergetes and the director of the Alexandrian Library, a principal storehouse of the literature and learning of antiquity.

AARON POOCHIGIAN earned a Ph.D. in classics from the University of Minnesota in 2006 and now lives and writes in New York City. His book of translations from Sappho, *Stung with Love,* was published by Penguin Classics in 2009. For his work in translation he was awarded a 2010–2011 grant in translation by the National Endowment for the Arts. His first book of original poetry, *The Cosmic Purr,* was published in 2012, and several of the poems in it collectively won the New England Poetry Club's Daniel Varoujan Award. His work has appeared in such newspapers and journals as the *Financial Times, Poems Out Loud,* and *Poetry.*

BENJAMIN ACOSTA-HUGHES is a professor of Greek and Latin at Ohio State University. He is the author of *Polyeideia: The Iambi of Callimachus and the Archaic Iambic Tradition* (2002) and *Arion's Lyre: Archaic Lyric into Hellenistic Poetry* (2010) and a coeditor, with Manuel Baumbach and Elizabeth Kosmetatou, of *Labored in Papyrus Leaves: Perspectives on an Epigram Collection Attributed to Posidippus* (P.Mil.Vogl. VIII 309). He is also a coeditor, with Luigi Lehnus and Susan Stephens, of *Brill's Companion to Callimachus* (2011).

APOLLONIUS
OF RHODES

Jason and the Argonauts

Translated by
AARON POOCHIGIAN

With an Introduction and Notes by
BENJAMIN ACOSTA-HUGHES

PENGUIN BOOKS

PENGUIN BOOKS

Published by the Penguin Group
Penguin Group (USA) LLC
375 Hudson Street
New York, New York 10014

USA | Canada | UK | Ireland | Australia | New Zealand | India | South Africa | China
penguin.com
A Penguin Random House Company

This translation first published in Penguin Books 2014

Translation copyright © 2014 by Aaron Poochigian
Introduction and notes copyright © 2014 by Benjamin Acosta-Hughes

LIBRARY OF CONGRESS CATALOGING-IN-PUBLICATION DATA
Apollonius, Rhodius, author.
[Argonautica. English]
Jason and the Argonauts / Apollonius of Rhodes ; translated by Aaron Poochigian ; with an introduction
and notes by Benjamin Acosta-Hughes.
pages cm—(Penguin classics)
ISBN 978-0-14-310686-9
I. Poochigian, Aaron, 1973– II. Acosta-Hughes, Benjamin, 1960– III. Title. IV. Series: Penguin classics.
PA3872.E5 2014
883'.01—dc23
2014016042

Printed in the United States of America
1 3 5 7 9 10 8 6 4 2

Set in Sabon

Contents

Introduction

1. THE POET

Apollonius of Rhodes was a poet and scholar who lived under the rule of the early Ptolemies in Alexandria, Egypt, in the third century BCE. Alexandria was a new city; founded by Alexander in the course of his Egyptian conquest (331 BCE), the city was drawn up on one of the mouths of the river Nile near Naucratis, an early Greek *emporion,* or trading post, on the Mediterranean. Thus, unlike Pharaonic cities such as Thebes (Luxor) or Memphis, Alexandria looked to the north, and the history of this city under Ptolemaic rule was one of engagement with the Mediterranean world. The Macedonian general, now king, Ptolemy I Soter made Alexandria his capital around 300 BCE, transferring there the body of Alexander the Great from Memphis, capital of the Pharaonic New Kingdom. The movement both toward Europe and from Egypt is representative of the mixed cultural heritage that quickly characterized the new city, and that has recently been confirmed by a series of spectacular maritime archaeological discoveries in the Mediterranean off the Egyptian coast. To Alexandria came settlers from many parts of the ancient Mediterranean world, the larger groups being from Macedon, home of Ptolemy I and much of his soldiery; Cyrene, an old Greek city-state some five hundred miles to the west (in modern Libya); the Aegean islands; the Peloponnese; and Athens. Unlike earlier Greek *poleis,* or city-states, this new, post-Alexander capital consisted from its instantiation of people from a variety of backgrounds, bringing with them the cultural memory of their own dialects, religious festivals, and local heroes. Much like a modern metropolis, Alexandria was something of a melting pot of a variety of ethnic groups and a blending of disparate traditions. One exemplary product of this new world, a world of a new kind of multicultural syncretism and new geopolitical spaces, is Apollonius' modern "take" on an age-old saga, the *Argonautica*.

Our knowledge of Apollonius' biography comes primarily from two much later *Lives* that are included in the manuscript tradition of scholia (learned notes) to the *Argonautica*, circumstantial evidence, and a good deal of speculation, some of which has (unfortunately, in some regards) passed into conventional scholarship and is easily accessible to the modern student. What we know more or less for certain is that Apollonius was a tutor to Ptolemy III Euergetes, who succeeded to the Egyptian throne on the death of his father, Ptolemy II Philadelphus, in 246 BCE. According to the ancient testimony, he also served as the second royal appointed head of the Alexandrian Library, although we have no way of knowing exactly what the title τῆς βιβλιοθήκης προστάτης ("figure in charge of the library") may actually have entailed, and recently some of the ancient evidence has been contested. Apollonius is thought to have been born in Alexandria. Why he acquired the epithet "the Rhodian" is a matter of speculation. The ancient lives reference a close relationship to his fellow Alexandrian poet Callimachus (he is said to be the latter's μαθητής or "student"), with whom he certainly has a much intertwined artistic rapport (see further below).

Only one of Apollonius' poetical works, his *Argonautica*, has survived intact (it has come to us in a manuscript tradition, i.e., a heritage of texts that were copied for many hundreds of years by hand, that includes the *Homeric Hymns*, Callimachus' *Hymns*, and the much later *Orphic Argonautica*). Of his other poetic output, we know of a *Canopus*. This presumably dealt with the legend of Canobus, helmsman of Menelaus, and the foundation of a city with his name east of Alexandria, which now lies underwater (the Bay of Aboukir). Apollonius also authored several foundation poems, one of Alexandria, one of Naucratis, and one of Rhodes (this may have had to do with the epithet "of Rhodes," which conveniently now differentiates our poet from a later "librarian," Apollonius the Eidographer ("compiler of forms"). There are extensive scholia that have survived with the *Argonautica* (originally these were written on separate papyrus rolls, but with the appearance of the codex, more like the modern book in form, they came to be included in the margins of the text). These scholia reference, for several lines in the first book of the four-book poem, a *proekdosis,* or "previous version," of at least this first book, and give alternate readings. We don't, in fact, know enough about the circumstances of publication in third-century Alexandria to be able to say that we are talking about an earlier "edition," only that there was some sort of "previous version" of the poem's first book.

The knowledge of an earlier version of the *Argonautica,* and of some sort of close relationship with his near (if somewhat older) contemporary Callimachus, gave rise early on to a narrative of rival artists and rival art forms. In fact, the two poets show a remarkable awareness of each other's work, apparently over a considerable period of time. It may be more helpful for the modern reader to consider their similarities rather than their differences, particularly in the case of Apollonius' extant four-book hexameter poem, his *Argonautica,* and Callimachus' fragmentary four-book elegiac poem, the *Aetia* ("Origins" or "Causes"). Both poems transform a vast amount of earlier material, from both poetry and prose, into a new or different use of a traditional poetic form (whether hexameter or elegy). Both poems are interested in *aetia,* in the limits of Ptolemaic geography, and in divine retribution of human transgression. In terms of their poetic forms, both poems recast a traditional relationship of poet and source(s) of divine inspiration, markedly eschew a purely linear narrative, and close with the type of hymnlike language that is traditionally characteristic of hymn. The points of contact between the two poems, whether shared subject, shared source of allusion, or cross-reference between the works, are legion. It is clear that the two poets knew each other's work in the course of composition and over a period of time, though many details of how this dynamic worked remain unknown. In some respects the association of contemporary artists today in other media, whether painting or music, provides a helpful model for thinking of the interrelationship of these contemporary Alexandrian court artists: at issue is contemporaneity rather than chronology.

We find a similar situation with another contemporary poet, Theocritus, who is of Sicilian origin but spent much of his artistic career in Alexandria. Theocritus clearly paid great attention to Apollonius' poem. Two of Theocritus' *Idylls,* 13 and 22, respond to episodes that occur at the end of *Argonautica* 1 and the beginning of *Argonautica* 2, respectively. I would argue that the relationship is closer than has been previously understood. Theocritus' *Idyll* 2 is another instance of this close response (here to Medea's infatuation with Jason, and specifically to Apollonius' use of the lyric poet Sappho), and also there is a close relationship between the narrative frame of exchange and the *ecphrasis* (description of an art object) in *Idyll* 1 and the opening of *Argonautica* 3. Again thinking in terms of tight chronology here, albeit a traditional approach to these artists, may not be the right paradigm. At issue seems to be a close association and awareness of each other's creative activities over time, which, given the context of a royal court with extensive royal patronage, is perhaps unsurprising.

2. THE POEM

The saga of the *Argo* and its heroic voyage is of great antiquity, and may go back to an earlier period than even the Homeric poems, to ancient Near Eastern narratives of sea voyages around the Black Sea. At the heart of the saga, as the German scholar Karl Meuli observed in his 1921 study of the *Odyssey* and the *Argonautica,* is a simple folk-tale motif, the young prince sent on a dangerous journey to the land of the Sun (i.e., to the farthest east) to achieve a heroic end, which he can only do through the aid of a local princess. The *Odyssey* is the earliest Greek text that is aware of this legend: in the opening of the twelfth book, as the magical enchantress Circe recounts Odysseus' future journey to him, she tells him of the Clashing Rocks (lines 69–72) through which only one ship has ever passed before, the *Argo,* "subject of care for all," because of Hera's love for Jason. Yet although the saga itself, with its motif of a hero aided by a goddess sent on a daunting quest, would seem an ideal theme for heroic epic, no known epic *Argonautica* has survived, and, given the silence on earlier epic poems in the rich Apollonius scholia, it is possible that none had survived to the time of Apollonius. It is not inconceivable that, for Apollonius, the composition of an *Argonautica* in hexameter may have been more of an innovation than a gesture toward established tradition, thus making the poem as an artistic composition, like Virgil's *Aeneid,* something quite new.

Earlier treatments of episodes, or more, of the *Argonautica* in other poetic forms certainly did exist, however. Jason figures in Hesiod's fragmentary hexameter *Catalogue of Women,* and treatments of the legend in lyric poetry are remarkable. These include extensive fragments of the poets Ibycus and Simonides, and particularly Pindar, whose fourth *Pythian Ode* has a lengthy treatment of the myth at its center. As the one extant lyric treatment, the influence of this model on Apollonius' poem can be traced in considerable detail. All three of the major tragedians treated material from the *Argonautica* narrative. Aeschylus composed a number of plays that treated themes from this narrative, among others an *Argo,* a *Lemnian Women,* a *Phineus,* and an *Hypsipyle.* Sophocles composed a *Medea,* a *Lemnian Women,* and a *Phrixus.* A lost play of particular interest for reading our poem would have been Sophocles' *Women of Colchis.* Euripides composed a *Hypsipyle,* of which considerable fragments survive, and of course his fully extant *Medea.* This last often reflects back on the journey of the *Argo,* famously in the tragedy's opening lines, but Apollonius was not composing his *Argonautica* with this play alone or particularly in mind. The long fame of Euripides' *Medea* is another story—it is one of many possible tragic models for the Alexandrian poet.

Among the many sources Apollonius interweaves into his epic poem are historical and philosophical ones. The former include Herodotus on Egypt (the second book of Herodotus' *Histories*) and Xenophon's description of Black Sea geography in *Anabasis* Book 5. Several images in Apollonius' poem implicate the pre-Socratic philosopher Empedocles, and, like other Hellenistic poets, Apollonius appears to be particularly drawn to Plato's erotic dialogues.

Apollonius was not only a careful reader of Homer, but a Homeric scholar: his knowledge of and sensitivity to the Homeric epics is pervasive throughout the *Argonautica,* and this manifests itself in a variety of ways. His poetic language is replete with rare Homeric words, including those whose meaning was doubted by Apollonius' contemporaries. His use of these Homeric words is

frequently his own way of asserting their correct definition. Apol-
lonius' similes are his own elaborations or variations on Homeric
ones. And Apollonius is acutely aware of Homeric narrative lines
in constructing his own. Let us consider one example, the sixth
book of Homer's *Odyssey*. The narrative of this book is fairly lin-
ear. Odysseus arrives at Scheria (land of the Phaecians) and, at the
end of *Odyssey* 5, burrows down, alone, like an animal (his low-
est point before he begins his reintegration into human society),
by the riverside. Book 6 opens with Athena appearing in a dream
to the daughter of the local king and queen, Alcinous and Arete;
the dream compels the princess Nausicaa to take the washing to
the river. There the princess and her maids play with a ball and the
poet compares the girl to Artemis amid her attendant nymphs. A
ball thrown and then missed wakes Odysseus. He then suppli-
cates the young princess, and compares her to a tree. She tells him
that only on his kneeling as a suppliant to her mother, the queen,
Arete, can he be safely accepted among the Phaecians. Apollonius
reworks every moment of this episode into *Argonautica* 3–4. At
the conclusion of *Argonautica* 2 the Argonauts wait among the
reeds at the river Phasis. At the opening of *Argonautica* 3 the gift
of a ball is the original cause that sets the erotic narrative in mo-
tion. Medea goes forth from town with her attendants, and the
poet compares her to Artemis with her nymphs. Medea awaits her
first meeting with Jason as her maids play, and here there is no
ball, as that figured earlier in this book of the poem. In their first
meeting the poet compares the two to silent trees. Later in the
poem they come to the island of Aia, where Circe (enchantress of
the *Odyssey,* and Medea's aunt), on having a nightmare, comes to
the water to wash her clothing. On arrival at Scheria in flight from
the Colchians, it is through Arete's actions that Medea's safety is
ensured.

One area where we repeatedly observe Apollonius' own en-
hancement, or variation, on Homer is in his similes. Similes are a
central feature of Homeric narrative. Plainly put, similes make the
intangible tangible for the poem's audience. For example, the mili-
tary prowess of a mythohistorical hero, a figure distant in time
and space, when compared to a ferocious beast that preys on
flocks and terrifies shepherds, becomes more "vivid," or "pres-
ent," for the narrative's listener, who can, through the comparison

to what he or she knows through experience, or through common knowledge, then better imagine what is going on in the narrative. Similes in Homeric poetry are of many kinds, among them human to nature, human to art object, human to divine, and human to human (Odysseus' weeping in *Odyssey* 8 compared to the weeping of a woman widowed in war and about to be led off to slavery). Some are simple, and easily repeated (e.g., military hero to lion); others are rather more complex both in composition and in their meanings (the previously cited comparison at the end of *Odyssey* 8 would be a good example of the latter). In Apollonius' poem, which, unlike the Homeric poems, is *not* the product of an oral poetic tradition, and lacks many of the features of that tradition (repeated epithets, formulaic lines, repeated short similes), similes are not only complex but also generally are implicated in multiple ways in the surrounding narrative.

Let us consider two examples. The comparison of Jason as Medea beholds him at *Argonautica* 3.1239–50 to Sirius, the Dog Star of late summer, not only emphasizes his physical beauty in the girl's eyes, but at the same time denotes great foreboding for her; this love has great destructive force. The comparison at *Argonautica* 4.203–18 of Jason cavorting with the golden fleece to a young girl admiring her dress in the moonlight not only highlights sensual pleasure in material in both cases, but both emphasizes Jason's physical allure and also brings his stature *qua* hero into an odd light. While the heroic Medea pacifies the horrific monster, Jason prances in the moonlight. The moon, Medea's companion throughout the narrative of her nights troubled by erotic visions, and the scornful celestial body that watches over her night-time flight from home and family earlier in the book, here reappears in a comparison that likens Jason's radiance to that of a young girl's dress, and frames an epic hero in a setting of sensuality and something rather like decadent irresponsibility.

There are many individual moments throughout the poem, both larger and smaller, that recall moments in the Homeric epics. Apollonius can certainly be read as an extraordinary act of reception of Homeric epic, but he is not derivative (and here some prejudices of earlier scholarship on the Alexandrian poem continue to echo in modern criticism). His engagement with Homer is anything but one-sided: the *Argonautica* questions, furthers, enhances, alters its Homeric models; its reading next to Homer is at once an act of attraction and disjunction.

Modern criticism of the *Argonautica* has foundered on several of the poem's novel features. One is of course the "difference" from Homer. Many of the standard features that the Homeric poems owe to an oral narrative tradition, formulaic epithets and repeated set scenes among others, are missing in Apollonius' poem. As already observed, there is a distinctly different mechanism in the use of simile. The portrayal of the gods, and their appearance in the poem, is markedly different from Homer. In the Homeric poems the gods serve a variety of functions within the poem, as metaphor, as directional movement (the passage of a divine figure from Olympus to Earth and vice versa changes the scene of narrative focus), and in the *Iliad* in particular as lighter and deathless contrast to the grim realities of war on the battlefield. Generally gods in the Homeric poems interact with mortals in disguise, even in dream sequences. Appearances of the gods in the *Argonautica* are quite different, and consciously play on Homeric convention. The one extended scene on Olympus (the opening of Book 3), in some ways a reworking of several scenes from the *Iliad* and the *Odyssey*, is at the same time unlike any scene in Homer: Homeric Olympus does not allow for this kind of portrayal of domestic intimacy. There are two extraordinary moments in the poem when the heroes actually see the god Apollo *as* the god Apollo. And when gods intervene in the Apollonian narrative, as Athena does when holding back the Clashing Rocks, they do so as anthropomorphized divine forces.

A major problem for modern criticism of the poem is the portrayal of Jason. Admittedly our first encounters with Odysseus in the *Odyssey* (the hero on the beach weeping with longing for his homeland) and Achilles in the *Iliad* (the hero on the beach lamenting to his mother of his mistreatment by Agamemnon) are not high moments in epic heroism, but these moments fit within a code of epic-heroic expectations: the hero in isolation, the hero dishonored. Jason is more complex, and, quite arguably, more problematic. The Argonauts' initial choice of Heracles to lead the expedition is only the first of a series of moments in which Jason's leadership is cast in doubt either by other Argonauts or by the poet's descriptive language. Jason is frequently characterized as *amekanos,* "resourceless," "at a loss." His first action in battle is to kill his host Cyzicus, king of the Doliones, albeit in error, but the action remains problematic. The hero who steps forward to fight the savage Amycus at the opening of Book 2 is not Jason but Polydeuces. Jason *does* succeed at the superhuman tasks assigned by the Colchian Aeëtes, but only through Medea's magic. And, as already observed, Jason's prancing about with the golden fleece is an odd reflection of traditional heroism.

To be sure, Jason has his defenders. Indeed, defenses of Jason are something of a small industry in Apollonian scholarship.[1] And the argument can indeed be made that here, as with Aeneas (though in some ways differently), at issue is a more modern, more complex type of epic hero. Certainly there are some factors that set Jason rather apart from his Homeric predecessors. One is without doubt the role of Jason's erotic appeal, already present in the Lemnian episode in Book 1, and at the center of the drama of Medea's psychological struggle in Book 3 and the opening of Book 4.[2] Only Paris in the *Iliad* is similarly characterized, but he has a somewhat circumscribed role in that poem.[3] Jason's beauty is the object of an eroticized female gaze, and, particularly in the case of Medea, this leads to extensive internal psychological reaction.

Jason is also a different kind of leader, one whose diplomacy is called repeatedly into action. Here one reading of Jason would be not so much as a hero of traditional epic as a reflection of the needs, and realities, of a modern monarch. Apollonius is a court poet who composed his poetry at the court of one of the successor kings who followed Alexander's campaigns, which transformed the ancient Mediterranean world into a series of competing dynastic monarchies. The *Argonautica,* and the figure of Jason himself, can be read against this immediate historical backdrop, and the relations of the male power figures in the poem can be understood in light of the political and military struggles of the Ptolemies, the Seleucids, the Antigonids, and other successor kings.

Similarly Medea's character, and the dominant role that she takes in the last half of the poem, can be read against a recent history where powerful women, among them Olympias, Alexander's mother, play central roles in the unfolding of political and dynastic (and even military) events that are far different from those of the archaic and classical periods. A recently discovered text from this period, a series of epigrams now attributed to Apollonius' near contemporary poet Posidippus of Pella,[4] is of particular interest here. The collection of hitherto almost entirely unknown short poems focuses largely on women in a variety of conquests, including as queens and subjects of victory celebrations. As several scholars have observed, Medea becomes a different sort of hero in the latter half of the poem. Whereas Jason's psychological processes are rarely touched on, the inner workings of Medea's mind, her dreams, her fears, her frightened inability to control her emotions, are all given considerable scope in the poem's third and fourth books. A particularly revealing moment is her interchange with the enchantress Circe in the fourth book, where Medea and Circe communicate in their own language. This moment sets Medea in the role of Odysseus, who seeks Circe's aid and whose particular relationship with Circe sets him apart from his followers. In the final combat with an otherworldly figure, the giant Talus, it is Medea whose magical knowledge is victorious, as is true with the dragon that guards the golden fleece, and of her "creation" of Jason as the hero who slays the earthborn men.

At the time of the *Argonautica*'s composition, the Ptolemaic Empire covered a vast geographical space, extending from the Cyreneica in the west (modern Libya) to Coele-Syria (modern Israel, Palestine, Lebanon) in the east, much of southern Asia Minor, and many Aegean islands.[5] The Ptolemies were further major players in the political world of mainland Greece, where they served as a counterweight to Macedon. The new epigrams attributed to Posidippus include a number of poems dedicated to early Ptolemaic queens, several of which, poems that celebrate victory in horse racing at Nemea in the Peloponnese, attest to the actual presence of individual royal family members at the games. Apollonius' *Argonautica* can be understood in one sense as a four-book travel narrative, one that takes its point of departure from a long-ago saga that told of a journey from Thessaly through the Propontis and around the Black Sea (an older trajectory). The poem then, in its long last book, brings the poem's audience (the newer trajectory) along the Danube, then down the western Adriatic coast, back up the Adriatic to the Po in Italy, to the Rhône in France, to Libya (importantly, the setting of the prophetic oracle of Zeus-Ammon at the Oasis of Siwah, where Alexander had been proclaimed son of Zeus), to Crete, and thence back to the Greek mainland. Apollonius' mapping of the Argonauts' return brings the heroes of the *Argo* through areas that were relevant to the Ptolemaic Empire with its vast naval fleet, a different Greek world from that imagined in the ancient saga tradition.[6] From the perspective of the ancient saga, this return involves a journey into the unknown. This journey may be in part a reflection of the expeditions that took place under the Ptolemies to Nubia, and particularly the Arabian Sea. The quest narrative of the original legend (a young prince is sent to the land of the Sun in search of a magical object, and is aided in that quest by a local princess) finds real-life parallel, as it were, in the early Ptolemaic quest for more widespread hegemony and control of the import of luxury goods.

While the *Argonautica* is, on the one hand, an epic hexameter poem heavily imbued throughout by Homeric and Hesiodic tradition, it is, in other ways, quite new, and to a modern reader, particularly one coming to the poem without much experience of its earlier models, may read much more like Tolkien in poetic form than anything else. And this would perhaps be right. In its combination of the real and the fantastical, its engagement with traditions of medicine, astronomy, and science, its magical vessel that speaks and yet serves as the plaything of water nymphs, heroes that have wings, and a king whose grandfather is the center of the solar system, it is truly without exact parallel in previous or contemporary Greek literature. The *Argonautica* has its detractors, and has long had its detractors, but for those who admire the poem, even on multiple rereadings, it is an experience close to magical.

BENJAMIN ACOSTA-HUGHES

Notes

1. Clauss 1993 is an excellent and accessible study of this issue.
2. There are a number of studies on the role of Eros in the *Argonautica*. A particularly good one is the second chapter of Richard Hunter's 1993 literary studies of the poem.
3. Here the portrayal of Paris in two poems of the Trojan cycle, the

Cypria and the *Little Iliad,* may have been contributing factors to Apollonius' portrayal. Neither poem, however, has survived.

4. These are available in English in the translation of F. Nisetich in Gutzwiller 2005.

5. On the Ptolemaic naval empire see now Bursalis, Stefanou, and Thompson 2013.

6. Thalmann 2011 is an excellent and proactively new study of the poem in these terms.

References Cited

Bursalis, Kostas, Mary Stefanou, and Dorothy J. Thompson, eds. *The Ptolemies, the Sea and the Nile: Studies in Waterborne Power*. New York: Cambridge University Press, 2013.

Clauss, James J. *The Best of the Argonauts: The Redefinition of the Epic Hero in Book 1 of Apollonius'* Argonautica. Berkeley: University of California Press, 1993.

Gutzwiller, Kathryn, ed. *The New Posidippus: A Hellenistic Poetry Book*. New York: Oxford University Press, 2005.

Hunter, Richard. *The* Argonautica *of Apollonius: Literary Studies*. New York: Cambridge University Press, 1993.

———. *The Shadow of Callimachus: Studies in the Reception of Hellenistic Poetry at Rome*. New York: Cambridge University Press, 2006.

Leitao, David. *The Pregnant Male as Myth and Metaphor in Classical Greek Literature*. New York: Cambridge University Press, 2012.

Loraux, Nicole. *Tragic Ways of Killing a Woman*. Cambridge, Mass.: Harvard Unversity Press, 1987.

Meuli, Karl. *Odysee und Argonautika: Untersuchungen zur griechischen Sagengeschichte und zum Epos*. Berlin: Weidmann, 1921.

Mori, Anatole. *The Politics of Apollonius Rhodius'* Argonautica. New York: Cambridge University Press, 2008.

Stephens, Susan A. *Seeing Double: Intercultural Poetics in Ptolemaic Alexandria*. Berkeley: University of California Press, 2003.

Thalmann, William G. *Apollonius of Rhodes and the Spaces of Hellenism*. New York: Cambridge University Press, 2011.

A Note on the Text
and Translation

Based on the edition of Francis Vian and Émile Delage (published from 1974 to 1999), this is an unabridged English translation of Apollonius of Rhodes' ancient Greek epic *Argonautica* (*Jason and the Argonauts*). My intention with this project was to create the most engaging and readable translation of the poem available.

Given its large cast of characters and vast geographic scope, *Jason and the Argonauts* is rich in proper nouns. I opted for the Latin spellings of Greek names because they look less foreign to the reader and are more likely to be recognized. Thus, Zeus' father is "Cronus" and not "Kronos," and Aphrodite is given the title "Cypris" instead of "Kypris" so that her connection to the island Cyprus would be clear. I translated Greek names that end in the letter *eta* with the Latin *a* ("Athena" instead of "Athene" and "Zona" instead of "Zone," for example) to clarify their syllable counts. I did, however, allow for exceptions where the names are standard in English with an *e* ending: Alcimede, Antiope, Aphrodite, Arete, Ariadne, Chalciope, Circe, Cleite, Cyrene, Dicte, Hecate, Helle, Hypsipyle, and Terpsichore. I include diaeresis (¨) in some names, again to assist with pronunciation and clarify syllable counts: Aeëtes, Alcinoös, Calaïs, Danaë, Laocoön, Nausithoös, Peirithoös, and Phaëthon.

In the lengthy roster of heroes (Book 1, lines 35–322), the names of the Argonauts are presented in boldface to make them stand out from the names of their fathers, grandfathers, mothers, home cities, and homelands. Furthermore, whereas editions of the Greek original present the reader with thousand-plus-line columns of text broken only at the ends of books, this translation takes the editorial license of breaking up the text into stanzas, easily digestible units of sense. I have also inserted, I hope unobtrusively, in-text translations of Greek words and word roots in the few cases where they are essential to understanding the surrounding passage. Line numbers are provided every five lines, and every fifteen lines line numbers for the Greek original are provided in parentheses to facilitate cross-reference. In short, I have done all that I could to make this translation as reader- and scholar-friendly as possible.

I have felt for years that *Jason and the Argonauts* needed a verse translation in which the poetic rhythms reinforce syntactic units, as do the rhythms of the original, and in which the electricity of language we expect in poetry is sustained. I hope I have achieved these goals. My models were the great blank verse epics of the English language: John Milton's *Paradise Lost* and Alfred Lord Tennyson's *Idylls of the King*. Iambic pentameter has the advantage of being familiar to the English ear, as dactylic hexameter, the meter of the original, was to the ancient Greek one. Given the longer lines of the original and the compression of ancient Greek, my translation averages fifteen lines for every twelve of the Greek.

Again and again in *Jason and the Argonauts,* poetry works magic and effects rapture. For example, Apollonius informs us that, while Zethus, one of the founders of Thebes, struggled under the rock he was lugging to build the city walls, his brother Amphion "simply strolled along behind him / and strummed his golden lyre, and a boulder / twice as gigantic followed in his footsteps" (Book 1, 994–96). The mythic father of poets, Orpheus, is, in fact, one of the Argonauts, and we are told that he could "soften stubborn / mountain boulders and reverse a river's / current with the seduction of his songs" (Book 1, 39–41). The effect of his music on humans and animals is mesmerizing. We learn that, when Orpheus strummed his lyre from the deck of the *Argo*, "fish both big and small came leaping out of / the sea to revel in the vessel's wake" (Book 1, 774–75). At the conclusion of his song to the Argonauts around the campfire, we find the following description:

> So Orpheus intoned, then hushed his lyre
> at the same time as his ambrosial voice.
> Though he had ceased, each of his comrades still
> leaned forward longingly, their ears intent,
> their bodies motionless with ecstasy.
>
> (Book 1, 696–700)

John Milton was so smitten with this passage that he all but trans-
lated it for *Paradise Lost:*

> The Angel ended, and in Adam's Ear
> So Charming left his voice, that he a while
> Thought him still speaking, still stood fixt to hear.
>   (Book VIII, 1–3)

Apollonius is himself subject to the same rapt amazement. In what
is, perhaps, his most emotional insertion of himself into the epic,
he expresses awe at the fact that his character Medea is able to
cast a spell that brings down bronze giant Talus:

> Father Zeus, profound astonishment
> has stormed my mind—to think that death can come
> not only through disease and injury,
> but people can undo us from afar,
> just as that man, though made of bronze, surrendered
> and fell down underneath the far-flung onslaught
> of that ingenious conjurer, Medea.
>   (Book 4, 2158–64)

Thus I found justification for a verse translation of the epic within
the epic itself—a prose version would have captured the meaning but
left out the magic. Though Orpheus, Medea, and Apollonius himself
are stiff competition, I can console myself with the knowledge that I
did my best to make my translation a tribute to their powers.

In addition to being thoroughly endearing, Apollonius' voice is
elastic—it rises to Homeric heights, slips into the "storybook" tone
of fairy tale and indulges in genealogical, mythological, and geo-
graphic asides, to which it enjoys calling attention ("wait, why
have I digressed so widely, talking / about Aethalides?", Book 1,
874–75). Furthermore, though he was head librarian at the Great
Library of Alexandria, Apollonius is no mere pedant. He is as
much a psychological realist as Henry James when it comes to
matters of love and sex ("devastating / affection crept up over him,
because / she was a maiden, crying," Book 3, 1391–93), and his
characters, especially the females, are capable of operatic pathos.
Take, for example, Medea's contemplation of suicide as she decides
whether to help Jason win the contest of the bulls:

> I cannot hope that, even when he dies,
> I will be free from anguish. He will be
> a curse on me when he has lost his life.
> So good-bye, modesty. Good-bye, fair name.
> Once I have saved him, let him go unharmed
> wherever he desires while I, the day
> that he completes the contest, leave this life
> by dangling my body from a rafter
> or taking drugs, the kind that kill the heart . . .
>
> (Book 3, 1032–40)

Unlike Homer, Apollonius provides occasional comic relief, and sexual innuendo is not too lowbrow for his Muse. We are told that, when Medea's handmaids teased the Argonauts over the paltry offerings they were giving the gods, "the men responded / with crude suggestions, and delightful insults / and sweet harassment sparkled back and forth / among them" (Book 4, 2227–30). It took perseverance to find a voice that could accommodate this range of modes, tones, and character voices, but I am confident the voice I found is Apollonius' own.

For as long as I have known the ancient Greek language, I have been certain that Apollonius is a great poet and that *Jason and the Argonauts* is a great epic. My translation, a labor of love, is an attempt to convince Greekless readers that this is so. I hope that the poem becomes, like Homer's *Iliad* and *Odyssey*, essential reading for a cultured individual. This project would have been much slower reaching completion without the financial support of the National Endowment for the Arts, to which I am very grateful.

AARON POOCHIGIAN

Jason and the Argonauts

BOOK 1

Taking my lead from you, Phoebus Apollo,
I shall commemorate the deeds of men
born long ago. King Pelias insisted,
so they drove the tautly fitted *Argo*
up through the narrows of the Pontic Sea   5
and past the Cobalt Clashing Rocks to win
the golden fleece.
             Pelias had received
a prophecy: a miserable doom
awaited him, a murder brought about
by someone he would see come from the country   10
wearing a single sandal. Soon thereafter
the prophecy came true: that winter Jason
was fording the Apidanus at flood time
and only saved one sandal from the mud—
the river current snatched the other one.   15 (11)
He simply left it in the depths and strode on
straight to the court of Pelias to take
a portion of the feast the king was hosting
in honor of his father lord Poseidon
and all the other sacred gods, excepting   20
Hera the goddess of Pelasgia,
to whom he paid no mind.
                  Soon as the king
saw Jason, he was sure he was the man
and right away contrived a labor for him,
a cruel voyage, in the hope that he   25
would die at sea or fighting savages
and never make the journey home to Greece.

Past poets have already told in song
how Argus with Athena's guidance built
a ship, the *Argo*. I intend to tell you   30 (20)
the names and lineages of the heroes,
their travels on the wide-paved sea, and all
that they accomplished in their wanderings.
Come, Muses, be the surrogates of my song.

Orpheus is the first we should remember.   35
They say it was Calliope that bore him
beneath the peak of Mount Pimpleia after
she coupled with Oeagrus king of Thrace.
The legends say their son could soften stubborn
mountain boulders and reverse a river's   40
current with the seduction of his songs.

The wild oaks his lyre charmed and marched
down out of Mount Pieria still today
are flourishing in dense, well-ordered ranks
at Zona headland on the Thracian coast—   45 (29)
clear proof of what his music could accomplish.

Such, then, was Orpheus, the king of all
Bistonian Pieria, and Jason
invited him to join the expedition
just as the Centaur Cheiron had advised.   50

Cometes' son **Asterion** arrived
without delay. He hailed from Peiresiae
under Mount Phylleius on the banks
of the sublime but wild Apidanus
right where it weds the noble Enipeus.   55
(Both rivers travel far to reach that union.)

Next **Polyphemus,** offspring of Eilatus,
forsook his native Larissa to join them.
Back in his adolescence he had fought
beside the mighty Lapiths when they waged   60 (41)
war on the Centaurs. Though his limbs had since

grown burdensome, his heart remained as keen
for battle as it had been in his prime.

Since he was Jason's uncle, **Iphiclus**
did not remain at leisure in Phylaca.   65
Aeson, you see, was wedded to the sister
of Iphiclus (and daughter of Phylacus),
and ties of blood and marriage left no choice—
Iphiclus had to be included, too.

Nor did **Admetus**, king of sheep-rich Pherae,   70
hang back beneath the peak of Chalcedon.

Echion and **Erytus**, both ingenious
at artifice, both sons of Hermes, rushed
to leave behind the wheat fields of Alopa.
As they were setting out, **Aethalides**,   75 (54)
half brother to them on their father's side,
ran out to catch their march and be the third
in their brigade. Phthian Eupolemeia,
Myrmidon's daughter, bore him on the banks
of the Amphryssus, and Menetes' daughter   80
Antianeira bore the other two.

Next Caeneus' son **Coronus** left
Gyrton, a wealthy town, to make the journey.
Yes, he was brave, but not his father's equal.
Poets recount how Caeneus went down,   85
while still alive, beneath the Centaurs' clubs.
All alone, separated from his comrades,
he still routed the Centaurs from the field.
When they stampeded back, they failed to break
or slay him, so he sank into the earth,   90 (63)
invincible, triumphant, hammered down
by a relentless rain of pine-wood clubs.

Mopsus the Titaresian also joined them.
Leto's son had taught him how to read
the sacred signs exhibited by birds   95
better than any other man alive.

Eurydamas the son of Ctimenos
came, too. He left a home in Dolopian
Ctimena beside lake Xynias.

Actor allowed his son **Menoetius**   100
to leave their home in Opus, so that he
could see the world with distinguished men.

Eurytion and valiant **Eurybotes**
were also quick to join. One was the son
of Iros son of Actor; one the son   105 (72)
of Teleon. (In all truth Teleon
had sired world-famous Eurybotes,
and Iros had begot Eurytion.)
Oileus joined them as a third, a man
of giant strength and matchless at harassing   110
foes from behind once he had turned the lines.

Euboean **Canthus** joined them next. His father
Cerinthus son of Abas gave him leave
since he insisted on the quest. But no
homecoming had been fated for him, no   115
return to fair Cerinthus. Fate had ruled
that he and the distinguished seer **Mopsus**
would wander to the farthest ends of Libya
and perish there. Wherever people travel,
catastrophe is waiting—so those two   120 (82)
were laid to rest in Libya, a land
as far from Colchis as the space between
the rising and the setting of the sun.

Next came those wardens of Oechalia,
Clytius, Iphitus, sons of cruel Eurytus,   125
to whom Far-Shooting Phoebus gave his bow.
Eurytus, though, did not enjoy it long
because he dared defy the god who gave it.

Aeacus' two sons arrived at different
times and from distant points of origin.   130
You see, they accidentally had murdered

their brother Phocus and had fled at once
to separate exiles outside Aegina:
while **Telamon** had claimed the Attic Island,
Peleus had erected walls in Phthia.   135 (94)

Next, from the land of Cecrops came the soldier
Boutes, the son of noble Teleon,
and with him came the staunch spearman **Phalerus.**
His father Alcon let him go. Although
there were no other sons to tend his age   140
and mind the homestead, Alcon all the same
sent him—his only heir, his best beloved—
to win renown among courageous heroes.

(Though Theseus was mightier than all
the other offspring of Erechtheus,   145
he never came. Invisible restraints
detained him in the earth beneath Taenarus
where he had traveled with Peirithoös—
a wasted trip. They would have made this quest
much easier for everyone who sailed.)   150 (104)

Tiphys the son of Hagnias forsook
Siphae, a Thespian harbor town, to join
the heroes' party. When it came to knowing
when breakers would disturb the sea's expanse,
anticipating stormy gales and plotting   155
course headings by the sun and stars, he was
a mastermind. Tritonian Athena
had packed him off to join the expedition,
and his arrival cheered a crew in need
of naval knowledge. After she designed   160
the speedy ship, Argus, Arestor's son,
had worked with her and built it to her order,
and that is why, of all the watercraft
that ever challenged ocean with their oars,
the *Argo* was the most remarkable.   165 (114)

Pleias, the next to join them, had forsaken
Araethyraea where he had been living

in luxury because he was the son
of Dionysos. The estate he left there
was very near the source of the Asopus.   170

Talaus and Areios, sons of Bias,
marched out of Argos, and beside them marched
courageous Leodocus. Pero, daughter
of Neleus, had borne all three of them—
this was the Pero for whose sake Melampus,   175
Aeolid Melampus, had endured
hard sorrow in the stalls of Iphicles.

No story claims strong-willed, invulnerable
Heracles failed to answer Jason's summons.
When he got word the heroes were assembling,   180 (124)
he was just crossing from Arcadia
into Lyrceian Argos, on his shoulder
a big live boar that had of late been grazing
the meadows of Lampeia all along
the Erymanthian swamp. He slid it down,   185
netted and muzzled, from his massive back
there in the Mycenaeans' meeting place
and freely hastened off to join the quest
against the orders of Eurystheus.
With him went Hylas in the prime of youth,   190
a noble squire, to bear his bow and arrows.

Next came divine Danaus' descendant
Nauplius. As the son of Clytonaeus,
he was, of course, grandson to Naubolus.
Naubolus had been sired by Lernus, Lernus   195 (135)
by Proteus, and Proteus in turn
by Nauplius the Elder. Long ago
Amymona the daughter of Danaus
had lain in love beneath the god Poseidon
and borne this Nauplius, and Nauplius   200
had bested all men in the art of sailing.

Of all the heroes reared in Argos, Idmon
came latest. Though he had foreseen his death

in bird signs, he enlisted all the same
so that his town would not deny him glory.   205
Idmon was not, in fact, the son of Abas—
Apollo had begotten him on one
of far-famed Aeolus' many daughters.
Phoebus himself had taught him to divine
future events by closely studying   210 (145)
bird omens and the flames of sacrifice.

Leda of Aetolia dispatched
thick-sinewed **Polydeuces** and his brother
Castor, master of swift-hoofed steeds, from Sparta.
She bore her much-beloved sons together   215
as twins in King Tyndareus' palace
and, when they begged to go, she gave them leave
to prove Zeus was their sire by worthy deeds.

Two sons of Aphareus, **Lynceus**
and firebrand **Idas,** marched out of Arena,   220
both of them glorying in boundless courage.
Lynceus also was endowed with vision
keener than that of any man alive.
They say that he could easily project
his eye beams even underneath the earth.   225 (155)

Periclymenus, Neleus' son,
joined up as well. He was the eldest born
of all the offspring Neleus had fathered
at Pylos, and Poseidon had bestowed
infinite strength upon him and the power   230
to change into whatever shape he wished
so that he could survive the shock of battle.

Next, **Cepheus** and **Amphidamus** left
Arcadia and came. Sons of Aleus,
they marched out of a home in Tegea,   235
Apheidas' estate. Their elder brother
Lycurgus had released his son **Ancaeus**
to be the third man in their company.
Yes, though Lycurgus stayed behind at home

to tend Aleus who was weak with age,   240 (166)
he couldn't keep his son from setting out.
The boy wore only a Maenalian bearskin,
lugged only a gigantic ax. You see,
his grandfather had hidden all the other
arms and armor in the granary,   245
hoping to keep the lad from going, too.

Augeas also joined the voyage. Fame
pronounces him the son of Helius.
King over Elis, he enjoyed his wealth
but greatly wished to see the Colchian land   250
and King Aeëtes of the Colchians.

Next came **Asterius** and **Amphion**,
both sons of Hyperasius. They forsook
Pellena in Achaea to enlist—
the same Pellena that their grandsire Pellen   255 (178)
had founded on the brow of Aegialus.

Euphemus, next, came to them from Taenarus.
He was the fleetest-footed man alive.
Europa, lordly Tityus' daughter,
had borne him to Poseidon. He could dash   260
across the whitecaps of the dull gray sea
without submersing his precipitate feet.
Only his toes would touch the liquid path.

Two other of Poseidon's sons arrived—
Erginus who had left the citadel   265
of glorious Miletus, and superb
Ancaeus who forsook Parthenia,
cult center of Imbrasian Hera. Both
exulted in their sea- and battlecraft.

From Calydon came Oeneus' son,   270 (190)
strong **Meleager**, with **Laocoön**
Oeneus' half brother. (Yes, the men
had different mothers, since Laocoön
had been begotten on a serving maid.)

Oeneus sent him forth, old as he was,   275
to chaperone his son. Thus Meleager,
young as he was, made one among the heroes.
I suspect that, barring Heracles,
none of the men who went would have surpassed him
if only he had stayed another year   280
back in Aetolia and reached his prime.
His mother's brother came along as well—
Iphiclus son of Thestius, a man
skilled equally in close- and long-range combat.

Palaemonius was next to come   285 (202)
and join the expedition. Though reputed
the son of Lernus of Olenia,
he was in fact the offspring of Hephaestus.
His feet, therefore, were hobbled like his father's,
but no one ever dared to slight his brawn   290
and battle skills, and so he made the roster
and added more renown to Aeson's son.

Next came Phocaean **Iphitus**, the son
of Naubolus and grandson of Ornytus.
This Iphitus, you see, had played the host   295
when Jason went to Delphi to consult
the Pythian oracle about the voyage—
yes, it was there at Delphi he received
the hero at his palace as a guest.

Zetes and **Calaïs** were next to join.   300 (211)
Orithyia had borne them to the Northwind
on the frontier of blizzard-haunted Thrace.
You see, while she was whirling in a dance
beside the eddying Ilissus River,
he snatched her up out of the land of Cecrops,   305
whisked her far away, and set her down
near the Erginus River on a crag
called "Rock of Sarpedon" today—that's where
he blanketed the maiden in a mist
and ravished her.

          Their sons arrived on flapping,   310
dusky wings that grew out of their ankles
(a wonder to behold)—those golden scales,
those feathers shimmering. The jet-black braids
that sprouted from their heads and tumbled down
across their backs kept swaying in the wind.   315 (223)

Even **Acastus**—yes, the very son
of stubborn Pelias!—refused to miss out
by staying safely in his father's palace.
Argus, the shipwright of Athena, too.
Both of them claimed their places on the roster.   320

Such were the men who rallied to assist
the son of Aeson. People took to calling
these heroes "Minyans," since most of them
(and many of the stronger fighters) claimed
descent from Minyas' daughters. Jason   325
was Minyan himself: Alcimede
his mother was the daughter of Clymena,
and she, in turn, was Minyas' daughter.

After the slaves had placed those goods aboard
that ships require when business forces men   330 (235)
to sail abroad, the heroes strode through town
to where the *Argo* stood upon a shorefront
known as Magnesian Pagasae. Though crowds
of giddy citizens had gathered round them,
the heroes shone like starlight between clouds.   335
The men who watched them marching under arms
stood wonderstruck and muttered to each other:

"King Zeus above! what's Pelias' plan?
To what wild tract outside Achaean lands
has he dispatched this large brigade of heroes?   340
Well, let's assume they're sailing to Aeëtes.
Even if he refuses them the fleece,
they could destroy his palace with consuming
fire in a single day. But, ah, the voyage—

that's the hard thing, not to be avoided,   345 (246)
a chore impossible to all who try."

Thus were the townsmen talking, while the women
raised their hands and asked that heaven grant
a heartwarming conclusion to the voyage.
Tears flowed as they lamented to each other: 350

"Poor Alcimede, anxiety
has come to you as well, however late.
No, you have not concluded life in splendor.
And Aeson, too—he's terribly unlucky.
The honest truth is it would have been better   355
if he had wound up shrouded long ago
and stowed in earth and so remained unwitting
of this atrocious quest. I wish the waves
had swallowed, darkly, Phrixus and the ram
along with that girl Helle when she drowned.   360 (256)
That baneful beast spoke with a human voice
only to cause Alcimede distress
and countless sorrows in the days to come."

So they commiserated as the heroes
marched to the launch.
                        At Jason's home a crowd   365
of serving men and women had assembled.
When his mother poured her arms around him,
poignant grief pierced every woman's bosom.
Aeson was lying on a cot, wrapped up
in shawls because of his decrepit age,   370
groaning among the women.
                        After Jason
had done his best to soften their distress,
he bade the slaves collect his battle gear.
They heeded the command in perfect silence,
eyes averted. But Alcimede,   375 (268)
who had embraced him when he first appeared,
refused to let him go, and only sobbed
with greater violence.

                           As a lonely maiden
clings desperately to a gray-haired nurse,
her last remaining friend, and weeps because   380
she lives a heavy life without protectors,
only a stepmother who so assails her
with fickle insults and relentless scorn
that she cannot stop weeping, and her heart
is bound and gagged by all this misery,   385
and she cannot sob out the countless sorrows
that throb within her, so Alcimede
was weeping, weeping, and she couldn't stop.
Squeezing her son, she wailed in despair:

"I wish that on the day when I first heard   390 (278)
Pelias, much to my dismay, pronounce
his cruel commandment, I had left off living
and blacked out all my woes. Then, oh, my son,
you could have buried me with your own hands.
That was the sole remaining expectation   395
I had of you, since I had long enjoyed
all other joys of motherhood. Though once
the envy of Achaean woman, I
shall now be left here like a slave to tend
an empty palace, withering away   400
with missing you, the son because of whom
I had such fame and glory in the past.
For you alone, my first and last, I loosened
my bridal sash. The goddess Eileithuia
begrudged me many children. Ah! not ever,   405 (289)
not even in my dreams, did I imagine
that Phrixus' escape would prove my ruin."

So, sobbing, she exclaimed and heaved a groan,
and all her handmaids wailed in turn, but Jason
soothed her with sympathetic words:
                                        "Please, Mother,   410
don't lay such bitter pains upon yourself,
since you will not drive off distress with tears
and may well end up heaping further sorrow

upon your sorrows. Sudden are the woes
the gods allot to mortals. Strive to bear   415
your portion of them, though it pains your heart.

Take courage from Athena's covenants,
from oracles (since Phoebus has delivered
highly favorable prophecies),
and from the strength of heroes. Now stay calmly   420 (303)
here among your handmaids. Don't become
a bird of dire omen for the ship.
My friends and slaves will walk me to the shore."

So he proclaimed and set out from his home
to make the quest. Think of Apollo striding   425
out of a fragrant temple and parading
through holy Delos or through Claros, Pytho,
or level Lycia along the Xanthus—
that is how Jason strutted through the crowd.

The townsfolk with a single voice let out   430
a cheer, and venerable Iphias,
priestess of Artemis the Town Protectress,
came shuffling up to him and kissed his hand.
Try as she might, she never got a word in
because the crowd kept pressing close around him,   435 (310)
and she was left behind them on the roadside,
an old woman abandoned by the young,
and there was Jason shrinking in the distance.

And so he left the well-paved streets of Iolcus
and came down to the beach at Pagasae,   440
and all the heroes waiting there for him
beside the *Argo* welcomed his arrival.
He stopped above the launch, and they assembled
opposite. Soon they glimpsed two men together—
Argus! Acastus!—marching from the city.   445
Everyone was amazed to see them coming
in spite of Pelias' orders. Argus,
Arestor's son, had thrown around his shoulders

a rough dun-colored ox hide that was flowing
down to his feet; Acastus, an exquisite,   450 (325)
two-layered cloak his sister Pelopeia
had given him. For all of his excitement,
Jason restrained himself from asking questions
and called for order, and the men sat down
upon the furled sails and level mast,   455
and he proposed the course he thought most prudent:

"All the gear a ship requires for travel
has now been snugly stowed, and there's no reason
for more delay. We will be setting forth
soon as the proper winds are blowing. Comrades,   460
because our journey homeward will be shared,
and shared our voyage to Aeëtes' realm,
choose freely, now, and without prejudice
who in the crew you wish to be your leader—
some man to manage details and engage in   465 (339)
wars and alliances with foreigners."

So he submitted, and the young men swiveled
their eyes and stared at mighty Heracles
sitting among them, and they all insisted
he lead the quest. He stayed right where he sat, though,   470
held his right palm out, and said in answer:

"No, no, let no one offer me this honor.
I won't accept. What's more, I will prevent
the rest of you from standing for the job.
The man who called us here should lead our party."   475

Such were his mighty words, and all the heroes
assented with a single voice because
Heracles was the one who had proposed it.
The son of Aeson jumped up and addressed
his eager comrades:
                          "Men, if you have truly   480 (351)
entrusted this position to my care,
let nothing more delay our expedition.
Come, let us first propitiate Apollo

with sacrifices, then at once prepare
a feast. While we are waiting for the servants   485
who oversee my cattle stalls to drive
the largest of them here, let's drag the *Argo*
down to the sea, stow all the gear aboard her,
and settle which of us will take which bench
by drawing lots. We also should construct   490
a seaside shrine in honor of Apollo,
the God of Embarkation, since it was
his oracle that vowed to send me signs
and teach me all the highways of the sea,
so long as I began my expedition   495 (362)
by giving sacrifices in his name."

So he proposed and was the first to take up
the tasks at hand. The others duly rose,
stripped off their clothes, and laid them, piece by piece,
above the surf upon a flat smooth stone   500
sea storms had long since scoured clean.
                                        First off,
with Argus in the background shouting orders,
the heroes ran a triple-braided cable
snugly around the ship and pulled it taut
from either end so that the bolts would stick   505
faithfully in the planking and withstand
whatever violence the sea swell sent them.

Next, they industriously dug a trench
wide enough to receive the vessel's keel
the whole way down into the sea (that is,   510 (373)
the total breadth of beach the ship would travel
pulled by their hands). As they approached the surf
they dug the channel deeper than was needed
to house the keel, inserted polished rollers
into the extra space, and tipped the vessel   515
onto the rollers so that she would coast
oceanward while gliding over them.

Next, they reversed the oars that stuck out starboard
and port so that the blades were on the inside

and handles sticking out a cubit's length.   520
After the stems were fastened to the oarlocks,
they stood on either side between the oars,
their hands and torsos pressed against the hull.

Tiphys had climbed on deck to tell the crew
when it was time to push. He bellowed hugely—   525 (382)
that was the signal. One concerted heave,
and they had loosed the vessel from the props,
feet dancing as they pushed and pulled it seaward.
Pelian *Argo* followed in a rush,
the men on each side boisterously shouting   530
as they were swept up in its course. The rollers
squealed as the sturdy keel scraped over them.
Friction and torsion sent up coils of smoke.

After the ship had rolled into the surf,
they yanked landward upon the lines to check   535
its forward motion. Then they snapped the oar pins
into the holes, locked them, and lugged aboard
the mast, the well-sewn sails, and all the gear.

Once they had scurried back and forth and seen
to each detail, they turned to divvying   540 (395)
the benches up by lot, two men per bench.
Straight off, though, separate from the lottery,
they gave the center bench to Heracles
to work beside Ancaeus the Tegean.
After the berths were set, they gladly handed   545
Tiphys the tiller of the well-keeled *Argo*.

Then they heaped some stones up on the beach
to make a seaside altar for Apollo
God of the Beachfront, God of Embarkation.
Dried olive boughs were quickly laid upon it.   550
Meanwhile, Jason's herdsmen had selected
two bulls out of the herd and led them back.
Some younger heroes tugged them toward the altar,
others lugged in grain and lustral water,

and Jason duly summoned with a hymn   555 (409)
Phoebus Apollo, his ancestral god:

"Hear me, O lord, O power who inhabit
Pagasae and Aesonia, the city
that bears my father's name. When I came seeking
a prophecy at Pytho, you assured me   560
you would reveal the methods of success
and all the courses of my quest, since you
were equal partner in this enterprise.
Therefore, I ask you please to guide our vessel
there and back again to Greece; please keep   565
my crew alive and healthy. Afterward,
to do you honor, I shall once again
heap up this altar with the sacrifice
of just so many bulls as men of mine
have safely made the journey. Furthermore,   570 (418)
I shall deliver countless other gifts
to Pytho and Ortygia.
                              Far shooter,
come to us now; accept these sacrifices,
the first of many, that we offer asking
for an auspicious boarding of our ship.   575
Lord, when I loose the hawsers, may I find
a future free of harm, and all because
of your assistance. May the gale be gentle,
the weather always favorable for sailing
as we pursue our quest across the sea."   580

So he intoned and tossed the barley offering.
Heracles, then, and proud Ancaeus stepped up
to slay the bulls. Heracles with his club
struck one of them dead center on the brow.
It lay there in a heap, all crumpled up.   585 (429)
Ancaeus with a bronze ax hacked the other,
chopped clean on through the strained and stubborn sinew
that stuck out of its neck. It toppled forward
onto its horns. The other heroes all
jumped in and slit the throats, stripped off the hides,   590

and made the cuts. While divvying the portions,
they set aside the sacred thighbones, wrapped them
snugly in fat, and roasted them on spits,
and Jason poured a gift of unmixed wine
into the fire. Idmon was delighted   595
to see the blaze enkindling the bones
and favorable coils of thick black smoke
ascending. He divulged Apollo's will
straight off with perfect clarity:
                                    "The gods
by harbinger and oracle have promised   600 (440)
you shall return here with the fleece in hand
despite the countless labors that await you
on both the outward and the homeward journey.
The gods have also specified that I
must perish somewhere on the Asian mainland   605
far from home. Although I learned my fate
some time ago from inauspicious bird signs,
I left my homeland, all the same, to join
the quest and win a name that would survive me
among my people."
                                    So the seer spoke   610
and, when the heroes heard the prophecy,
they reveled in the news of their return
even as they succumbed to grief at learning
of Idmon's doom.
                                    Already at the hour
when sunlight starts to slant toward evening   615 (450)
and mountain ridges fill the fields with shadows,
the men had heaped up leaf beds on the beach
and lay there side by side above the surf.
Abundant food was waiting near at hand,
and, as the stewards poured them unmixed wine   620
from jugs, they told each other different stories,
the sort that young men tell to give amusement
over a meal or at a drinking party
when insult and offense are far away.

Jason, however, like a man in sorrow,   625
minutely scrutinized within himself

all that might leave him feeling still more helpless.
Idas leered at him awhile, then ribbed him
in an obnoxious voice:
                              "Jason, what plan
is spinning in your mind? Come now and share   630 (464)
what you are thinking. Has dismay, the monster
that panics cowards, shambled up and mauled you?
I'll swear an oath and wager as a pledge
the spear with which, above all other heroes,
I win renown in combat (no, not even   635
Zeus backs me up as well as my own spear):

no trouble you encounter will be fatal,
no task you try will go unfinished—no,
not even if a god should block the path—
so long as you have Idas on your side.   640
Just such a champion you are bringing with you
in me, your great salvation from Arene."

So he proclaimed and picked a full bowl up
with both his hands and swilled the sweet neat wine.
He came up with his lips and black beard dripping.   645 (474)
While others muttered curses in the background,
Idmon called him out for all to hear:

"Idiot, have you always cherished wicked
presumptions such as these or is it rather
the unmixed wine that has incensed your heart   650
with recklessness and pushed you to offend
the gods? There are a thousand heartening words
a man can say to urge a comrade on,
but you have blurted out offensive ones.

They say Aloeus' gigantic sons   655
sputtered such stuff against the blessed gods,
and you're not half their valor. All the same,
the two of them, courageous as they were,
went down beneath the arrows of Apollo."

As soon as Idmon finished speaking, Idas   660 (485)
the son of Aphareus, burst out laughing,
glared slantwise at the seer and answered sharply:

"Come now and forecast with your prophet's art
whether the gods shall work the same destruction
upon me as your father Phoebus wrought   665
upon the offspring of Aloeus—stop
and think, though, how you will escape my clutches
when you are caught predicting utter nonsense."

So Idas raged and threatened, and the quarrel
would certainly have come to blows, had Jason   670
and all the others not rebuked and checked them.
Orpheus also did his best to calm them.
He took his lyre up in his left hand
and played a song he had been working on.

He sang of how the earth and sea and sky   675 (496)
were once commingled in a single mass
until contentious strife divided each from other
in ordered layers,
                    how the stars and moon
and sun's advance consistently provide
clear beacons in the firmament,
                                and how   680
the mountains rose, and roaring watercourses,
each with a nymph, started into existence,
and animals began to walk on land.

He sang of how, back in the world's beginning,
Ophion and Eurynoma, the daughter   685
of Ocean, ruled on snow-capped Mount Olympus
till Ophion released the throne perforce
to strong-armed Cronus, and Eurynoma
gave way to Rhea, and the vanquished gods
went tumbling into the ocean waves,   690 (507)
and the usurpers ruled the Titans, happy
so long as Zeus was still a child, still growing
in thought, still hidden in a cave on Dicte.
The earthborn Cyclopes had not yet fashioned
the lightning bolt, the source of Zeus' power.   695

So Orpheus intoned, then hushed his lyre
at the same time as his ambrosial voice.

Though he had ceased, each of his comrades still
leaned forward longingly, their ears intent,
their bodies motionless with ecstasy.   700
Such was the magic of the song he cast
upon them. After they had mixed libations
for Zeus, they rose and dutifully poured them
over the victims' simmering tongues, then turned
their minds toward sleeping through the night.
                                                As soon   705 (519)
as radiant Dawn with her resplendent gaze
looked on the steep cliff face of Pelion,
and day broke fair, and breezes stirred the sea
that dashed, in turn, upon the headlands, Tiphys
awoke and roused the dozing crew and bade them   710
hasten aboard and man the oars. The harbor
of Pagasae called out, urging departure,
and, yes, the ship itself, Pelian *Argo,*
called to them also, since its hull contained
a talking plank. Athena had herself   715
cut it from a Dodonan oak to serve
beneath them as the keel. And so the heroes
headed to the benches single file
and duly took their seats beside their weapons
in just the places they had been assigned.   720 (531)
Ancaeus and colossal Heracles
were seated at the center bench. The latter
set down his club beside him, and the keel
sank deep beneath his feet. The mooring ropes
were drawn in, and the heroes poured libations   725
of wine into the bay, and Jason, weeping,
turned his eyes from his ancestral home.

When dancing for Apollo at Ortygia
or Pytho or along the Ismenus,
young men will sway around a shrine together   730
heeding the lyre's rhythm as their nimble
feet beat time—in just that way the heroes
slapped the choppy water with their oars,
churning the sea as Orpheus' harp
accompanied their strokes. The billows surged   735 (541)

around the oar blades, and to port and starboard
the dark brine boiled in foam, its spray excited,
stirred up by the thrusts of mighty men.
Their armor shone like fire in the sunlight,
and *Argo* plunged onward, its long white wake   740
most like a pathway through a grassy plain.

And on that day the gods looked down from heaven
upon the ship and demigods within it—
the finest heroes ever to have sailed.
Nymphs of the mountains on the topmost peak   745
of Pelion stood wonderstruck, admiring
the craft work of Itonian Athena
and all those heroes with their hands working
the *Argo*'s oars. Cheiron, Phillyra's son,
strode from a mountain summit to the sea   750 (554)
and wet his fetlocks where the brackish surf
churns on the shore. Waving a mighty hand,
he wished them all a safe return. Beside him
his wife was holding up infant Achilles
so that Peleus, the loving father,   755
could see his son.
                    Under the tutelage
of prudent Tiphys, Hagnias' son
(the master hand who gripped the sanded tiller
and kept the vessel steady on her course),
the heroes left the curved shore of the bay   760
behind them. When they reached the open sea
they stepped the giant mast up in the mast bed
and pulled the forestays taut on either side
to hold it upright. Then they bent the sail on
and draped it from the masthead. When a shrill   765 (566)
wind found and filled it, they were quick to fix
the sheets to polished bollards on the deck.
Finally idle and at ease, they skirted
the long headland of Tisae.
                              Orpheus meanwhile
plucked his lyre and sang a lovely hymn   770
to honor Artemis, the Sailors' Savior,

the Potent Father's Daughter, since she guarded
the cliffs beside them and the coast of Iolcus.
Fish both big and small came leaping out of
the sea to revel in the vessel's wake.   775
In just the way innumerable sheep,
after a satisfying meal at pasture,
tread the footsteps of their rustic guide
back to the paddock, and he leads by playing
shepherd music on a bright-pitched pipe,   780 (577)
the shoal of fish accompanied the ship.

And still a stiff wind bore the heroes onward.
Pelasgia and its abounding wheat fields
vanished in mist and, as they coasted farther,
they passed the rugged cliffs of Pelion,   785
and soon the spit of Sepae sank from view.
Sciathus rose out of the sea and then
more distant Peiresiae and, beyond it,
mainland again, the coastline of Magnesia,
and Dolops' barrow under sunny skies.   790

That afternoon a stiff wind rose against them,
and they were forced to run the ship ashore.
Then, as they roasted joints of sheep at twilight
to honor Dolops, surges riled the sea.
Two days and nights they idled on the beach   795 (588)
and on the third again launched *Argo*, spreading
her ample sail. That shore is known today
as *Argous Aphetai* (or "*Argo*'s Launch").

From there they sped along past Meliboea,
marveling at the cliffs and storm-swept shore.   800
They spotted Homola at dawn, a city
slanted toward the sea, and sailed on past it.
A little farther, and they would have skirted
the mouth of the Amyrus. Next they spotted
Eurymenae and the eroded gorges   805
of Ossa and Olympus. As they sped
that night before the panting of the wind,

they passed the Pallenean cliffs beyond
the headland of Canastra, and at dawn
they still were dashing onward.
                              There was Athos,   810 (601)
the Thracian mountain, rising up before them.
The shadow from its utmost summit reaches
eastward to Myrina Promontory
on Lemnos—leagues a well-trimmed ship would need
from dawn to noon to travel. All day long   815
a mighty wind was blowing, and the sail
rippling, but the gale expired at sunset.
So the heroes rowed to rugged Lemnos,
land of the venerable Sintians.

Here, in the previous year, the womenfolk   820
had mercilessly slaughtered all the menfolk—
inhuman massacre! The men, you see,
had come to loathe and shun their lawful wives
and suffer a persistent lust instead
for captive maidens they themselves had carried   825 (611)
home across the sea from raids in Thrace.
(This was the wrath of Cyprian Aphrodite
exacting vengeance on the men because,
for years, they had begrudged her any honors.)
Stricken with an insatiable resentment   830
that would destroy their way of life, the women
cut down not only their own wedded husbands
and all the battle brides who slept with them
but every other male as well, the whole
race of them, so that no one would survive   835
to make them pay for their atrocious slaughter.

Hypsipyle alone of all the women
thought to save her father—aged Thoas
who, as it chanced, was ruler at the time.
She hid him in an empty chest and cast him   840 (622)
into the ocean, hoping he would live.
Fisherman caught him off an island called
Oenoa then but later on Sicinus

after the child Sicinus whom Oenoa
(a water nymph) conceived from her affair   845
with Thoas.
        Soon enough the women found
animal husbandry, the drills of war,
and labor in the wheat-producing fields
easier than the handcrafts of Athena
to which they were accustomed. Often, though,   850
they scanned the level sea in grievous fear
that Thracian soldiers would descend upon them.
So, when they saw the *Argo* under oar
and heading toward their shore, they dressed in armor
and like a mob of Maenad cannibals   855 (637)
dashed through Myrina Gate onto the beach.
They all assumed the Thracians were at hand.
Hypsipyle, the child of Thoas, joined them,
and she had donned the armor of her father.
There they mustered, mute in their dismay,   860
so great a menace had been swept against them.

Meanwhile the heroes had dispatched ashore
Aethalides, the posthaste messenger,
whose work included overtures and parleys.
He held the scepter of his father Hermes,   865
and Hermes had bestowed on him undying
memory of whatever he was told.

Although Aethalides has long since sunk
under the silent tide of Acheron,
forgetfulness has never seized his spirit—   870 (645)
no, he is doomed to change homes endlessly,
now numbered with the ghosts beneath the earth,
now with the men who live and see the sun . . .
wait, why have I digressed so widely, talking
about Aethalides?
        On this occasion   875
his overtures convinced Hypsipyle
to grant his comrades harbor for the night,
since it was getting on toward dusk. At dawn, though,

the heroes still had not unbound the hawsers
because a stiff north wind was blowing.
                                    Meanwhile,   880
the Lemnian women all throughout the city
had left their homes and gathered for assembly.
Hypsipyle herself had summoned them.
When they had found their places, she proposed:

"Dear women, come now, let us give these men   885 (657)
sufficient gifts, the sorts of things that sailors
stow in the hold—provisions, honeyed wine—
so that they will remain outside our ramparts.
Otherwise, when they come to beg supplies,
they will discover what we've done, and thus   890
a bad report of us will travel far and wide.
Yes, we have done a horrid, horrid thing,
and knowing it would hardly warm their hearts.

This is the plan before us. If some woman
among you can propose a better one,   895
come, let her stand up and reveal it now—
that is the reason I convened this council."

So Hypsipyle proclaimed, then settled
again upon her father's marble throne,
and her beloved nurse Polyxo stood up,   900 (669)
using a cane to prop her palsied legs
and shriveled feet, since she was keen to speak.
Around her sat four women who, although
they still were maidens and had never married,
were garlanded with heads of pure-white hair.   905
Steady at last and facing the assembly,
Polyxo strained to lift her neck just slightly
above her stooping shoulders and proposed:

"Let us by all means send the strangers presents,
just as Hypsipyle has recommended.   910
It's best that way. But as for all of you,
what plan do *you* have to defend yourselves
if, say, a Thracian army or some other
enemy force invades? Out in the world

such raids are common. Witness, for example,   915 (680)
this group that has arrived out of the blue.

Furthermore, even if some blessed god
should drive them off, a thousand other troubles
worse than war await you in the future.
When all us older women pass away   920
and you, the younger ones, attain a childless
and cruel dotage, how will you get by?
Poor women. Will the oxen yoke themselves
as favors to you in the loamy fields?
Will they pull the furrow-cleaving harrow   925
over the acres of their own volition?
And who will reap the grain when summer ends?

My case is different. Though the gods of death
thus far have shuddered at the sight of me,
I'm certain that before the next year's out,   930 (691)
long, long before such troubles come about,
I will have drawn a gown of earth around me
and earned my share of reliquary honors.
Still, I entreat you girls to think ahead.
Right now a perfect means of upkeep lies   935
before your feet. All you must do is hand
your houses, property, and dazzling city
over to the strangers to maintain."

So she proposed. A murmur filled the assembly:
her speech made sense. As soon as she was finished,   940
Hypsipyle stood up again and answered:

"If all of you approve of this proposal,
I shall be so immodest as to send
an envoy to their ship at once."
                                    So spoke she
and told Iphinoa, who was at hand: 945 (702)

"Please go and ask the man that leads their party
(whichever he might be) to come and visit
my royal palace so that I may make him

a proposition that will warm his heart.
Also, be sure to ask his comrades please   950
to come inside our land and city walls
without concern, provided they are friendly."

Once she had sent the message, she dissolved
the council and departed toward the palace.

Iphinoa sought out the Minyans,   955
and, when they asked why she had come, she greeted
her questioners at once with this announcement:

"Queen Hypsipyle the heir of Thoas
has sent me here to summon your commander
(whichever he might be), so she can make him   960 (713)
a proposition that will warm his heart.
Also, she wishes to invite you others
to come inside our land and city walls
without concern, provided you are friendly."

So she announced, and all the men approved   965
of the auspicious overture. You see,
they all assumed Hypsipyle was queen
because she was the only child of Thoas
and he had passed on. So they sent her Jason
and started getting ready for their visit.   970

Over either shoulder Jason pinned
a double-woven, vivid-purple mantle,
the handwork of Itonian Athena.
Pallas had given it to him when first
she propped up trusses for the ship and taught   975 (723)
the men to measure out the beams by rule.
You could more comfortably stare upon
a sunrise than this mantle's rich resplendence.
The center was a fiery red, a violet
border ran around it, and embroidered   980
illustrations, subtly stitched vignettes,
stood side by side along its top and bottom:

The Cyclopes were seated in it, plying
their endless trade. The stunning thunderbolt
that they were forging for Imperial Zeus   985
was all but finished, all but one last tip.
Their iron mallets pounded at it, giving
shape to a blast of molten, raging fire.

Antiope's twin sons were featured, too,
Zethus and Amphion, and Thebes was there,   990 (736)
unfortified as yet, but they were raising
the circuit walls. While Zethus seemed to stagger
under the mountain peak upon his back,
Amphion simply strolled along behind him
and strummed his golden lyre, and a boulder   995
twice as gigantic followed in his footsteps.

Next appeared thickly braided Cytherea,
the shield of Ares in her hand. Her gown
had come unfastened, tumbled from her shoulder
down to her forearm, and exposed a breast,   1000
and in the shield's polished bronze a mirror
image admired her, a true reflection.

Next, there were cattle on a tufted grange,
and Taphian marauders, Teleboans,
fighting the offspring of Electryon   1005 (748)
to win the herd. The latter strove to fend off
the former, who were bent on taking plunder.
Dew dampened the enclosure, dew and blood,
and there were many brigands, few herdsmen.

A race came next, a pair of chariots,   1010
and Pelops flicked the reins and held the lead,
Hippodameia standing at his side.
Myrtilus whipped his horses in pursuit.
Beside him Oenomaus rode in state,
his long spear pointed forward. But the axle   1015
snapped in his hub just as he lunged to pierce
Pelops' back, and he went tumbling sideways.

Apollo was embroidered in it, too,
a strong youth, not yet fully grown, and launching
a shaft at giant Tityus, who was rashly   1020 (761)
tearing the veil from Apollo's mother—
Tityus whom divine Elara carried
but Earth brought forth and suckled like a midwife.

Phrixus the Minyan was there as well,
depicted as if he were giving ear   1025
to what the ram was saying. Yes, the ram
seemed to be speaking. If you watched the scene
you would be mute with wonder, duped by art,
intent on overhearing something wise.
And you would gaze a long time waiting for it.   1030

Such was the gift of the Itonian goddess
Athena. In his right hand Jason gripped
the long-range throwing spear that Atalanta
once gave him as a gift on Maenalus.
She had been pleased to meet him and was eager   1035 (771)
to undertake the quest, but he decided
against her in the end, because he feared
the ugly rivalries that lust provokes.

He strode on toward the city like the star
young brides who are confined to new-built chambers   1040
watch rising radiantly above their houses.
They stand adazzle as its twinkling crimson
shines through the dark-blue night and charms their eyes.
As it ascends, the virgin, too, delights
in longing for a youth, the groom for whom   1045
her parents have preserved her as a bride.
But he is off somewhere, some distant city,
dealing with strangers. Brilliant like that star,
Jason came marching in the envoy's tracks.

When they had passed the gates into the city,   1050 (782)
the females all came swarming up behind him,
admiring a strange new male. He fixed

his gaze steadfastly on the ground until
he reached Hypsipyle's sunlit abode.

At his approach, the serving women parted   1055
a pair of finely chiseled double doors.
Iphinoa then led him through a courtyard
and seated him upon a shining couch
facing her mistress, who, with eyes downcast,
released a blush across her maiden cheeks.   1060
For all her modesty, she told him lies:

"Why, stranger, have you sat so long outside
our circuit walls? As you can see, no males
inhabit here. They up and emigrated
and now are furrowing the harvest-bearing   1065 (796)
fields of the Thracian mainland. I shall tell you
truthfully all about our whole misfortune
so that you know the facts as well as I.

Back when my father Thoas ruled this city
our men would sail abroad and from their ships   1070
pillage the dwellings of the Thracian tribes
who hold the mainland opposite the island.
And when they sailed back home to us, they brought
countless spoils, including captive girls.

This was a plot, though, working toward fulfillment,   1075
a vicious plot of Cypris. Yes, she struck them
with heart-corrupting madness. Husbands started
spurning their wedded wives and went so far,
once they had given way to the affliction,
to drive us from our homes and sleep instead   1080 (806)
with women captured by their spears. The fiends!
We let it go for quite some time indeed,
thinking they would come to change their minds,
but their diseased condition only worsened
and soon was twice as shameless as before.   1085

Legitimate descendants were compelled
to yield pride of place in their own homes.

A bastard populace was rising up.
Maidens and widowed housewives were abandoned
to walk the streets just as they were, disowned.   1090
A father never showed the least concern
for his own daughter, even if he saw her
brutalized by a merciless stepmother
before his very eyes, and sons no longer
avenged disgraceful slander of their mothers,   1095 (816)
and brothers cut the sisters from their hearts.
At home, at dances, feasts, and the assembly
the captive girls held sway, and so it went—
until a god inspired us to vengeance
and we barred the gates against our husbands   1100
when they returned from pillaging the Thracians.
We told them they must change their ways or pack up
their concubines and settle somewhere else.

After demanding all the children—all
the boys, that is—within our walls, they left   1105
and settled on the snowy plains of Thrace,
where they are living still. And that is why
you and your men should settle down with us.

If you are willing and would find it pleasant
to stay with us, you could assume the kingship   1110 (829)
and honors of my father Thoas. You
will not be disappointed in our soil,
I think. Ours is the richest, the most fruitful
of all the islands riding the Aegean.
Go now and tell your friends what I propose—   1115
and please do not remain outside the city."

So she proposed, with half-truths glossing over
the massacre that had been perpetrated
against the Lemnian males. Jason replied:

"Hypsipyle, we gratefully accept   1120
the heartfelt aid that you are offering
to ease our desperate need. After reporting
the details to my men, I will return here.

But let the royal scepter and the island
remain in your possession. I am not   1125 (840)
refusing them from scorn, no, but because
pressing adventures speed me on my way."

With this he clasped her right hand and at once
went back the way he came. Around him maidens
from all directions gathered in excitement,   1130
a swarm of them, until he passed the gate.
Later, once Jason had reported all
Hypsipyle had told him at the palace,
another company of girls arrived
in smooth-wheeled wagons, bearing countless tokens   1135
of friendship to the heroes on the shore.
Eagerly, then, the females led the males
into their homes for entertainment. Cypris,
you see, had roused them all with sweet desire—
she did this as a favor for Hephaestus,   1140 (851)
so that the isle of Lemnos might again
fill up with men and rest secure thereafter.

The son of Aeson sought Hypsipyle's
royal estate, and his companions each
landed wherever chance received them—all   1145
but Heracles. He of his own free will
remained beside the *Argo* with a few
select companions. Soon the city turned
to dancing, banqueting, and pleasure. Incense
of offerings suffused the atmosphere,   1150
and all their songs and prayers celebrated,
before the other gods, famous Hephaestus
Hera's son and Cypris Queen of Love.

And so from day to day the journey languished.
The heroes would have idled there still longer   1155 (863)
had Heracles not called them all together,
without the women, and reproached them thus:

"Fools, what prevents us from returning home—
what, have we shed our kinsmen's blood? Have we

set sail to seek fiancées in contempt   1160
of ladies on the mainland? Are we planning
to divvy up the fertile fields of Lemnos
and settle here for good? We won't accrue
glory while cooped up here with foreign girls
for years on end. No deity is going   1165
to nab the fleece in answer to our prayers
and send it flying back to us. Come, then,
let's each go off and tend his own affairs.
And as for *that* one—leave him to enjoy
Hypsipyle's bedchamber day and night   1170 (873)
until he peoples Lemnos with his sons,
and deathless glory catches up with him."

So he condemned his comrades. None of them
dared meet his gaze or make excuses, no,
they hurried as they were from the assembly   1175
to get the *Argo* ready for departure.

The women ran to find them when they heard.
As bees swarm from a rocky hive and buzz
about the handsome lilies, and the dewy
meadow itself rejoices as they flit   1180
from bloom to bloom collecting sweet fruition,
so did the women press around the men
and weep as they embraced them one last time,
entreating all the blessed gods to grant them
safe passage home. So, too, Hypsipyle   1185 (886)
took Jason's hands in hers and prayed, and tears
were tumbling for her lover's loss:
                                    "Go now,
and may the gods protect you and your comrades
from harm, so that you live to give your king
the golden fleece. That is your heart's desire.   1190
This island and my father's royal scepter
will still be yours if, after you are home,
you ever wish to come back here again.
How easily you could amass a vast
following out of the surrounding cities!   1195

But you will not desire this future, no,
my heart foresees that it will not be so.
Promise that, both abroad and safe at home,
you will remember me from time to time—
Hypsipyle. But, please, what should I do   1200 (898)
if the immortals grace me with a child?
I shall obey your will with all my heart."

Stirred to esteem, the son of Aeson answered:

"Hypsipyle, I pray the blessed gods
accomplish everything as you desire it.   1205
Still, you must check your wild expectations
where I'm concerned, since it will be enough
for me to live again in my own land
at Pelias' mercy. All I ask
is that the gods preserve me on my quest.   1210

But if my fate forbid that I return,
after a lengthy journey, home to Greece,
and you have borne a son, hold on to him
until he comes of age and send him then
to Iolcus in Pelasgia to ease   1215 (906)
my parents' grief (if they are still alive),
so that they may be safe in their own home,
comfortable and far from Pelias."

He spoke these final words and was the first
to board the ship. The other heroes followed,   1220
took up their oars, and manned the benches. Argus
loosed the hawser from a sea-washed rock,
and soon the heroes were exuberantly
slapping the water with their lengthy oars.

At Orpheus' bidding they debarked   1225
that evening on the island of Electra,
Atlas' daughter, so that they might suffer
gentle induction, learn her secret rites,
and cruise more safely through the chilling sea.

But I shall speak no further of such matters.   1230 (919)
Farewell, Electra, and farewell, you powers
whose task it is to guard and keep the secrets
of which it is forbidden me to sing.

Off Samothrace they briskly pulled their oars
over the Black Gulf's depths. The land of Thrace   1235
was larboard, and the isle of Imbros starboard
there on the seaward side, and just at sunset
they reached a finger of the Chersonese.
A stiff south wind was blowing for them there,
so they unfurled the canvas to the gale's   1240
beneficence and soon approached the roiling
narrows of Helle daughter of Athamas.
By morning they had left the sea astern.
(They had, in fact, been sailing all night long
within a farther sea between the headlands   1245 (929)
of Rhoeteum.) The land of Ida starboard,
Dardania abaft, they passed Abydos,
Percota, sandy beaches in Abarnis,
and holy Pityeia. Thus they crossed
by oar and sail before the next sunrise   1250
the whole length of the Hellespont and all
its dark whirlpools.
                              There is a lofty island
that slopes on all sides down to the Propontis.
A steep and sea-washed spit of land connects it
to mainland Phrygia and a wealth of grain.   1255
Two of its shores are welcoming to ships,
both of them north of the Asepus River.
The island had the name of Black Bear Mountain,
and there were savage Earthborn Giants on it,
great wonders for the locals to behold: 1260 (943)
six rippling arms grew out of each of them—
two sprouting out of their colossal shoulders,
four farther down along their frightening flanks.
The Doliones dwelled there, all the same,
along the spit and island's rim. Their king was   1265
Cyzicus son of Aeneus. Aeneta,

daughter of divine Eusorus, bore him.
Though wild and violent, the Earthborn Giants
never attacked the Dolionan people
because they were descended from Poseidon—   1270
he guarded them.
           A Thracian gale impelled
the *Argo* toward this island, and the heroes
moored in a harbor called the "Handsome Port."
Here it was that, at Tiphys' suggestion,
they cut the stone that served as anchor loose,   1275 (957)
dropped it into the stream Artacia,
and chose a larger one to suit their needs.
Years later, to fulfill Apollo's plan,
the sons of Neleus (that is, the ones
that settled Asia Minor) set apart   1280
the very stone abandoned by the heroes
as sacred in the temple of Athena,
Helper of Jason, and the gift, of course,
was quite appropriate.
                The Doliones
and Cyzicus their king received the heroes   1285
and, after finding out their names and mission,
warmly invited them to stay as guests.
Cyzicus urged them please to row in farther
and make their mooring in the city harbor,
and so they did and, after raising there   1290 (965)
an altar to Apollo God of Landings,
busied themselves preparing sacrifices.

The king himself supplied what they required—
some sweet wine and a flock of sheep. You see,
Cyzicus had received a prophecy   1295
that claimed a godlike crew would land one day,
and he should rush warmly to welcome them
and take no thought of war. His beard was downy,
like Jason's, and had only lately sprouted,
and fate had not yet graced him with a child.   1300
Cleite, his plush-tressed, newly wedded wife,
daughter of Merops of Percota, shared

a chamber with him in the royal palace,
but labor pains were still unknown to her.
Cyzicus only recently had led her   1305 (978)
out of her home on the opposing coast,
and he had paid her father many gifts
to buy the right to wed her. Nonetheless,
he brought himself to leave the marriage chamber
and bridal bed and entertain the heroes.   1310
He had dismissed suspicion from his heart.

They asked each other questions at the feast—
Cyzicus learned of Pelias' bidding
and the objective of their quest. The heroes,
in turn, inquired about the neighboring cities   1315
and the whole basin of the vast Propontis,
but Cyzicus' knowledge ranged no further,
much as they wished to learn what lay beyond.

So half the heroes set about ascending
Dindymum at dawn to see firsthand   1320 (985)
what waters they would cross, and to this day
the path they took is known as Jason's Way.
The other half, however, stayed behind
and rowed the *Argo* from her former mooring
over to Chytus Haven.
                        All at once   1325
the Earthborn ones came down around the mountain
and tried to block the exit from the harbor
by dropping countless rocks into the water,
the way men catch sea creatures in a pool.
Heracles and the younger men, however,   1330
had stayed back with the ship, and Heracles
nocked arrows nimbly on his back-bent bow
and dropped the giants freely one by one
since they had focused all their strength on heaving
and hurling jagged rocks into the sea.   1335 (995)
No doubt the goddess Hera, Zeus' consort,
had reared these horrid things as yet another
labor for Heracles. The other heroes
turned back before they reached the mountaintop

and joined their comrades, and they all got down   1340
to slaughtering the Earthborn Giants, routing
by shaft and spear their reckless, headlong charges
till each and every one of them was dead.

As woodcutters, once they have finished felling
colossal old-growth trees, proceed to lay them   1345
side by side along the surf to soak
and soften and receive the dowels, the heroes
laid out the Earthborn Giants one by one
along the shorefront of the choppy harbor—
some headfirst in the brine, their tops and torsos   1350 (1008)
submerged, their legs protruding landward; others,
conversely, had their feet out in the deep
and heads out on the beach. Both groups were doomed
to serve as meals for fish and birds alike.

After the men returned, unscathed, from battle,   1355
they loosed the hawsers, and the wind came up,
and they pursued their quest across the swell.
All day the *Argo* coasted under sail.
At evening, though, the wind became unsteady.
Gusts from the opposite direction seized her   1360
and blew her back until she reached once more
the island of the kindly Doliones.
They disembarked at midnight, and the rock
to which they hastily attached a line
is called the Sacred Outcrop to this day.   1365 (1019)

But none among them was astute enough
to notice they had stopped at the same island.
Since it was night the Doliones failed
as well to mark their friends come back again,
no, they assumed Pelasgian invaders,   1370
Macrian men, had breached their beach instead,
and so they took up arms and started fighting.

Their shields and ash-wood lances clashed as swiftly
as fire that has sparked on arid brushwood
leaps aloft in crested conflagration.   1375

Battle, horrible and unforgiving,
befell the Doliones. Cyzicus
was not permitted to escape his doom
or go home to enjoy his bridal bed.
Just as he joined the battle, Jason ran up   1380 (1032)
and stabbed him in the center of the chest.
Ribs shattered round the spear tip, and he crumpled
upon the beach and met his destined end.

Mortals can never sidestep fate; the cosmic
net is extended round us everywhere.   1385
And so it was that, on the very night
Cyzicus had assumed that he was safe
from bitter slaughter at the heroes' hands,
destiny snared him, and he joined the fray.

Many others on his side were slain: 1390
Heracles clubbed the life from Megabrontes
and Telecles; Acastus slaughtered Sphodris;
Peleus vanquished battle-keen Gephyrus
and Zelys; and that mighty ash-wood spearman
Telamon triumphed over Basileus.   1395 (1043)
Idas in turn disposed of Promeus; Clytius,
Hyancinthus; and the brothers Castor
and Polydeuces slew Megalossaces
and Phlogius. Beside them Meleager
son of Oeneus dispatched Artaces   1400
leader of men and bold Itymoneus.
Still today the locals venerate
the men who perished in that fight as heroes.

The remnants of the Doliones turned
and fled like doves pursued by swift-winged hawks.   1405
After they stumbled, hoarse and helter-skelter,
into the city, cries of lamentation
erupted—yes, its soldiers had retreated,
retreated from a dismal fight.
                               At daybreak
both parties recognized the fatal error,   1410 (1053)

but nothing could be done to make it right.
Violent sorrow gripped the Minyans
once they had spotted Aeneus' son
Cyzicus lying, bloody, in the dust.

Three days the heroes and the Doliones   1415
tore out their hair and mourned the loss together.
Then, after putting on their bronze war gear,
they marched three times around the corpse, entombed it,
and filed away to the Leimonian plain
to hold memorial games, as is the custom.   1420

Cleite, however, Cyzicus' wife,
refused to stay behind among the living
now that her man was dead. She heaped a further
sorrow on top of what had gone before
by fastening a noose around her neck.   1425 (1065)
Even the woodland nymphs bewailed her passing.
In fact, these deities collected all
the tears that tumbled earthward from their eyelids
into a spring called Cleite—the "Renowned"
name of the ill-starred widow.
                              Zeus had never   1430
dropped a more heart-devastating day
upon the Dolionan men and women.
None of them could enjoy the taste of food
and, far into the future, sorrow kept them
from working at the mill, and they subsided   1435
on raw provisions. Still today, in fact,
when the Cyzician Ionians
make yearly sacrifices to the dead,
they always use the public stone, and not
the stones they keep at home, to grind the meal.   1440 (1072)

And then stiff winds arose and blew, preventing
the heroes from departing, twelve nights, twelve days,
but on the thirteenth night, when all their comrades
had yielded to exhaustion and were sleeping
heavily through the final watch, two men—   1445

Ampycus' son Mopsus and Acastus—
were standing sentry, and a halcyon
appeared and fluttered round the golden hair
of Jason son of Aeson, prophesying
with strident voice the calming of the gales.   1450
As soon as Mopsus heard and apprehended
the seabird's joyous news, some higher power
dispatched it fluttering aloft again
to perch atop the *Argo*'s sculpted stern post.
Mopsus immediately ran to shake   1455 (1090)
Jason sleeping under soft sheep fleeces.
Soon as his captain was awake, he said:

"You, son of Aeson, must ascend to where
a temple stands on rugged Dindymum
and soothe the Mother of the Blessed Gods   1460
upon her shining throne. Once you have done this,
the stormy gales shall cease. Such is the message
I heard just now. You see, an ocean-dwelling
halcyon fluttered round your sleeping head,
revealing everything that must be done.   1465

The winds, the ocean, and the earth's foundations
all depend upon the Mother Goddess,
as does the snow-capped bastion of Olympus.
When she forsakes the mountains and ascends
the mighty vault of heaven, Zeus himself,   1470 (1101)
the son of Cronus, offers her his place,
and all the blessed gods bow before her power."

Such were his words, and Jason welcomed them,
vaulted for joy out of his bed, and ran
to rouse his comrades. Once they were awake,   1475
he told them what the offspring of Ampycus,
Mopsus, had ascertained.
                              The younger heroes
hurried to drag some oxen from the stalls
and drive them all the way up Dindymum's
precipitous ascent. After detaching   1480

the hawsers from the Sacred Rock, the others
rowed into the so-called "Thracian Harbor,"
picked out some few to stay and guard the ship,
and went to scale the mountain.
                                    From the peak
the Macrian massifs and all the Thracian   1485 (1112)
coastline stretching opposite them seemed
almost within arm's reach. They also spotted
the misty entrance to the Bosporus,
the Mysian hills, and there, across the strait,
Asepus River and its namesake city   1490
and the Nepeian plain of Adrasteia.

There in the forest was an old vine stump,
stubborn and dry. They cut it out to make
a sacred image of the Mountain Goddess.
Artful Argus carved it, and they set it   1495
atop a rugged outcrop in the shade
of lofty oaks, which shoot their taproots deeper
than any other tree.
                          They built an altar
of fieldstone, garlanded their brows with oak leaves,
and offered sacrifice, invoking Mother   1500 (1125)
Dindymena, Dweller in Phrygia,
and Queen of Many Names. They also summoned
Titias and Cyllenus who, alone
of all the Dactyls bred on Cretan Ida,
have earned the titles "Destiny Assessors"   1505
and "Confidants" of the Idaean Mother.
A nymph named Anchiala brought them forth
in the Dictaean Cave while squeezing fistfuls
of Oaxian earth to ease the pain.

The son of Aeson poured libations over   1510
the blazing victims and implored the goddess
with various prayers to turn the storms away.
Under the tutelage of Orpheus
the younger men performed the Dance in Armor,
leaping and pounding swords on shields so that   1515 (1135)

any unlucky cry of grief the locals
might possibly be making for their king
would vanish in the din. From that day on
the Phrygians have always celebrated
Rhea with tambourine and kettledrum.   1520

These flawless sacrifices clearly won
the goddess' approval. Signs appeared,
conclusive proof: fruit tumbled from the trees
in great abundance, and beneath their feet
the earth spontaneously sprouted flowers   1525
out of the tender grass, and savage creatures
forsook their dens and thickets in the wild
to fawn and beg with wagging tails around them.

Later, another marvel came to pass:
water had never flowed on Dindymum   1530 (1147)
but on that day it sprang forth on its own
ceaselessly from the barren mountaintop,
and locals from that day have called the spring
"The Font of Jason." Then they held a feast
in honor of the goddess of that mountain,   1535
the Mountain of the Bears, and sang the praises
of Rhea, Rhea, Queen of Many Names.

The storm winds died by daybreak, and they left
the island under oar. And then a spirit
of healthy competition spurred the heroes   1540
to find out which of them would weary last.
The air had calmed around them, and the waves
fallen asleep. Trusting in these conditions,
they heaved the *Argo* on with all their might.
Not even lord Poseidon's tempest-footed   1545 (1158)
stallions could have outstripped them as they dashed
across the sea.
                    But when the violent winds
that rise up fresh from rivers in the evening
had riled the swell again, the heroes tired
and gave up trying. Heracles alone,   1550

he and his boundless strength, pulled all those weary
oarsmen along. His labor sent a shudder
through the strong-knit timbers of the ship,
and soon the *Argo* raised Rhyndacus strait
and the colossal barrow of Aegaeum.   1555

But as they passed quite near the Phrygian coast
in their desire to reach the Mysian land,
Heracles, in the very act of plowing
deep furrows through the sea swell, broke his oar
and toppled sideways. While the handle stayed   1560 (1169)
locked in his fist, the ocean caught and carried
the blade off in the *Argo*'s wake. He sat up,
dumbstruck, silent, swiveling his eyes:
his hands were not accustomed to disuse.

At just the hour when a field hand,   1565
a plowman, gratefully forsakes the furrows
to head home hungry for his evening meal
and squats on weary knees, sun-burned, dust-caked,
before the door, eying his calloused hands
and calling curses down upon his belly,   1570
the heroes reached the land of the Cianians
who dwell beneath Mount Arganthonia
along the delta of the Cius River.

Since they had come in peace, the local people,
Mysians by race, received them warmly   1575 (1179)
and gave provisions, sheep and ample wine,
to satisfy their needs. Some of the heroes
collected kindling; others gathered leaves
out of the fields to make up mattresses;
still others grated fire out of sticks,   1580
decanted wine in bowls, and, after giving
due offerings at dusk to Lord Apollo,
the God of Embarkation, cooked a feast.

After encouraging his friends to banquet
heartily, Heracles the son of Zeus   1585

set out into the woods to find a tree
to carve into an oar that fit his hands.
He wandered for a while until he spotted
a pine with few boughs and a dearth of needles,
most like a poplar in its height and girth.   1590 (1190)

He set his bow and arrow-bearing quiver
straightway upon the ground and laid aside
the lion skin. Then, leveling his club,
a great big bronze-encinctured log, he loosened
the trunk inside the soil. With all his faith   1595
placed in his strength, he wrapped his arms around it,
squared his shoulder, braced his feet, pulled tight,
and heaved it, deeply rooted though it was,
out of the earth, with big clods dangling from it.

In just the way that, after dire Orion   1600
has made his stormy setting in the sea,
a sudden bluster from above assails
a ship's mast unexpectedly and snaps it
free of the stays and wedges, Heracles
ripped out the pine. Afterward he retrieved   1605 (1205)
his bow and arrows, lion skin, and club
and went galumphing shoreward.
                                    Meanwhile Hylas
had taken up a pitcher cast in bronze
and wandered far from his companions, seeking
a holy flowing river, so that he   1610
might draw off water for the evening meal.
He wanted to get everything in order
promptly, before his lord came back to camp.

Such were the habits Heracles himself
had fostered since he first took Hylas, then   1615
a toddler, from the palace of his father,
the noble Theodamas, whom the hero
ruthlessly slew among the Dryopes
in a dispute about a plowing ox.
You see, this Theodamas had been poor,   1620 (1213)

so he was furrowing his fields himself
when Heracles commanded him to yield
the plowing ox or else. The hero did this
only to find a pretext for a war
against the Dryopes because they lived   1625
scornful of justice—but this tale would steer
my song too far from its purported subject.

Soon Hylas happened on a spring called Pegae
among the locals. As it chanced, the nymphs
were just then gathering to dance. In fact,   1630
the nymphs who dwelled upon that lovely summit
convened each night to honor Artemis
in song. All those whose haunts were peaks and torrents—
the guardian forest nymphs—were in the woods
chanting their hymns.
               But one, a water nymph,   1635 (1228)
had surfaced from the sweetly flowing spring,
and she could see the boy, how flush with beauty
he was, how captivating in his sweetness,
because the moon shone full and clear above them
and cast its beams on him. The goddess Cypris   1640
so roused the nymph that she could hardly keep
her heart together. Rapture struck her helpless.

As soon as he was laid at length and dipping
the pitcher in the spring, just as the surface
water came rushing in and gurgled echoes   1645
inside the bronze, she threw her left arm up
around his neck. An urgent need to kiss
his plush lips moved her, so her right hand tugged
his elbow closer, closer—down he plunged
into the swirling water.
             Polyphemus   1650 (1240)
son of Eilatus was the only one
of all the crew to hear the boy cry out.
He had been walking down the path to greet
colossal Heracles on his return.
He dashed toward Pegae like some savage beast   1655

that baas and bleats have summoned from afar.
On fire with hunger, it pursues the sheep
but never reaches them because the shepherds
already have enclosed them in the fold.
Just as that creature snorts and roars horribly   1660
until he tires, so did Polyphemus
groan horribly and range about the place
hallooing, but his shouts were all in vain.

So, whipping out his broadsword with dispatch,
he hurried farther down the path, afraid   1665 (1250)
that wild animals were mangling Hylas
or kidnappers had lain in ambush for him
and were that moment dragging him away,
an all-too-easy prey. As, sword in hand,
he ran along, he spotted Heracles   1670
and recognized at once what man it was
galumphing through the twilight toward the ship.
Breath laboring, heart pounding, Polyphemus
divulged at once the dire calamity:

"Poor friend, I shall be the first to tell you   1675
news of a shocking loss. Though Hylas left
to fetch some water, he has not come safely
back to us. Bandits nabbed him and decamped
or beasts have eaten him. I heard his cry."

So he explained, and at his words abundant   1680 (1261)
sweat tumbled down from Heracles' temples,
and bad blood boiled blackly in his guts.
He hurled the fir tree to the ground in rage
and set out running, and his feet impelled him
at top speed down the path.
                              As when a bull   1685
that has been goaded by a gadfly bolts
out of the meadows and the fens and, heedless
of herd and herdsmen, rushes here and there,
and only stops to rear his thick dewlap
and roar in vain at the relentless stinging,   1690
so in his frenzy Heracles at one time

worked his frantic knees incessantly
and at another paused the search to heave
a mighty bellow far into the distance.

Soon the morning star had risen over   1695 (1273)
the highest summits, and a breeze got up,
and Tiphys promptly roused the crew to clamber
aboard and take advantage of the wind.
Straightaway they embarked and with a will
pulled up the anchor stone and hauled the cables   1700
astern. The mainsail bellied with the gale,
and they were happy to be far from shore
coasting around the Posideian headland.
Only after Bright-Eyed Dawn had risen
from the horizon to the middle sky,   1705
and all the seaways were distinct and vivid,
and the dew-wet plains were spangling bright,
did they discern that they had accidentally
abandoned Heracles and Polyphemus.

Fierce was the quarrel that erupted then,   1710 (1284)
an ignominious row, since they had left
the bravest of the company behind.
Jason was so dumbstruck and at a loss
he uttered nothing one way or the other—
no, he just sat there gnawing at his heart,   1715
feeling the burden of catastrophe.
Rage laid its hands on Telamon, who told him:

"Go on, keep sitting there at ease like that
because you are the one who benefits
from leaving Heracles behind. You hatched   1720
this little scheme so that his fame in Greece
would not eclipse your own, that is, if ever
the gods consent to grant us passage home.
But what's the use in words? No, I will go
and bring him back, even if I must do it   1725 (1294)
without your claque of co-conspirators."

So he accused them all, then charged at Tiphys
the son of Hagnias. His eyes were blazing

like twists of flame inside a raging bonfire.
They would have all sailed back across the gulf   1730
and braved its constant gales and deep-sea swell
to reach again the Mysian dominions,
had not the sons of Thracian Boreas
broken in and with harsh reproaches stopped
Telamon short—a ruinous decision!   1735
Terrible vengeance later came upon them
at Heracles' hands because they chose
to halt the search for him: when they were heading
home from the funeral games of Pelias,
he killed them on the isle of Tenos, heaped   1740 (1305)
barrows above them, and erected two
pillars on top (one of the pillars swivels
in answer to the breath of Boreas—
a clever thing, a wonder to behold).

Out of the salt sea's depths appeared, just then,   1745
Glaucus, the eloquent interpreter
for holy Neleus—a shaggy head
emerged, and then a torso to the waist.
His right hand resting on the *Argo*'s keel,
he bellowed at the agitated sailors: 1750

"Why, in contempt of mighty Zeus' will,
have you resolved to drag bold Heracles
the whole way to Aeëtes' citadel?
Heracles' lot is bound to Argos: heavy
toil for presumptuous Eurystheus   1755 (1317)
until he finishes the full twelve labors—
and he will sit at the immortals' banquet
if only he completes a last few more.
So let his loss occasion no regret.

Likewise with Polyphemus, who is destined   1760
to build beside the Cius River's mouth
a famous citadel among the Mysians
and then go off to meet his destiny
in the unbounded Chalybian waste.

As for the loss of Hylas, here's the cause: 1765
a holy nymph has dragged him off as husband
because she loves him. When those heroes ran
to rescue Hylas, they were left behind."

After these words he dove and cloaked his body
in the unresting swell. The dark-blue wake   1770 (1327)
that boiled out of his plunge rose up behind
the hollow ship and drove it through the waves.
The men took solace in the prophecy,
and Telamon went running up to Jason,
gripped his hand, embraced him, and proclaimed: 1775

"Do not be angry with me, son of Aeson,
if, in my thoughtlessness, I gave offense.
Overwhelming sorrow made me utter
a rash, insufferable accusation.
Let us cast that error to the winds   1780
and be as friendly as we were before."

Jason replied with due consideration:

"You certainly accused me, dear old friend,
of dirty dealing when you claimed, in public,
I had betrayed a man that loved me well.   1785 (1338)
Still, I shall foster bitter wrath against you
no longer, grossly slandered though I was,
since it was not for wealth or flocks of sheep
that you succumbed to rage, but for a man,
your comrade. No, no, I sincerely hope   1790
that you would fight like that on my behalf,
should such a thing befall me in the future."

After these words they both sat down together,
side by side and friendly as before.

As for the two who had been left behind   1795
(as Zeus himself intended), Polyphemus
son of Eilatus was indeed predestined

to found among the Mysians a city
named from the Cius River; Heracles
was bound as well to heavy labor under   1800 (1347)
Eurystheus' thumb. Before he left, though,
he threatened to annihilate the Mysians
right then and there if they did not divulge
the fate of Hylas, whether he was dead
or living. They selected and surrendered,   1805
in pawn, the children of their noblemen
and promised they would never give up searching.
Still today the Cianian people
ask after Hylas son of Theodamas
and recognize a bond with well-built Trachis,   1810
the town where Heracles immured the boys
they gave as pledges to be led away.

All day, all night a stiff wind kept on blowing,
pushing the *Argo* onward, but by dawn
nothing was stirring, not the slightest breeze.   1815 (1359)
They spotted on the coast a jutting headland
which, from the gulf, looked wide and welcoming
and, as the sun came up, they rowed ashore.

BOOK 2

Haughty Amycus, the Bebrycian king,
kept farms and cattle paddocks near the shore.
Begotten by Poseidon Patriarch
on a Bithynian nymph named Melia,
he was the most obnoxious man alive.   5
It was his savage custom to permit
no visitors to exit his dominions
until they met him in a boxing match,
and he had beaten many of his neighbors
to death.
            On this occasion King Amycus   10
came strutting straight up to the heroes' ship
and scornfully dispensed with asking them
who they might be and why they made the journey.
No, he just dropped a challenge on them all:

"Listen to me, you seaborne derelicts,   15 (11)
and learn what you most certainly should know.
The law here stipulates no foreigner
that comes ashore upon Bebrycian land
may ever leave again until he holds up
his fists against my fists and fights with me.   20
So quick, now, pick the strongest man among you
and let him step right up and face the challenge.
Be warned, though: if you spurn our laws, brute force
will grab you, and the outcome will be dire."

So snarled he, certain he was tough, and wild   25
resentment gripped the heroes at his words.

The challenge wounded Polydeuces most,
and he leapt up to represent his comrades:

"Hold on. Whoever you presume to be,
it's hardly necessary to insult us   30 (23)
with crass displays of force. We shall obey
your laws and customs. I myself am eager
to satisfy your challenge on the spot."

Such was his blunt rejoinder, and Amycus
swiveled his eyes and glared at Polydeuces,   35
just as a lion wounded by a spear
and hemmed around by men on every side
focuses solely on the one that first
struck him but failed to land a fatal blow.

Tyndareus' son then laid aside   40
the lightweight cloak one of the girls of Lemnos
gave him as a parting gift. Amycus
undid, in turn, his doubly thick black mantle
clasp by clasp and threw his notched and knotted
olive-wood crook of kingship to the ground.   45 (34)

As soon as they had found a spot nearby
to function as a ring, they sat their rival
companies separately from one another
along the sand. The two contestants differed
greatly in stature and physique: Amycus   50
looked like the monstrous spawn of grim Typhoeus
or even one of the abominations
Earth herself had brought up long ago
to challenge Zeus. Tyndareus' son,
in contrast, shimmered like the star of heaven   55
that shoots its brightest beams against the darkness
at evening time. Yes, he was Zeus' son—
a soft down sprouting on his cheeks, his eyes
aglint with joy, he gloried like a beast
in godlike strength. Whereas he shadowboxed   60 (45)
to prove his fists were sportive as before

and not benumbed by handling an oar,
Amycus scorned such exercise. He simply
stood there in silence, glaring at his foe,
heart pounding with the urge to shatter ribs   65
and spatter blood.
               Amycus' assistant
Lycoreus set down before their feet
two pairs of tanned and toughened rawhide straps.
Haughtily, then, the king addressed his rival:

"No need to bother drawing lots. Go on   70
and pick whichever set of straps you like—
that way you cannot say I tricked you later.
Go on, now, wrap them round your hands and then
learn well and tell all other men how skilled
I am at toughening and cutting ox hide   75 (58)
and spattering the cheeks of men with blood."

So spoke the braggart king. But Polydeuces
did not respond in kind, no, he just smiled
and chose the straps that lay before his feet.
Castor and Talaus the son of Bias   80
jogged in and tied the straps on, all the while
pumping him up with fervor for the match.
Aretus and Ornytus did the same
for King Amycus, nor did they suspect,
poor fools, his highness was a doomed man facing   85
his final match.
             Soon as the straps were wrapped
around their hands, they squared off toe-to-toe,
hefted their huge fists up before their faces,
and charged in, bringing all their weight to bear
each on the other. On a choppy sea   90 (70)
a violent wave will rear above a ship,
then, just as it is poised to swamp the deck,
the helmsman's skill will save her by a hairsbreadth,
and off she glides unscathed. Just so Amycus
pounded and pounded and allowed no respite,   95
while Polydeuces with superior skill

baffled the onslaught and remained uninjured.
Once he had learned the strengths and weaknesses
of his opponent's brutish fighting style,
he stood his ground and gave him blow for blow.   100
Imagine shipwrights' hammers, how they pound
tapering dowels into sturdy planks—
the thumping sounds incessantly—that's how
the cheeks and chins of both opponents sounded.
Teeth shattering with constant horrid cracks,   105 (83)
the men did not stop pummeling each other
until sheer lack of breath had overcome them.

They drew apart a spell and, panting, woozy,
wiped streams of perspiration from their brows.
Soon, though, they charged again, like bulls in heat   110
fighting to win a pasture-fattened heifer.
Amycus stretched his torso, stood on tiptoe
like a butcher poised to slay an ox,
then brought the weighty bottom of his fist
hammering down. But Polydeuces tilted   115
his head in time and dodged the brunt of it.
The heavy blow went glancing off his shoulder.
Then Polydeuces leaned in closer, locked
his leg behind his foe's, and with a swift heave
haymakered him above the ear. The skull   120 (95)
cracked, and Amycus crumpled to his knees
in agony. The Minyan heroes cheered
when life came spurting from the big man's head.

Far from abandoning their king, however,
his loyal soldiers took up gnarled clubs   125
and hunting spears and charged at Polydeuces
in one mad rush. The heroes interlocked
their shields before him and unsheathed their swords.

Castor was first to strike. A man ran up,
and Castor axed him in the head, the head   130
split down the middle, and the halves flopped over
onto his shoulders. Straight out of his triumph

Polydeuces felled Itymoneus
and Mimas: with a flying leap he struck
the one beneath the chest and knocked him flat;   135 (106)
then, when the other made a rush, he struck
his left eye with his right hand, tore away
the eyelid, and the eyeball stood there naked.

Amycus' hotheaded squire Oreides
wounded Talaus the son of Bias   140
but missed the kill, because his brazen spear tip
merely grazed the skin beneath the belt
and wholly missed the vitals. Then Aretus
leveled his weather-hardened club and thumped
Iphitus, rugged scion of Eurytus.   145
But Iphitus was not yet doomed to die,
and soon enough Aretus was himself
cut down by Clytius' sword. Ancaeus,
the dauntless son of King Lycurgus, took up
a massive ax and, with his left arm swinging   150 (119)
a shield of black-bear hide before him, leapt
fiercely into the fray. When Telamon
and Peleus, offspring of Aeacus, rushed in
behind him, warlike Jason joined their charge.

Imagine how, upon a winter's day,   155
gray wolves will suddenly descend, unmarked
by herdsmen and precision-sniffing hounds,
to terrorize a flock of countless sheep—
how, as the wolves glare back and forth deciding
which one to pounce on first and carry off,   160
the sheep stand clumped together, tripping over
each other—that's the way the heroes sent
grim panic through the proud Bebrycians.

And as when beekeepers or herdsmen smoke
a giant hive concealed in a rock,   165 (131)
the bees at first are crowded and confused,
abuzz with rage, and then the sooty coils
of vapor suffocate them, and they all

dart from the rock and scatter far and wide,
so the Bebrycians did not hold firm   170
for long, but fled in all directions, bearing
news of Amycus' demise. The fools
had not yet realized another crushing
disaster was at hand. That very day,
now that their king was dead, the hostile spears   175
of Lycus and his Mariandynians
were pillaging their villages and vineyards
(the two were rival peoples, always feuding
over a territory rich in iron).

So the heroes raided all the stalls   180 (142)
and rounded up vast flocks and, as they did it,
this was how they were talking to each other:

"Just think of how those cowards would have fallen
if Zeus had somehow left us Heracles.
I am quite sure that, had he been at hand,   185
the boxing match would not have taken place.
No, when Amycus swaggered up to us
to bray his laws, a thumping would have made him
forget his pride and all his proclamations.
We did a thoughtless thing indeed by leaving   190
that man behind and heading out to sea.
Each one of us will come to know death ruin
intimately, now that he is gone."

That's how they talked, but Zeus, of course, had brought
the loss of Heracles to pass on purpose.   195 (154)

The heroes spent the night there, bound the wounded,
and, after making sacrifice, prepared
a mighty banquet. After dinner, though,
slumber was far from holding sway beside
the wine bowl and the blazing sacrifices.   200
Once they had crowned their golden hair with laurel
that grew along the same shore where the cables
were bound, the heroes sang a victory ode
in harmony with Orpheus' lyre,

and the unruffled shore enjoyed their singing,   205
since they were celebrating Polydeuces,
the boy whom Zeus had fathered in Therapna.

But when the sun came over the horizon,
lit the dewy hills and roused the shepherds,
the heroes lugged aboard the spoils that seemed   210 (166)
most useful, loosed the cables from the laurel,
and coasted with a friendly wind behind them
into the roiling Bosporus.
                                      There wave
on wave, like heaven-climbing mountains reaching
above the clouds, shoot up before a ship's prow,   215
hover a while and then come crashing down.
One would assume no vessel could endure
so dire a doom suspended like a savage
storm cloud above the mainmast. But these threats
are navigable to a hardy helmsman.   220
So, guided by the skillful hands of Tiphys,
they coasted onward, frightened but alive,
and lashed their cables on the following day
to Thynia on the opposing coast.

Phineus the son of Agenor   225 (178)
was living in a house there near the shore,
suffering more than any man alive
because of the prophetic skill Apollo
had granted him some years before. You see,
he never paid due reverence to the gods,   230
not even Zeus himself, since he divulged
their sacred will too thoroughly to mortals.
Zeus smote him, therefore, with a long old age
and plucked the honeyed sunlight from his eyes.
Still worse, he never could enjoy the lavish   235
banquets the locals heaped up in his house
when they arrived to ask their fortunes. Harpies
would always swoop down with rapacious maw
and snatch the food out of his hands and lips.
Sometimes they left behind no food at all   240 (189)

and sometimes just a morsel, so that he
might go on living in despair. Still worse,
they left a foul stench on the leftovers,
and no one dared to lift them to his mouth
or even stand nearby, because they reeked   245
so hideously.
           As soon as Phineus
discerned the heroes' footsteps and halloos,
he knew what men had come—those at whose coming
the oracle of Zeus had prophesied
he would again be able to enjoy   250
comfortable meals. He struggled out of bed
like an ethereal dream and then, propped on
a walking stick, tapped over to the door
by fingering his way along the walls.
His joints were trembling with age and weakness   255 (200)
as he divined the exit. Scabrous skin
coated in dirt was all that held his bones
together. Once he reached the door, his knees
buckled. He crumpled on the courtyard threshold.
Dark dizziness enveloped him. The ground,   260
it seemed, was spinning, and he slipped away
into a torpor, helpless, speechless, still.

Soon as the heroes spotted him, they gathered
around in awe. After a while he sucked
a rasp up from the bottom of his lungs   265
and uttered prophecy unto them:
                        "Hear me,
bravest of the Hellenic heroes—that is,
if you are actually the men whom Jason
leads in the *Argo* questing for the fleece
under the orders of a ruthless king.   270 (210)
Yes, it is you. My mind has grasped the fact
through divination. Racked by miserable
afflictions though I am, I still shall give
Apollo son of Leto proper credit.

By Zeus the guardian of suppliants   275
and sternest judge of sinful men, by Phoebus,
by Hera, too, who most of all the gods

protects your quest, I beg you, help me please!
Save an accursed man from degradation.
Please, oh, please, do not just sail away   280
and with indifference leave me as I am.
Not only has a Fury dug her feet
into my eyes, not only must I drag out
old age interminably day by day,
but, in addition to these woes, a still   285 (222)
more bitter evil lurks above me: Harpies
swoop down from some exotic nest of spite
and rip the food out of my mouth. I know
no way I can relieve myself of them.
When famished for a meal, more easily   290
could I escape from my own mind than them,
so swiftly do they plummet through the air.

And even when they leave some scrap behind,
it breathes an odor putrid and unbearable.
No mortal could endure approaching it,   295
not even if his heart were forged of iron.
But bitter, cruel necessity compels me
to stay there all the same and, while I'm there,
force it into my miserable stomach.

An oracle holds the sons of Boreas   300 (234)
shall stop the Harpies' aerial thefts and, trust me,
whoever does so will be dear to me,
that is, if I am still that Phineus known
for wealth and seercraft, and if indeed
I am my father's son, and if indeed,   305
when king of Thrace, I purchased Cleopatra
(the sister of you sons of Boreas)
with bridal gifts and brought her to my home."

So spoke the son of Agenor, and deep
compassion worked its way through all the heroes,   310
especially the sons of Boreas.
As soon as Zetes had repressed his tears,
he went up to the venerable man,
a man of sorrow, took his hand and said:

"Sad old man, of all the men on Earth   315 (244)
not one, I swear, has suffered more than you.
Why have so many woes been heaped upon you?
Surely you must have uttered prophecies
in awful brashness to offend the gods
and make them rage so violently against you.   320
Nevertheless, keen as we are to help,
the minds within us are uneasy, wondering
whether some god has truly offered us
this special honor. Here among us mortals
gods' punishments hit all too close to home.   325
So, though we long to help you, we shall not
drive off the Harpies till you promise us
that we shall not incur the gods' disfavor
because of it."
    So Zetes sought assurance.
The old man opened up his empty orbs,   330 (254)
swiveled them round to him and answered,
           "Hush,
my child. Don't fill your head with thoughts like those.
I call as witness Leto's son, the god
who kindly taught me the prophetic art;
I call the dismal fate that is my lot,   335
to wit, this smoky cloud upon my eyes;
I call as well the Gods of Underground
(when I am dead, may they be kind to me)—
yes, in the names of all these powers, I swear
the gods will not resent the help you give me."   340

After this oath the sons of Boreas
were keen to drive the Harpies off. Straightway
the younger heroes put a feast together,
the Harpies' final meal, and Calaïs
and Zetes stood on either side of Phineus,   345 (265)
ready to snatch their weapons up as soon as
the Harpies swooped.
       At just the very moment
the old man laid his hands on food, the Harpies
descended without warning from the clouds,

like gales, like lightning, shrieking out their hunger.   350
The heroes shouted when they saw them coming
but, even as they shouted, *whoosh*! the creatures
had gobbled up the banquet and were gone
far, far away across the sea. The stench
they left behind them was insufferable.   355
Nevertheless, the sons of Boreas
took sword in hand and flew off in pursuit.
Zeus gave them boundless speed. Without his help,
they never could have kept up since the Harpies
had always outstripped even Zephyr's gales   360 (277)
both when they dived for Phineus and left him.
Imagine mastiffs on a mountainside,
pedigreed trackers, chasing goats and deer—
how, when their muzzles near the quarry's haunches,
their fangs can snap and snap to no avail,   365
that's how the brothers Calaïs and Zetes
swooped in behind the Harpies' tail feathers
and grazed them with their fingertips in vain.
They were at last quite close to catching them
way out above the Ever-Floating Isles   370
and surely would have cut the fiends to pieces,
contrary to the gods' intent, had not
swift Iris seen them, streaked out of the sky,
and halted them with these imperious terms:

"Justice forbids you, sons of Boreas,   375 (288)
from touching with your swords almighty Zeus'
feathered hounds, the Harpies. But I here
do solemnly proclaim that they shall never
again return to bother Phineus."

She swore an oath upon the river Styx   380
(the gods' most firm and formidable pledge),
vowing the Harpies never in the future
would come and harry Phineus' house—
so had the Fates ordained. The brothers yielded
before the oath and turned around to fly   385
back to the ship, and still today men call

the islands where they turned the Turning Isles
and not the Floating Isles (their former name).
Then Iris and the Harpies parted ways:
the latter to Minoan Crete to find   390 (299)
their cage again; the former fluttering
on rapid wings back up to Mount Olympus.

The men meanwhile were scrubbing years of foulness
off the old man's hide and sacrificing
sheep taken from the plunder of Amycus.   395
Once they had cooked them up, they held a banquet.
Phineus ate as well, and ravenously,
sating his lust as people do in dreams.
When they had dined and drunk themselves to fullness,
the heroes stayed awake all night awaiting   400
Zetes and Calaïs. The aged seer
sat at the hearth among them, prophesying
how they should travel to complete their quest:

"Now heed me well. The gods do not permit you
to know in detail all that is to come,   405 (312)
but what they do permit I shall reveal.
You see, I made an error long ago
by rashly prophesying Zeus' plans
from start to finish. He himself insists
humanity possess, through divination,   410
abridged foreknowledge, so that we are always
lacking some portion of divine intent.

When you depart from me, you will discern,
first off, the Cobalt Clashing Rocks, two headlands
right where the estuary narrows. No one,   415
and I repeat, no one, has ever sailed
between them. Lacking deep bedrock to root them
into the ocean floor, they often crash
together into one, and briny spume
boils above them, and the rugged shores   420 (323)
roar hoarsely. Therefore, if you are endowed
with prudent thoughts and truly fear the gods,

if you are not mere reckless adolescents
heading for a self-assured destruction,
heed my instructions now:
                         Send out a dove   425
to fly before the ship and as an omen
test the Rocks. If it survives the flight
through them into the Pontus, all of you
no longer hold off on your outward journey
but grip the oars solidly in your hands   430
and cleave that narrow stretch of sea. Survival
will then depend less on how hard you pray
than on how strong your hands are. Scorn distraction
and heave, heave all your strength into the oars—
though, mind you, I do not forbid you prayer   435 (336)
before that time.
               However, if the dove
dies halfway through, you may as well start sailing
for home again, since it is far, far better
to bow before god's will. No, even if
your ship had iron planks, you couldn't then   440
escape a dismal fate between the Rocks.
Unlucky men, do not then disregard
my prophecy, not even if you think
the gods upon Olympus loathe me three times
more than in fact they do—no, even if   445
you think they loathe me more than that—do not
defy the dove and push the *Argo* onward.
What will come to pass will come to pass.

But if you do outrun the Rocks' concussion
and coast, unscathed, into the Pontic Sea,   450 (346)
sail with the land of the Bithynians
to port and guard against the barrier reefs
until you round the swiftly flowing Rhebas
and Sable Promontory and at last
make landfall on the Isle of Thynias.   455
From Thynias row out across the sea
and put in at the Mariandynian land
opposite. There a footpath switchbacks down

to Hades, and the Acherousian headland
pierces the sky, and Acheron's white spate   460
shoots out of an unfathomable chasm
and flows back down by cutting through the cape.
Once you have passed this river, you will pass
the uplands of the Paphlagonians.
Their patriarch was Enetean Pelops—   465 (359)
such is the blood that courses through their veins.

There, underneath the astral Bear Helica,
a headland rises steep on all sides round.
Carambis is its name. The seaward face
projects so high that Boreas' squalls   470
split on its summit. You will find the Long Shore
stretching beyond it. At the farther end,
beyond a jutting cape, the river Halys
disgorges a bewilderment of froth.
Not at all far from there, the Iris drains   475
its less tumultuously churning current
into the sea. Still farther on from there
a large, sharp cape projects out of the coast.
Beyond it you will find the Thermodon,
which, after wandering across the mainland,   480 (370)
ends in a tranquil harbor at the base
of the Themiscyreian promontory.
Here are the steppes of Doeas, and the three
forts of the Amazons that stand upon them.

Next you will reach those miserable wretches   485
the Chalybes who live upon a pinched,
illiberal soil. They are heavy drudges,
workers in iron. Tibarenians,
men rich in sheep, dwell on a plain nearby
beneath the Genetaen cape, a site   490
sacred to Zeus the God of Guests and Hosts.

Next in line and neighbors to these men
the Mossynoeci dwell on woodland plains
and mountain spurs and cols. They build their homes
from bark inside of towers made of timber,   495 (381)

rugged towers. They call the things 'mossynes'
and take their name from them.
                                        Once you have passed them,
make landfall on the barren isle nearby,
but only after using every means
to drive off the repugnant, homicidal   500
birds who nest on it in countless numbers.
Here Otrera and Antiope,
two Amazonian queens, once built a shrine
in Ares' name when they were on campaign.
Here from the unforgiving sea a boon   505
will come to you, a boon I dare not name.
Still, I exhort you with benign insistence
to harbor there. Why should I go too far
a second time with my prophetic art?
Why tell you everything from start to finish?   510 (391)

Beyond this island and the facing coastline
dwell the Philyres; the Macrones next,
and next in turn the multitudinous tribes
of the Becheirieans. Next in order
dwell the Sapeires, the Byzeri, then   515
the warlike Colchians themselves at last.

Still, you should travel farther on until
you reach the limit of the Pontic Sea.
Here on the mainland near the city Cyta
the raucous Phasis, after racing down   520
the Amarantian mountains and across
the plain of Circe, empties liberally
into the sea.
                    While rowing up that river
you will discern the towers of Aeëtes
at Cyta, and the gloomy grove of Ares   525 (403)
where a serpent dreadful to behold,
a monster, glares all round, forever guarding
the fleece that lies across an oak tree's crown.
Neither day nor night does honeyed slumber
vanquish the thing's insatiable surveillance."   530

Such was his prophecy, and terror gripped
the heroes. Long they stood there gaping, dumbstruck.
At last the son of Aeson, at a loss
before the terror of it all, spoke out:

"Venerable man, thus far you have foretold   535
the ways and worries of our quest's completion
and warned us of the omen we must heed
when passing through those dreadful Clashing Rocks
into the Pontic Sea. But I am eager
to learn as well if we must suffer through them   540 (414)
a second time while sailing back to Greece.
How can I do it? How can I survive
a second endless journey through the sea?
I am an untried man, my comrades, too,
are untried men, and Colchian Aea   545
lies at the limit of the Pontic Sea,
the far end of the earth!"
                                   So Jason spoke.
The hoary prophet uttered in response:

"Once you have passed those deadly Rocks alive,
my son, have confidence. Some god will guide you   550
along a different path out of Aea,
and on the way there you'll have guides enough.
But I advise you, friends, do not dismiss
the goddess Cypris and her slippery
assistance, since the glorious fulfillment   555 (424)
of your adventure lies with her. No further,
ask me no further questions on these matters."

So prophesied the son of Agenor.
Just then the sons of Thracian Boreas
came swooping down out of sky and brought   560
their feathered feet to rest upon the threshold.
All the heroes leapt out of their seats
at their return. Still panting from exertion,
Zetes informed his eager audience
how far they drove the Harpies, how the goddess   565

Iris had flown in, blocked the slaughter of them,
and kindly sworn an oath, and how the Harpies
had taken refuge in a giant cave
within Mount Dicte.
               Their report delighted
everyone, but Phineus most of all,   570 (436)
and Jason son of Aeson, overflowing
with kindliness, addressed the aged man:

"Phineus, certainly some god has looked
warmly on your distress and brought us here
from Hellas so that Boreas' sons   575
could save you. Now, if only light could shine
again within your eyes, I'd be as happy
as if I had returned to Greece in safety."

So he proclaimed, but Phineus glumly answered:

"My blindness, Jason, cannot be undone,   580
nor is there hope it will be in the future.
My eyes are void, completely withered. No,
I wish some god would grant me death instead.
When I am dead and gone, I shall be basking
in perfect brilliance."
               Thus the two men spoke,   585 (448)
and soon thereafter, while they were conversing,
Dawn the Early Riser came again,
and Phineus' neighbors gathered round him—
the men who, in the time before the Harpies,
came every morning, bearing him some food   590
out of their stores. An old man even then,
he gave his prophecies and heartfelt blessings
to all who came, even the poorest of them,
and soothed the woes of many with his art.
That's why the people came and cared for him.   595

Among them was a certain man, Paraebius,
Phineus' most devoted friend,
and he was glad to find the strangers there

because the seer had long ago proclaimed
a band of heroes on a voyage bound   600 (459)
from Hellas to Aeëtes' citadel
would tie their cables to the Thynian land
and, with divine approval, stop the Harpies
from landing there. Once Phineus had sated
these guests with prudent words, he sent them out   605
and asked Paraebius alone to stay
among the heroes. Then he sent him out
to lead the finest sheep out of the folds.
Once he had left them, Phineus explained
gently about him to the gathered oarsmen: 610

"My friends, not everyone is arrogant
and heedless of a favor done to him.
This man, such as he is, once came to me
to learn about his destiny. You see,
though he had labored much and struggled more,   615 (471)
an ever-growing scarcity of means
kept grinding him away. Day after day
matters were worse for him until no ease
relieved his toil.
                    In fact, he had been paying
the dire wages of his father's error.   620
One day his father, in the act of felling
trees in the mountains, scorned a wood nymph's plea.
You see, she had been weeping, begging him
please not to chop her oak tree down, her age-mate.
She had been living in its trunk and boughs   625
for many years. He was a young man, though,
and scornful, so he rashly cut it down.
The wood nymph fixed the fate of constant failure
on him and all his heirs as retribution.

When Paraebius, that fellow's son,   630 (484)
came to me, I discerned the curse and told him
to build an altar to that Thynian nymph
and lavish gifts upon it in atonement,
begging her, all the while, please to forgive
his father's malice. Ever since he slipped   635

that god-sent doom, he has remembered me.
In fact, whenever I excuse him for a time,
he grudgingly departs, so scrupulous
is he in standing by me in my troubles."

So Phineus explained, and there he was,   640
Paraebius, at hand again, returning
with two sheep chosen from his master's sheepfold.
Jason arose and, at the old man's bidding,
the sons of Boreas stood up beside him.
Then, calling on Apollo God of Prophets,   645 (493)
Phineus slew the victims on the hearth
just as the day was drawing to a close.
The younger men prepared a heartening feast
for their companions. When they all had eaten,
some went to sleep among the *Argo*'s cables,   650
others in clusters all throughout the house.

That morning the Etesian Winds arose.
These are the winds that blow throughout the world
with equal strength, at the behest of Zeus.
A maiden named Cyrene, it is said,   655
once tended sheep among the men of yore
along the flats of the Peneus River.
She plied this trade because virginity
was sweet to her, and an untainted bed.
One day, while she was pasturing her flocks   660 (503)
along the riverbank, Apollo snatched her
up from Haemonia and set her down
among the nymphs who dwell in Libya
beside the Hill of Myrtles. There she bore
Phoebus a child, a son named Aristaeus   665
(though men in barley-rich Haemonia
know him as Agreus and Nomius).
The god so loved Cyrene that he made her
an ageless huntress in her newfound land.
He carried off the child, though, to be brought up   670
in Cheiron's cave. When he was grown, the Muses
arranged his marriage and instructed him
in all the arts of prophecy and healing.

They also made him keeper of the sheep
that grazed the Athamantian plain of Phthia   675 (514)
beside steep Othrys and the holy-flowing
Apidanus.
                When down out of the heavens
the Dog Star Sirius was searing all
the isles of Minos, and for many days
the locals suffered but could find no cure,   680
they begged assistance from the oracle
of Phoebus, who commanded them to summon
Aristaeus to expel the drought.
So, at his father's bidding, he set forth
from Phthia, rounded up some Parrhasians   685
(who are, in fact, the heirs of Lycaon),
and settled them in Ceos. There he raised
a mighty shrine to Zeus the God of Rain
and duly offered on the mountaintops
sacrifice to the Dog Star Sirius   690 (524)
and Zeus the son of Cronus. That is why
Etesian winds descend from Zeus to cool
the earth for forty days, and still today
the priests in Ceos offer sacrifice
before the Dog Star Sirius appears.   695
So runs the story of the winds.
                                The heroes
were held up there awhile and, every day
they stayed, the Thynians sent them countless presents
to thank them for relieving Phineus.
Then, once the gales had calmed, they built an altar   700
in honor of the twelve immortal gods
on the opposing shore, heaped it with gifts,
boarded the *Argo,* and began to row.
And they did not forget to bring along
a bashful dove—Euphemus was the one   705 (536)
who seized it, frightened, trembling, in his hand.
Then they unbound the cables from the land.

Nor did Athena fail to mark their heading.
All in an instant she had set her feet

upon an airy cloudlet that provided   710
swift conveyance, weighty though she was,
and so she hastened to the Pontic Sea
to do the crew a favor. When a man
goes traveling outside his fatherland
(as we long-suffering mortals often do),   715
no land seems out of reach, the ways and means
shine in his mind, and he can see his house
and picture traveling by path and channel
and with his swift thoughts visit now one country
and now another in imagination,   720 (546)
so Zeus' daughter leapt out of the cloud
and instantly set foot upon the hostile
Thynian shore.

        Soon as the heroes reached
the narrows of the mazy strait, they found
sharp outcrops closing in on either side   725
and hectic whirlpools churning up white water
around the ship. They made their way in horror.
The rumble of the Clashing Rocks already
assailed their senses, and the sea-washed headlands
echoed the noise.

        Euphemus then ascended   730
the prow beam, dove in hand, and all the oarsmen,
under the orders of the steersman Tiphys,
rowed at their ease to save up strength enough
to pull them through the crisis. When the heroes
rounded the final bend, they saw the Rocks   735 (560)
dividing, and their spirit drained away.

Euphemus launched the dove, which on its wings
shot forth and flew between the ranks of oarsmen.
They turned their heads to watch it go, and then
the two rock faces crashed together. Spouts   740
of seething spray shot upward like a mist,
the sea was far from cheerful in its roaring,
and everywhere the mighty air was trembling.
Down at the Rocks' foundations hollow sea caves
boomed as the brine came boiling up within them.   745

The white spume of the falling waves erupted
above the Rocks, and riptides spun the ship.
Still, though the twin peaks nipped her hindmost feathers,
the dove got clear—she made it through alive.

The oarsmen raised a hearty cheer, and Tiphys   750 (573)
commanded them to row with all their strength
because the Rocks were opening again.
Trembling seized them as they heaved, but soon
the same wave as before propelled them forward,
with its returning wash, between the Rocks.   755
Insufferable dread took hold of them:
the doom impending there on either side
seemed inescapable. Though for a moment
the level Pontus shimmered far and wide
beyond the Rocks, a sudden wave arose   760
before them, vaulted like a steep cliff face.
They cocked their heads to duck because it seemed
that arching wall of froth would soon collapse
onto the deck and swamp them. Just in time, though,
Tiphys reined the ship in as it labored   765 (584)
under the oars. The great wave slithered off
beneath the keel but, with its passing, lifted
the stern into the air and dragged the *Argo*
back outside the Clashing Rocks.
                                        Euphemus
walked the deck commanding his companions   770
to pour their strength into the oars. Groaning,
they struck the water. But whatever headway
the *Argo* made by rowing, it retreated
twice as far, and, as the heroes heaved,
the oars bent under them like back-bent bows.   775
A sudden wave then rushed them from behind,
and *Argo* coasted on the crest as smoothly
as if it were a sanded wooden roller.
So they proceeded through the air until
a whirlpool sucked them in and spun them round   780 (595)
between the agitated Clashing Rocks.
The hull was sea-stuck.

                        So Athena braced
her left hand on a crag for leverage
and with her right shoved *Argo* from the stern.
The ship went flying like a swift-winged arrow,   785
and, when the Rocks came hurtling together,
they only nipped the stern post's tip abaft.

Once they had gotten through alive, Athena
flew back to Mount Olympus, and the Rocks
were rooted firmly in one place forever,   790
just as the gods had fated would occur
whenever someone saw them clash together
and still sailed through them to the other side.

The heroes caught their breath at last, shook off
the chill of horror, then surveyed the sky   795 (607)
and flat sea stretching eastward out of view.
They felt as if they had escaped from Hades.

Tiphys was first to find his voice again:

"It was the ship itself, I think, that pulled us
out of that pinch. Athena, though, deserves   800
the highest praise, since it was she who breathed
magical strength into the hull when Argus
was pounding dowels home into the planks.
Wrecking this ship would be like sacrilege.
Now that a god has helped us to escape   805
those dreadful Clashing Rocks, no longer worry
about fulfilling Pelias' demands.
Phineus son of Agenor predicted
that, after this, our voyage would be easy."

So Tiphys reassured them as he steered   810 (619)
the ship through open sea beside the land
of the Bithynians. But Jason answered
with subtle words and sidelong purpose:
                                            "Tiphys,
why are you trying to console my grief?

I've made a horrid and unpardonable   815
blunder. When Pelias proposed the challenge,
I should have turned this journey down at once,
even if death, a savage death by torture,
was waiting for me. Now I wear a shroud
of fear and dread past bearing—loathing travel   820
across the frigid sea but loathing, too,
the thought of landing, since the local tribesmen
are hostile everywhere. Night after night,
since first you all assembled for my sake,
I have been spending wretched hours obsessing   825 (631)
over these worries. Each of you can speak
with unencumbered ease because you fear
for your one life alone, while I, your leader,
don't care a whit about my own but worry
for each and every hero on this quest: 830
What if I fail to bring him back to Hellas?"

So he proclaimed to test his comrades' mettle.
When they responded with enthusiastic
bellows and whoops, the heart grew warm within him.
When he spoke again, he spoke with candor: 835

"Dear friends, my courage thrives on your devotion.
Even if I should now be traveling
into the mouth of Hades, fear would never
take hold of me, because you all have proved
steadfast in time of crisis. Now that we   840 (644)
have sailed beyond the Clashing Rocks, I think
no future threat will be as great, so long
as we abide by Phineus' instructions."

Thus he encouraged them, and they at once
gave over conversation and returned   845
wholeheartedly to rowing. Soon they passed
the rapid Rhebas and Colona's peak,
the Sable Promontory and at last
the Phyllis River's mouth where, years before,
Dipascus kindly welcomed to his halls   850

Athamas' son Phrixus who was fleeing
Orchomenus, his hometown, on the ram.
Because a meadow nymph had borne Dipascus,
weapons and war did not appeal to him,
no, he preferred to settle with his mother   855 (656)
beside the waters of his father's river
and graze his flocks along the shore.
                                        The heroes,
in passing, gazed upon his monument,
the wide banks of the Phyllis, then the plain
beside it and the roiling Kalpa River.   860
The sun set, and they spent the windless night
just as they had been, heaving at the oars.
Imagine oxen laboring to furrow
muddy acres, how a spume of sweat
drips from their necks and flanks: their eyes roll sideways   865
under the yoke, and constant panting scours
their arid throats and issues from their mouths.
All day they churn the earth, digging their hooves in—
that's the way the heroes heaved the oars
out of the ocean swell.
                              At just the hour   870 (669)
when ambrosial dawn has not quite come
but there is not full darkness, since a haze
has crept into the night (that is, the hour
that early risers call "the morning twilight"),
the heroes rowed up to the desert island   875
of Thynias and with an insurmountable
weariness slogged ashore. The son of Leto
revealed himself there. He was leaving Lycia
and striding far away toward the expansive
dominions of the Hyperboreans.   880
And, as he moved, clusters of golden hair
swung loose and swept down over either cheek.
His left hand brandishing a silver bow,
a quiver hanging from his shoulder down
across his back, he trod his course. The island   885 (679)
quaked with each footstep, and the breakers washed up
onto the beaches. As they watched him, helpless

amazement seized them all, and no one dared
to look directly at his dazzling eyes.
They stood a long time gazing at the ground,   890
while he, aloof, proceeded through the air
across the sea. Some minutes later Orpheus
found his voice and said to his companions:

"Come now, and let us dedicate this island
to Phoebus God of Dawn and name it for him   895
since it was here that we have seen him passing
before us as the sunrise. We shall build
a seaside shrine and give what offerings
we can procure. Afterward, if he grants us
a safe homecoming in Haemonia,   900 (690)
we shall repay him with the burned thighbones
of hornéd goats. Now we must satisfy him
as best we can, with liquid offerings
and the aroma of the roast. O god,
O revelation, please advance our quest."   905

So he instructed them. Some right away
went to construct an altar out of stones
while others scoured the island in pursuit
of goat and deer, the sorts that commonly
reside in forests. Leto's son provided   910
good hunting, and they duly immolated
two thighbones from each kill upon the altar.

Then, as the meat was cooking, they performed
a choral dance in honor of Apollo,
the little boy, the Shooter of the Arrow.   915 (702)
The admirable offspring of Oeagrus
plucked his Bistonian lyre and started singing
how long ago Apollo on Parnassus
felled the beast Delphina with an arrow,
and he did this while still a naked toddler,   920
still delighting in his curly hair
(Be gracious, lord, I beg you. Eternally
your tresses are unshorn, eternally.

It's sacred law that only Leto, daughter
of Coeus, strokes them with her loving hands),   925
and the Corycian nymphs, the seed of Pleistus,
over and over urged the toddler on
by shouting *Hie* ("Shoot"), from which derives
the lovely ritual cry to summon Phoebus.

After the heroes celebrated him   930 (713)
with choral song, they poured out pure libations,
laid their hands upon the festal meat,
and swore an oath always to aid each other
with singleness of purpose. Still today
the shrine of kindly Harmony remains there,   935
the very one the heroes instituted
in honor of a venerable goddess.

Then, when the third dawn broke, they left the steep-cliffed
island with a strong west wind behind them.
That day they passed on the opposing coast   940
the mouth of the Sangarius, the buxom
Mariandynian fields, the Lycus River's
ecstatic spate, and Lake Anthemoesis,
and all the halyards and the tackle strained
before the gale as they went sailing onward.   945 (725)
The wind, though, started flagging in the night
and they were much relieved to reach at dawn
a bay inside the Acherousian headland,
a steep cape facing the Bithynian Sea.

The surf rolls in uproariously around   950
the polished boulders rooted to its base,
and plane trees flourish all across the crest
from which a hollow dale slopes gently inland.
Within that dale a cave that leads to Hades
lurks behind rocks and shrubs, and from its depths   955
a chilling vapor rises every morning
and gathers in a glistening frost that thaws
beneath the midday sun. Never does silence
descend upon this gloomy cape because

the restless sea stirs up a constant murmur   960 (741)
and subterranean breezes rouse the trees.
A river has its mouth here—Acheron,
which, following the valley from the crest,
cuts through the middle of the cape and empties
into the Eastern Sea. Megarians   965
out of Nisaea later dubbed this cape
"The Sailors' Savior" since it saved their ship
from a horrendous storm when they were sailing
to colonize the Mariandynian land.

Because the wind had recently died down   970
the Minyans were keen to row the *Argo*
inside this breakwater and moor it there.
The Mariandynians and their leader Lycus
were not long unaware the soldiers anchored
upon their shores were those who killed Amycus,   975 (754)
or so they had been told, and for that reason
they struck a truce, saluted Polyedeuces,
and welcomed him as if he were a god.
They had, you see, for quite some time been waging
war on the insolent Bebrycians.   980

When the heroes came to town, they feasted
a whole day at the court of Lycus, forged
the bonds of friendship, and relieved their hearts
with conversation. Jason named the names
and pedigrees of each of his companions,   985
explained what mission Pelias had set them,
how the Lemnian women welcomed them,
and all that happened with the Doliones
and Cyzicus their king. He also told him
how, when they came to Mysia and the Cius,   990 (766)
they happened to abandon Heracles,
what prophecies the sea god Glaucus gave them,
and how they beat Amycus and his people.
Next he recounted Phineus' woes
and prophecies and how they had survived   995
the Clashing Rocks and, only lately, spotted
the son of Leto rising from an island.

King Lycus took heartfelt delight in hearing
all these adventures just as they had happened,
but sorrow gripped him when he heard the news   1000
of the abandonment of Heracles,
and he commiserated with the heroes:

"Friends, you have lost a great man's help by losing
Heracles the hero in the midst of
your lengthy voyage to Aeëtes' palace.   1005 (775)
Heracles was my friend, in fact. I met him
here in my father Dascylus' house
long, long ago when he was traveling
through boundless Asia on a quest to win
the belt of war-obsessed Hippolyta.   1010

I was a young man when we met. The down
had only freshly sprouted on my cheeks,
and funeral games were being held in honor
of Priolas my brother. (Mysians killed him,
and since his death the people here have sung him   1015
heartrending dirges.) In the boxing match
Heracles beat the dashing Titias,
who was supreme among us younger men
in strength and beauty. Yes, he knocked his teeth out
onto the ground.
                    Heracles subjugated   1020 (786)
the Mysians beneath my father's rule,
then the Mygdones who are neighbors to us,
then some Bithynians and their land as far as
the Rhebas River and Colona's peak.
In fact, the Paphlagonian heirs of Pelops   1025
(that is, those hemmed in by the dark Billaeus)
surrendered without putting up a fight.

Lately, with Heracles gone far away,
haughty Amycus and his subject soldiers
had started cheating me, for years now chipping   1030
such large tracts from my realm that they have pushed
their kingdom's borders to the grass that lines
the deeply flowing Hypius River.

                                Now, though,
they have received their punishment from you,
and I suspect the gods were there supporting   1035 (798)
Tyndareus' son the day he beat
Amycus and defeated all his henchman
in battle. Therefore I shall gladly give you
whatever help I can, since this is simply
what weaker men should do when stronger men   1040
have done a good turn first. And I shall order
Dascylus my son to join your quest.
With him among you, you should find the natives
you meet along the way hospitable
as far off as the river Thermodon.   1045

Furthermore, I shall build a lofty temple
atop the Acherousian heights to honor
Tyndareus' sons, and every sailor
who sees their shrine, even from far away,
will ask their aid. Once I have built the temple,   1050 (809)
I shall consecrate, outside the city,
some fertile acres in our well-tilled plains
to yield them honor as if they were gods."

All day the heroes took delight in feasting,
then bustled back down to the ship. King Lycus   1055
gathered his train to follow them and gave them
numberless gifts. What's more, he sent his son
to make the quest among them.
                                    It was then
that Idmon son of Abas reached his destined
demise. Though he excelled at seercraft,   1060
his seercraft did not protect him, no,
necessity was pushing him toward doom.

There was a meadow near a reedy river.
A white-tusked boar was lounging in it, cooling
its flanks and massive belly in the mud—   1065 (819)
a lethal beast. Even the marsh nymphs feared it
feeding alone along the river flats.
No mortal knew that it was there.

When Idmon
was strolling on the muddy riverbank,
it rushed out of some purlieu in the willows,   1070
gored his thigh, cut through cartilage and femur.
Idmon shrieked and fell. His friends called out,
and Peleus quickly loosed a spear and struck
the monster as it fled into the swamp.
When it returned and charged them, Idas pierced it,   1075
and it collapsed upon the sharp tip, squealing.
Leaving it thus impaled, they trundled Idmon
back to the *Argo* where he coughed up blood
and shortly died in his inconsolable
comrades' arms.
They thought no more of sailing   1080 (835)
but stayed there, grieving, to entomb the body.
Three days they wailed and on the fourth interred him
with hero's honors. Lycus and his subjects
joined in the mourning, slaughtered many sheep
as funeral offerings around the tomb,   1085
as is the custom for the dear departed.
So in a foreign country Idmon's barrow
was heaped up, and a marker planted on it
for future generations to admire—
a wild olive tree, the tree of shipwrights,   1090
a tree that still is flourishing today
under the Acherousian cliffs.
Because
I heed the Muses' will, I must declare,
upfront, this fact as well: Phoebus Apollo
commanded the Boeotians and Niseans   1095 (847)
to worship Idmon as a city founder
and build a town around his barrow tree.
Today, though, all the Mariandynians there
venerate Agamestor rather than
god-fearing Idmon, Aeolus' grandson.   1100

Who else died there? (The heroes surely raised
a second barrow for a fallen comrade
because two mounds are standing to this day.)

Tiphys it was, the son of Hagnias—
so runs the story. It was not his fate   1105
to steer the *Argo* farther toward its goal.
Once they had buried Idmon, a malignant
disease afflicted Tiphys, left him prostrate
and bedrid far, far, from his fatherland.
Struck by these dreadful blows, the men gave way   1110 (858)
to absolute despair. Once they had buried
this second fallen comrade, they collapsed
beside the sea in utter helplessness,
shrouded their bodies tightly in their cloaks,
and lost all love of food and drink. Grief-stricken,   1115
they threw their hearts away because returning
to Greece was now outside their expectations.

They would have stayed there, grieving, even longer
had Hera not stepped in and filled Ancaeus
with special bravery. Astypylaia   1120
conceived him underneath the god Poseidon
and birthed him next to the Imbrasus River,
and he was wise in all the ways of seacraft.
This fellow rushed to Peleus and said:

"Son of Aeacus, how can it be noble   1125 (869)
to rest a long time in a foreign land,
shirking our task? Surely the son of Aeson
recruited me out of Parthenia
to undertake this journey for the fleece
more for my expertise in steering ships   1130
than making war. Therefore, don't have the slightest
fear for the *Argo*. There are expert sailors
among us, none of whom would wreck the voyage
if we should set him at the helm. Go swiftly,
tell our comrades all these things, be firm,   1135
force them to think again about the quest."

So he explained, and Peleus' spirit
leapt with delight, and he was quick to shout:

"Why, comrades, are we clinging to a sorrow
as profitless as this? These two have died,   1140 (881)

I think, the death they were allotted. Think, now,
there are other steersmen in our crew,
a number of them, so stop wasting time,
cast off your woes and rouse yourselves for labor."

Jason had nothing but despair to offer: 1145

"Son of Aeacus, where are all these helmsmen?
Those we regarded as our guides and experts
are lying there more dead to hope than I am.
Thus I foresee an evil ending for us
beside our fallen friends if we can neither   1150
reach the city of extreme Aeëtes
nor pass beyond the Rocks again and back
to Greece. An evil fate, one without glory,
will hide us here to age in idleness."

So he lamented, but Ancaeus promptly   1155 (894)
offered himself as helmsman of the *Argo*.
A god's encouragement had urged him on.
Next, Nauplius, Erginus, and Euphemus
stood up in eagerness to man the tiller,
but others held them back because Ancaeus   1160
was favored by the bulk of the assembly.

Therefore at sunrise, after twelve days mourning,
they boarded, since a stiff west wind was blowing.
Quickly they rowed out through the Acheron,
then trusted in the wind, unfurled the canvas,   1165
and, with the sail spread taut, went coasting onward,
cleaving their way in favorable weather.
Soon they passed the mouth of Callichorus,
"River of Gorgeous Dancing."
                               It was here,
they say, that the Nysaean son of Zeus,   1170 (905)
after departing from the Indic tribes
and settling at Thebes, initiated
secret rites and set up choral dances
before the cave where he had once spent mirthless,
unearthly nights. Ever since then the locals   1175

have called the nearby river "Gorgeous Dancing"
and the cave "The Hostel."
                                        Next they sighted
the tomb of Sthenelus the son of Aktor.
While he was marching homeward after waging
glorious war upon the Amazons   1180
(he had gone there with Heracles), an arrow
struck him and laid him dead upon the beach.
The heroes sailed no farther for a time
because Persephone herself had sent up
Sthenelus' shade. With tears and wailing   1185 (917)
the ghost had begged her, please, please, let him see,
just for a little, soldiers like himself.

Watching them from the barrow's crest, he seemed
such as he was when first he went to war—
a four-billed, formidable helmet gleaming   1190
upon his head, its crest a deep dark red.
Then he descended back into the gloom.
The heroes marveled at the vision. Mopsus
son of Ampycus saw it as a sign
and urged the men to beach the ship and honor   1195
the hero with libations.
                                So they furled
the sail, ran the hawsers to the beach,
and paid homage to Sthenelus' tomb
by pouring offerings and sacrificing
sheep to his shade. They also raised, nearby,   1200 (927)
an altar to Apollo Ship-Preserver
and burned thigh pieces on it. Orpheus
enshrined a lyre there as well—that's why
the spot is known as Lyra to this day.

Then, since the wind was calling, they embarked,   1205
unfurled the sail, and used the sheets to pull it
taut, and the *Argo* coasted out to sea
with bellied canvas, as on lofted wings
a hawk goes coasting swiftly through the air,
its pennons poised and level. Like a hawk, then,   1210

the *Argo* passed the seaward-flowing stream
Parthenius, a very gentle river.
Artemis often stops there after hunting
and bathes her body in its soothing waters
before she joins the gods upon Olympus.   1215 (939)

They coasted without pausing all night long,
skirting Seisamus, rugged Erythini,
Cromna, Crobialus, tree-lined Cytorus.
Just as the sun first cast its beams they rounded
Carambis and were pushing past the Long Shore   1220
the whole day through, the whole night under oar,
until they beached on the Assyrian coast.

Here Zeus himself had settled Sinopa
the daughter of Asopus and allowed her
lasting virginity, but only after   1225
she hoodwinked him with his own lover's oaths.
When he was aching for her love, he promised
to give her anything her heart desired,
and, clever girl, she asked for maidenhood.
When Phoebus tried in turn to lie with her,   1230 (952)
she tricked him in the same way, then deceived
Halys the River God as well. What's more,
no mortal ever stole her innocence
with vehement caresses.
                            On this coast
three sons of brave Deimarchus the Triccean—   1235
Deileon, Phlogius, and Autolycus—
had camped out ever since they lost their comrade
Heracles. As soon as they discerned
the party of heroic men, they ran
to meet them and explain their destitution.   1240
They did not desire to be marooned there
forever, so they climbed aboard, and soon
a stiff nor'wester started blowing.
                            So,
with new recruits, the heroes took to sea
before the eager gale and coasted past   1245 (962)

the Halys River, then the nearby Iris,
then the sandy delta of Assyria.
That day they also rounded, at a distance,
the cape that guards the Amazonian harbor
where the hero Heracles once ambushed   1250
Melanippa daughter of the war god
when she went traveling abroad. Her sister
Hippolyta was quick to pay the ransom,
and he returned her safe and sound.
                                          Because
the sea had turned too turbulent for travel,   1255
the heroes anchored at the harbor where
the Thermodon goes down into the sea.
There is no river like the Thermodon,
none that divides into as many branches.
Reckon them up, the tally would be only   1260 (974)
four shy of a hundred. But the true
headwater is a single stream that tumbles
down mountains called the "Amazonian Heights"
onto a lowland where it multiplies,
its rills meandering this way, that way,   1265
one near, one far, each seeking lower ground.
Most of them dissipate anonymously,
but several merge to form the Thermodon,
which hurls itself, a vaulted span of froth,
into the Hostile Sea.
                        The men might well   1270
have lingered for a time there, making war
upon the Amazons, and they would surely
have suffered losses if they had because
the Amazons in the Doean plain
were not at all docile and civilized.   1275 (987)
Savage aggression and the works of Ares
were all their care. In fact, they claimed descent
from Ares and the nymph Harmonia.
She bedded down beside him in a dale
in the Acmonian woods and bore him daughters   1280
that dote on war.
                    But, under Zeus' sway,
the northwest wind returned and pushed the heroes

beyond a cape where other Amazons,
Themiscyreans, girt their loins for battle.
The Amazons, you see, did not inhabit   1285
one city but were settled separately
in three tribes scattered all throughout the land:
those called Themiscyreans lived in one part
under the warrior queen Hippolyta,
the Lycastians settled in another,   1290 (999)
and the spear-mad Chadesians a third.

During the next day and the following night
the heroes skirted Chalybian country.
Pushing teams of oxen through the fields
and sowing thought-sweetening plants and trees   1295
hold no appeal for the Chalybes.
They cleave dense, iron-bearing soil instead
and barter what they find for wares and produce.
Dawn never rises for them without toil,
more toil, unending toil in soot and smoke.   1300

After the Chalybes, the heroes rounded
the Cape of Zeus God of the Genes River
and passed the country of the Tibarenians.
Here, when a women is with child, her husband
wraps his own head in towels, lies in bed,   1305 (1013)
and howls, and his woman brings him food
and draws and boils a childbirth bath for him.

After the Tibarenians they passed
a sacred mountain and the country where
the Mossynoeci dwell along the slopes   1310
in towers or the "mossynes" they take their name from.
Odd laws and customs mark their way of life.
Everything that we do out in the open
either in council or the marketplace,
they find some way to do inside their homes,   1315
and all the things we do inside our homes,
they do out in the middle of the street
without the least compunction. Public sex
is not disgraceful there. Like boars in heat,
they feel not even slight embarrassment   1320 (1024)

with others present but engage their women
in open copulation on the ground.
Their ruler sits inside the highest tower,
rendering personal verdicts to his subjects—
poor wretch, since, if his rulings seem unfair,   1325
they lock him up in prison for a day
without a meal.
              After the Mossynoeci,
they labored dead ahead toward Ares' Island,
hacking their course with oars all day because
the gentle breeze had left them in the night.   1330
And then they spotted one of Ares' birds,
the special breed indigenous to the island,
flitting back and forth above their heads.
With one wing pump above the moving ship,
it launched a tapered feather dart, which struck   1335 (1036)
the left shoulder of noble Oileus.
Injured, he dropped his oar, and his companions
sat awestruck gaping at the tufted shaft.
His bench mate Eurybotes yanked it out,
unhitched the sword belt running through his scabbard,   1340
and bound the wound. Soon, though, a second fowl
was circling like the first. This time the hero
Clytius, the offspring of Eurytus,
because he had his longbow nocked and ready,
released a speedy arrow, struck the bird,   1345
and brought it, spinning, down into the sea
beside the heaving *Argo*. Amphidamus
son of Aleus spoke his mind among them:

"Now the Isle of Ares is at hand.
You yourselves, doubtless, guessed the news already,   1350 (1047)
since we have met the birds. I doubt that arrows
will be enough to get us to the shore,
so let us come up with a plan—that is,
if you respect the words of Phineus
and still intend a landfall here.
                  Not even   1355
Heracles, when passing through Arcadia,

had strength enough to drive off with his bow
the birds that rode on the Stymphalian slough.
I saw it all myself. No, what he did
was stand atop a rock and make a racket   1360
by shaking copper rattles—all the birds
fled from the noise in terror and confusion.

We should devise some similar arrangement,
and I will tell you what I have in mind:
let's all set on our heads our high-plumed helmets,   1365 (1060)
and half our number, every other of us,
mind the rowing, while the other half
walls off the ship with polished spears and shields.
Then we should all raise so grotesque an uproar
that they scatter at the strangeness of it—   1370
the ruckus, bobbing crests, and brandished spears.
And if we make it to the island, then
make noise by clattering your shields together."

So he proposed, and everyone accepted
his prudent plan. They set atop their heads   1375
helmets forged from brightly glinting bronze
with crimson feathers flickering above them.
Half of the heroes plied the oars, and half
covered the *Argo*'s deck with shields and spears.
As when a fellow roofs his house with tile   1380 (1073)
to trim it and protect against the rain,
and each tile dovetails snugly with the next,
so half the heroes locked their shields together
and roofed the ship. The clangor that arose
from ship to air resembled the percussion   1385
that rises from opposing hordes when soldiers
dash together, and the ranks collide.
Soon enough, every single bird had vanished.

But when the heroes neared the shore and clashed
their shields, thousands of them of a sudden   1390
took to the air and flew in all directions.
Just as the son of Cronus shoots thick hail

down out of thunderheads onto the homes
of people sitting patiently inside,
listening to the rattle at their ease   1395 (1085)
because the stormy months are no surprise,
and they have wisely reinforced their roofs,
so did the birds rain feathered missiles down
as they went flying off across the ocean
toward the massifs that mark the world's end.   1400

But what did Phineus really have in mind
in telling that divine brigade of heroes
to anchor there? What benefit would come
to them thereafter, as they hoped it might?

The sons of Phrixus had embarked upon   1405
a Colchian ship and sailed out of Aea,
away from Cyta and Aeëtes, hoping
to reach the city of Orchomenus
and win the boundless riches of their father.
This voyage was his dying proclamation.   1410 (1096)

But, on the day they neared the Isle of Ares,
Zeus urged the potent north wind on to blow
and marked Arcturus' wet route with showers.
All day long he gently shook the topmost
leaves of the mountain forests but at night   1415
swooped monstrously down upon the sea
with shriek and bluster puffing up the tide.
A dark mist veiled the heavens, and the stars
did not shine anywhere beyond the clouds.
A murky gloom was brooding all around.   1420

Half-drowned and dreading an abysmal death,
the sons of Phrixus weltered at the waves' whim.
The gales had long since snatched their sails away,
the roll shaken the ship, the hull broken
in half, and now, just as the gods had planned,   1425 (1110)
the four of them were clinging to some flotsam

tightly fitted dowels had held together
when the ship broke up.
                    The wind and waves
carried the helpless men off toward the island,
and they were close to drowning. Then another   1430
horrendous squall erupted, and the rain
assailed the sea, the island, and the whole
coastline opposing it as far away
as where the haughty Mossynoeci dwelt.

The swollen tide threw all the sons of Phrixus,   1435
together with the planks, onto the shore.
The night had been a black one, but the torrents
Zeus had been hurling at them ceased at dawn,
and soon the two groups happened on each other.
Argus the son of Phrixus called out first: 1440 (1122)

"Please, in the name of Zeus of Supplication
we beg of you, whoever you might be,
to take us in and help us in our need.
The dire storm winds, you see, roughed up the sea
and broke apart the wretched ship on which   1445
we had embarked out of necessity
to carry us across the swell. Therefore,
as suppliants we beg you please be kind
and give us clothes, enough to shield our skin.
Please be compassionate and rescue men   1450
like you, your age-mates, who are in distress.
Yes, honor us as guests and suppliants,
since guests and suppliants belong to Zeus,
and he, I hope, is watching over us."

Though Jason was suspecting all the while   1455 (1134)
that Phineus' words were being fulfilled,
he tactfully inquired in response:

"Yes, we are well-disposed. We shall provide you
with all you need. But tell me where you hail from,

what circumstances drove you on this voyage,   1460
and what good names and pedigrees are yours."

All desperation in his shipwrecked state,
Argus replied:
              "Not many years ago
a son of Aeolus named Phrixus traveled
from Hellas to Aea—I suspect   1465
you know the tale. He rode a flying ram
(and golden, too, since Hermes gilded it)
the whole way to the city of Aeëtes,
and still today the fleece is lying spread
across the crown of a luxuriant oak.   1470 (1145)
The ram, you see, could talk as well and ordered
Phrixus to slaughter it in sacrifice
to Zeus the Exiles' God, the son of Cronus,
before the other gods. Aeëtes welcomed
Phrixus into his court and gave his daughter   1475
Chalciope to him, without the bride-price,
out of the kindness of his heart.
                      We four
are products of their love. But Phrixus, old
already at the time of his arrival,
died at Aeëtes' court. We have resolved   1480
to satisfy our father's dying wish
by sailing to Orchomenus to claim
Athamas' estate. If you would like
to know our names, this here is Cytissorus,
this is Phrontis, this is Melas here,   1485 (1155)
and you may call me Argus."
                       So he told them.
The heroes in delight and wonder greeted
the strangers, and the son of Aeson answered:

"It is as kinsmen on my father's side
that you entreat us to relieve your plight: 1490
Cretheus was the brother of Athamas,
and I, the grandson of that Cretheus,
am sailing from the very Greece you speak of

to King Aeëtes' city. We shall talk
among ourselves about our kinship later.   1495
Put on some clothing now. I do believe
you were marooned here by some god's design."

So he proclaimed and gave them clothes to wear
out of the *Argo*. Linked in friendship, then,
they strode to Ares' shrine to slaughter sheep   1500 (1170)
and offer them in sacrifice. Assembled
before the roofless temple, they assumed
their places round an altar built of fieldstone.
A black stone lay half-buried in the earth
within the precinct. It was to this stone   1505
the Amazons had once all prayed. In fact,
whenever they would venture from the mainland,
their laws prevented them from burning oxen
or sheep as sacrifices on this altar;
rather, they butchered horses, giant horses   1510
they fattened for a year. Only after
the heroes had performed the sacrifice
and dined upon the feast they had prepared,
did Jason speak among them. He began:

"Zeus truly must be minding these affairs.   1515 (1179)
Whether devout or cruel and sacrilegious,
we mortals never can escape his gaze.
Zeus, for example, saved your father Phrixus
from murder at his mad stepmother's hands
and gave him boundless wealth besides. So, also,   1520
he brought you safe out of the deadly storm.

Our ship can sail wherever one might wish—
Aea or that rich and holy city
Orchomenus. Athena planned it out
and with a bronze ax on the peak of Pelion   1525
felled trees for planks, and Argus built it with her.

Your ship, though, cracked beneath the savage swell
before it even reached the Rocks that run

crashing together in the Pontic strait.
Come, then, and be our helpers, too: we seek   1530 (1192)
the golden fleece to bring back home to Hellas.
Come, guide our course. I'm going to atone for
Phrixus' forced escape, which is the reason
Zeus has been angry with the Aeolids."

So Jason solaced them. The brothers, though,   1535
cringed upon hearing of the quest. They thought
Aeëtes was unlikely to be gentle
with men that sought to take the fleece from him,
and Argus tried to talk them out of it:

"My friends, whatever strength we have to help you   1540
shall never fail to serve your cause. We shall assist you
whenever need arrives. Aeëtes, though,
has fortified himself in dreadful fashion
with savage cruelty, so I greatly doubt
your quest will be successful.
                            King Aeëtes   1545 (1203)
boasts he was born the son of Helius,
and countless tribes of Colchians support him.
The man could rival Ares with his war cry,
muscle, and vigor. Nor would it be easy
to steal the fleece without Aeëtes' knowledge.   1550
The dragon standing sentinel before it
is of the worst sort—deathless, never-sleeping.
Mother Earth begot it on the slopes
of the Caucasus, on the Rock of Typhon—
you know, where Typhon with his mighty hand grip   1555
climbed up to challenge Zeus. The legends tell us
Cronian Zeus' lightning blasted him
right there atop the jagged peak, and steamy
blood came welling up out of his head.
He dragged himself, then, wounded, toward
    the mountains   1560 (1214)
and reached the plain of Nysa where he lies
submerged beneath the tide of Lake Serbonis
down to this very day."

So Argus warned them.
When the heroes learned what was before them,
terror blanched their cheeks, that is, the cheeks   1565
of all but Peleus. He answered Argus
straight off, with resolution in his voice:

"My friend, don't try to spook us with your talk.
We're not so inexperienced in warcraft
that we would fall beneath Aeëtes' arms.   1570
No, we are heading in prepared, I think,
since we are offspring of the blessed gods.
So, if the king will not do us a favor
and offer up the fleece, I doubt his countless
Colchians will be much assistance to him."   1575 (1225)

So they conversed awhile among themselves,
then feasted once again and went to sleep.

A breeze was blowing when they rose that morning,
so they set forth, the sail stretched taut before
the onrush of the wind, and soon enough   1580
they left the Isle of Ares in their wake.
That night they passed the island of Philyra.
Here, back when Cronus, Ouranos' youngest,
ruled his Titan kin on Mount Olympus
(and infant Zeus was in a cave on Crete   1585
tended by the Idaean Curetes),
Cronus went off to meet up with Philyra
behind his consort Rhea's back. When Rhea
caught them in the act of making love,
he changed himself into a long-maned horse,   1590 (1237)
kicked himself out of bed, and galloped off.
Philyra, daughter of the Ocean, left
her dear old home and island in disgrace
and settled down among the lofty mountains
of the Pelasgians, and there it was   1595
she foaled at length Cheiron: half man, half horse,
product of an extra-species union.

From there they sailed on, skirting the Macrones,
the never-ending land of the Becheiri,
the proud Sapeires, even the Byzeri.   1600
So, swept along by favorable winds,
they ever onward cleaved their course. And now
the far end of the Pontic Sea appeared
before their rapid progress. Now arose
the summits of the sheer Caucasus Mountains   1605 (1247)
where Prometheus was hung, his limbs
fixed to a rough cliff face by cuffs of bronze.
He served his liver to an eagle daily;
daily the bird returned to rip it out.
The heroes spotted outspread wings toward dusk   1610
passing above the masthead near the clouds.
The huge and churning pennons loudly whispered,
puffing the sails. No, this was not a normal
bird of the air, but bigger, and it worked
its feathered wings like smoothly polished oars.   1615
They soon discerned Prometheus' anguished
howl as, again, his liver was devoured.
The air was full of shrieks until they saw
the cruel eagle flying from the mountain
back the way that it had come.
                                    That evening,   1620 (1260)
under Argus' unfailing guidance,
they reached wide-flowing Phasis and the eastmost
edge of the Pontic Sea. Straightway they struck
the sail and yardarm, stowed them in the hold,
and then stepped down the mast and laid it out   1625
beside them. Quickly under oar, they entered
the river's mighty current, and it yielded,
foaming, before them. The sublime Caucasus
and the Cytaean city of Aea
were larboard, and to port the plain of Ares   1630
and Ares' sacred orchard, where the dragon
kept constant watch beneath the fleece spread out
across the crown of a luxuriant oak.

And Jason from a golden goblet poured
honey-sweet offerings of unmixed wine   1635 (1271)

into the river, asking that the Earth,
the local deities, and all the shades
of the indigenous departed heroes
please be kind, benign, and blameless helpers
and warmly welcome *Argo* to their shores.   1640

Ancaeus, then, announced:
                              "We now have reached
the river Phasis and the land of Colchis.
The time has come to plan among ourselves
whether to ply Aeëtes with persuasion
or whether other means will serve us best."   1645

So he announced. At Argus' suggestion
Jason told the crew to keep the ship
afloat at anchor after they had reached
a green lagoon inside the river's mouth,
and so they spent the night. A few hours later   1650 (1285)
day broke, the day that they had been expecting.

BOOK 3

Come now, Erato, stand beside me, tell me
how, through the passion of Medea, Jason
returned the fleece to Iolcus. Yes, you, too,
enjoy your share of Cypris' dominion.
Your magic spellbinds marriageable maidens   5
with thoughts of love, and that is why, Erato,
Eros is in the lovely name you bear.

We left the heroes hiding in a blind
among some thickly growing reeds. Athena
and Hera spotted them, despite their cover,   10
and slipped into a room to plait a plot
apart from Zeus and all the other gods.
Hera was first to ask what should be done:

"Since you are Zeus' daughter, you should be
the first to give advice. What should we do?   15 (12)
Can you devise some scheme by which the heroes
strip the golden fleece from King Aeëtes
and bring it back to Hellas? No, he's not
the sort they could persuade with honeyed phrases.
In fact, that man is such an awful bully   20
that we should shun no means of thwarting him."

So she confided, and Athena answered:

"Hera, I also have been meditating
upon this matter, but my mind, for all
the many tactics I have weighed and measured,   25
has failed to find one that will do the trick."

With that, they fixed their eyes upon the floor
and stood there each in her own world. Hera
first broke the silence to propose a plan:

"Come, let us go find Cyprian Aphrodite   30 (25)
and tell her that she must approach her son
and pressure him to sink a shaft into
Aeëtes' daughter, drug-adept Medea,
so that the girl is struck with lust for Jason.
I am quite certain that, with her assistance,   35
Jason will bring the fleece back home to Greece."

So she proposed. The shrewd scheme satisfied
Athena, and she uttered honeyed words:

"Hera, I am as my father made me—
oblivious to that little fellow's arrows.   40
Love charms and all such things are lost upon me.
Still, if you like this plan, I'll go along . . .
please, though, do all the talking when we see her."

So spoke she, and they rose and promenaded
over to Cypris' colossal palace   45 (36)
(the one her hobbled husband had constructed
before he led her out of Zeus' halls).
Once inside the walls, they reached a courtyard
and strode on to the chamber that the goddess
shared with her man Hephaestus. He himself   50
had gone at daybreak to his forge and anvils
in a vast cavern on a Floating Island
where he would daily cast with blasts of fire
ingenious miracles of metalwork.
So, left alone again, the goddess Cypris   55
was lounging on a couch inlaid with bronze.
Her mane of hair let down and dangling over
either spotless shoulder, she was using
a golden comb to work the tangles out
before she wove the tresses into braids.   60 (47)
Soon as she saw the goddesses before her,

she paused and bade them enter. Then she rose,
sat them on couches, sat herself back down,
and tied her hair above her head because
there still was brushing to be done. All smiles,   65
she greeted them with pointed deference:

"Dear ladies, welcome! Why, what pressing purpose
could bring such reverend matrons to my home?
What has come over you? Before today
you never over-often deigned to pay me   70
such honor, since you move in higher spheres."

Hera retorted then: "You mock us, dear.
But, seriously now, we face a matter
of life or death. Already Aeson's son
and all who follow questing for the fleece   75 (58)
at anchor ride beside the banks of Phasis.
Now that the crucial moment is at hand,
we're worried to distraction for them all,
but most for Jason. Though he chart a course
far off to Hades' palace to release   80
Ixion from his bondage, all my strength,
so long as strength remains, shall go to guard him.
Nor shall I suffer Pelias to shirk
a well-earned death and live to laugh at me.
Rash fool! To fail to pay my shrines their due!   85

But it was well before that king's neglect
that Jason proved his worth and won my favor:
when the Anauros crested, chest-high, over
the ford, he strode up glistening from the hunt,
and I was out inspecting men's behavior.   90 (69)
Snowy, the mountain summits shone; runoff
through channel and ravine rolled rushing, swirling,
tumbling down. He pitied at the crossing
the weathered flesh I wore as a disguise.
Once I was muscled up onto his back,   95
he shouldered me across the heaving rapids—
hence my unquenchable esteem for him.

But Pelias will not be forced to pay
for his atrocities unless you, dear,
contrive safe passage for the son of Aeson."   100

The queen had spoken. Cypris for a time
sat dumbstruck at the sight of Hera begging.
When she replied, she spoke in humbler guise:

"Queen, nothing would be more depraved than I,
if I make light of your appeal, denying   105 (80)
helpful suggestion or whatever labor
impotent hands could work on your behalf.
Nor do I ask a favor in return."

So Cypris spoke, and Hera in her turn
uttered a calculated repartee: 110

"We've not come for your brawn or broadsword, dear.
All you must do is tell your son to spark
passion for Jason in Aeëtes' daughter.
For if she takes an interest in the man,
she cherishes his cause and, when she does,   115
our hero will with trifling labor seize
the golden fleece and coast back home to Iolcus—
trust me, that girl was simply made for guile."

So Hera spoke her mind, and Cypris voiced
the following reply to both of them: 120 (90)

"But ladies, listen, little Eros sooner
would heed your will than mine. Brash as he is,
his eyes might show some glimmer of respect
before such stately figures as yourselves.
My discipline means nothing to him. Always   125
willful and wild, he cackles when I chide him.
Why, sick of all his antics, I once threatened,
in view of all the gods, to snap in half
his dismal-whizzing darts and short bow, too.
Only wound up the more, the little monster   130

menaced me thus: *If you don't keep your mitts*
far from my darts and let me get my way,
you might regret, Mommy, what you have done."

So she lamented. Hera and Athena
smiled and bandied glances back and forth,   135 (101)
so she exclaimed again in agitation:

"Yes, yes, the whole world titters at my troubles.
I shouldn't publish them to all and sundry.
My private misery already more than
suffices. All the same, because you both   140
have taken such an interest in the matter,
I shall sound him out, speak sweetly to him,
and never take his back talk for an answer."

So Cypris promised them, and Hera squeezed
her slender hand and spoke the final word: 145

"Accomplish now, forthwith, what we require
just as we said and just as you have promised.
And, dear, don't pout so, squabbling with your boy—
he will be all grown up before you know it."

She rose and, with Athena at her heels,   150 (111)
paraded back up to her husband's palace.
Cypris in turn wound around Mount Olympus,
searching the valleys for her wayward son.

The garden was blooming, and she found him there,
but not alone; there, too, was Ganymede   155
whose bloom had moved the king of gods to make
a home for him in heaven among the immortals.
Cozy as neighbor boys, they played at dice
(there even dice are golden). Little Eros
stood clutching greedily against his breast   160
fists full of winnings. An impassioned flush
seethed on his cheeks. His playmate, though, sat silent
and grimaced as he sent his two last dice

tumbling, one by one, into the dirt.
Ganymede frowned, Love cackled, and indeed   165 (124)
the last were lost as quickly as the rest.
The loser stalked off, cleaned out, empty-fisted,
failing to notice Cypris on the path.
She strode across the playground, chucked her son
under the chin and gently scolded him: 170

"Mischievous little imp, why are you smirking?
Have you been bad and tricked a toddler? Well,
if you are good and do what Mommy says,
she has a treat for you. A nice bright ball!
All striped and shiny! Once upon a time   175
Zeus was a baby in a cave on Ida
and liked to play, so Adrasteia, his nanny,
made him this pretty toy. Handy Hephaestus
himself could not devise a finer plaything:

Golden circlets hold the whole together.   180 (137)
Parallel hoops are sewn slantwise around them
to cinch them tight, and blue streaks round these hoops
in spirals wind and wander, hiding all
the seams and stitches. Toss it up, a train
trails after, glittering like a comet's tail—   185

this will be your reward, but not before
you shoot Medea full of love for Jason.
Now go and do the deed; don't drag your feet,
for Mommy's kindness, later, may be less."

So spoke she, and the words fell welcome on   190
his eager ears. Scattering dice before him,
he ran to hang upon his mother's skirts
with clenched fists and demanded his reward:
Now, Mommy, no, right now! To soothe the fit,
she pinched his cheeks and kissed him, hugged him close, 195 (150)
and, smirking, promised:
                          "Let your head and mine
attest the bargain: I shall not deceive you.

There—I have sworn. Now, if you want the toy,
go sink a shaft deep in Aeëtes' daughter."

So spoke she, and the god snatched up the dice,   200
reckoned the sum, and stuffed his mother's pockets
full of them. Then he ran and grabbed his quiver
from where it leaned, ready, against a tree,
slung it about him with a strap of gold,
and gathered up his crooked little bow.   205

Brilliant around him bloomed the garden of Zeus,
the groves and orchards, but the boy rushed on,
flew through the gates of high Olympus.
                                                   Thence
opens the downward path; there double peaks
like pillars of the earth vault ever upward   210 (162)
to keep the sky from falling; there the sun,
first upon rising in the morning, ruddies
the summits with extended beam. As Eros
was coasting unobstructed through the air,
plump tilth and bustling towns and nymph-abounding   215
waterways passed into his view and then
strange ridges and a rounded swatch of sea.

The heroes, though, remained apart, concealed
among the river rushes, strategizing.
Jason was speaking, and the men were seated   220
in order bench by bench, in silence, listening:

"Comrades, the plan I now shall lay before you
strikes me as wisest. Yours will be the task
of bringing it to pass. Our need is shared,
and counsel, too, is shared among us all.   225 (174)
The man who locks his thoughts and wisdom up
in reticence should know that he alone
is keeping all of us from heading home.

While you remain at ease but under arms
here on the *Argo,* I shall make my way   230

to King Aeëtes' palace—I myself,
the sons of Phrixus, and two other men.
Once I am granted audience, I shall test him
with words to find out whether he is willing
to give the golden fleece up out of friendship   235
or whether he will balk, trust in his strength,
and block our quest. Thus we can sound the depth
of our distress and next consider whether
the implements of war will serve us better
or double-dealing, if we rule out war.   240 (185)
We shouldn't simply take the man's possession
until we have at least assessed his mind.
Surely it's wiser to approach him first
and try to win him over with entreaties.
In rough spots words have often smoothed the way   245
and won what valor only could have won
with toil and sweat.
                      Consider this: Aeëtes
once welcomed worthy Phrixus when the latter
was running from his stepmother's deceit
and slaughter at his father's hands. All men,   250
even the most contemptuous of them,
dread and revere the covenants of Zeus
the God of Guest and Host."
                            So Jason spoke,
and all the heroes rushed to voice approval.
No one proposed a different course, so Jason   255 (195)
bade Telamon, Augeas, and the sons
of Phrixus join him in his embassy
and took the staff of Hermes in his hand.

They wasted no time disembarking over
the rushes where the upward sloping bank   260
afforded solid ground. This tract is known
as Circe's Plain, and tamarisks and willows
grow there in rows, and corpses wrapped in cables
dangle earthward from the overstory.
Down to this very day it is taboo   265
among the Colchians to cremate males

upon their death. Nor does their faith allow them
to lay the bodies in the earth and heap
barrows above them. Rather, they are shrouded
in uncured hide and dangled from the treetops   270 (207)
outside the city. Still, the earth receives
as many corpses as the air because
their females' bodies are, in fact, interred.
Such are the equitable customs there.

Hera helped the heroes travel safely   275
by casting thick mist down around the city
so that they would escape the notice of
the multitudinous throngs of Colchians.
Soon as the heroes passed out of the plain
into the town and palace, Hera scattered   280
the cloud away. They stood there in the entry
marveling at the royal court—the wide
gateways, the columns standing, rank on rank,
along the walls, and, higher up, the bronze
capitals holding up a marble cornice.   285 (218)

They softly crossed the threshold. All around them
high-climbing vines, prolific strands of leaves,
had broken into bloom. Beneath them bubbled
four ever-flowing springs for which Hephaestus
himself had dug the channels. One was flowing   290
with milk, and one with wine, a third contained
a stream of fragrant oil, and the fourth
was limpid water that, they say, ran hot
after the setting of the Pleiades
but at their rising jetted chill as crystal   295
out of the hollow rock. Such were the wonders
Hephaestus fashioned for Aeëtes' palace
at Cyta.
        He had forged for him as well
bronze-footed bulls with brazen mouths that breathed
shocking, abominable blasts of flame.   300 (231)
What's more, he made an indestructible plow
out of a single block of adamant
to pay a favor back to Helius

who had picked up Hephaestus in his war car
when he was faint from waging war at Phlegra.   305

A central iron door was built there, too.
Beyond it many sturdy double doors
and living chambers ran in both directions.
Along each side a fine arcade extended,
and crosswise to them in the wings loftier   310
apartments stood. In one of them, the highest,
Aeëtes slept beside his wife. Absyrtus,
his son, inhabited another of them.
Asterodeia, a Caucasian nymph,
bore him before Aeëtes wed Eidyia,   315 (243)
Tethys' and Ocean's youngest daughter.
The Colchians, however, took to calling
Absyrtus "Phaëthon" (the Shining One)
since he outshone the other boys his age.
In other lower rooms, Aeëtes' daughters   320
Medea and Chalciope resided,
along with all their maids.
                              It was Medea
that Jason and his party met by chance
when they were wandering from room to room
to find Chalciope. Hera had made   325
Medea stay at home that day on purpose.
The girl, you see, was rarely at the palace
but usually working all day long
as priestess at the shrine of Hecate.

Soon as the maiden saw that men were coming,   330 (253)
she shrieked. Chalciope could not but hear it,
and when her handmaids dropped their wool and spindles
and rushed out all together in a crowd,
she went as well and, when she saw her sons,
flung out her hands for joy. Her sons as well   335
flung out their hands for joy at seeing her
and hugged her warmly. Sobbing, she exclaimed:

"So, you were not, in fact, about to leave me
so thoughtlessly and travel far away.

Fate has returned you. How distraught I was!   340
A wild and senseless lust to sail to Greece
had taken hold of you, a dire delusion,
all at your father Phrixus' behest.
His dying proclamation to you tortured
my heart with netherworldly afflictions.   345 (265)
Why risk a voyage to the place they call
Orchomenus, whatever that might be,
to claim some King Athamas' estate?
Why leave me here to bear my grief alone?"

So she lamented. Last of all, Aeëtes   350
emerged from his apartment with the queen,
Eidyia, when they heard Chalciope.
A bustle filled the court, the sounds of servants—
some of them readying a massive bull
for slaughter, some with brazen axes splitting   355
wood for the fire, and others boiling water
for baths before the feast. Not one of them
was stinting in his service to the king.

And Eros was descending all the while,
descending through the lustrous air, unseen   360 (276)
but as rambunctious as the stinging fly
that oxherds call the "goad," the kind that nettles
heifers. In an instant he was there,
bracing his back against the antechamber's
doorpost. He deftly strung his little bow   365
and from the quiver chose a virgin arrow
laden with future groans. His speedy feet
whisked him across the threshold, he himself
unnoticed as he keenly scanned the scene.
Then, crouching low beneath the son of Aeson,   370
he nocked the arrow midway up the string,
and, parting bow and string with both hands, shot
Medea. Sudden muteness gripped her spirit.
The god, then, fluttered from the high-roofed hall,
cackling, and the arrow burned like fire   375 (286)
deep, deep down beneath the maiden's heart.

She fired scintillating glances over
and over at the son of Aeson. Anguish
quickened her heart and panted in her breast,
and she could think of him, him only, nothing   380
but him, as sweet affliction drained her soul.

As when a workwoman, a hireling drudge
whose livelihood is spinning yarn from wool,
piles kindling around a burning brand
so that there might be light beneath the roof   385
at night, since she has woken very early,
and from that one small brand a fire spreads
marvelously and eats up all the twigs,
so all-consuming Eros curled around
Medea's heart and blazed there secretly.   390 (296)
Her tender cheeks kept turning pale, then crimson,
pale, then crimson, in her mind's confusion.

After the slaves had laid the banquet out,
and all the guests had washed off their exhaustion
in nice warm baths, they satisfied their hearts   395
with meat and drink. Soon, though, Aeëtes questioned
his daughter's sons, addressing them just so:

"Sons of my daughter, offspring of that Phrixus
I honored more than any other guest
who lived at court, how has it come about   400
that you have made your way back to Aea?
Did some misfortune cut your voyage short?
No, no, you wouldn't listen when I warned you
about the endless distance of the journey.
I saw the whole route once while flying in   405 (309)
my father Helius' chariot.
We were resettling my sister Circe
way out west and flew a great long while
before we stopped at the Tyrrhenian coast
where she is living to this day, far, far   410
from Colchis. But what joy is there in stories?
Come, tell me what misfortune spoiled your trip,

who are these men attending you, and where
you beached your hollow ship on disembarking."

So he demanded. Argus answered first,   415
before his brothers, since he was the eldest
and most intent on aiding Jason's quest:

"Furious storms, Aeëtes, quickly splintered
our ship and, as we huddled on the wreckage,
a roller rose out of the night and swept us   420 (322)
ashore upon the Isle of Enyalius.
Clearly some god was guarding us, because
we never ran into the birds of Ares,
the ones that used to make that rock their home.
These men, you see, had scared the birds away   425
when they had disembarked the day before.
It must have been the will of Zeus, or Fate,
that pitied us and sent these men to save us.

As soon as they had heard the famous name
of Phrixus (and your name as well), they gave us   430
clothes and provisions, more than we required.
You see, they had been sailing to your city.
If you would like to know their journey's purpose,
it's not a mystery:
                    A certain king
passionately desired to drive this fellow   435 (334)
far from his homeland and estate because
he far surpassed all Aeolus' offspring
in battle prowess. So the king dispatched him
on an adventure, an impossible quest.
This king maintains the heirs of Aeolus   440
will not escape the heart-confounding grudge
and punishment of unrelenting Zeus,
nor Phrixus' insufferable sentence
and curse on them, until the fleece at last
returns to Greece.
                    Pallas Athena built   445
their ship, a ship unlike the vessels found

among the Colchians. I swear, we happened
to take the worst of these—the churning sea
and gale winds quickly battered it to pieces.
Their tight-knit ship, however, holds together,   450 (343)
even though every gale at once should storm her.
She runs with equal speed both under sail
and when the oarsmen with persistent strokes
muscle her onward. Here's the man who gathered
the mightiest warriors in Greece aboard her   455
and set out for your city. He has traveled
through many cities and unfathomed seas,
confident you will give the fleece to him.

Their quest will turn out just as you decide
because this man has not arrived among us   460
with outrage in his hands, but eager, rather,
to offer fitting payment for the gift—
he heard from me about the Sauromatae,
your fiercest rivals, and would gladly force them
under your scepter.
                              If you wish to know   465 (354)
their names and pedigrees, I shall be happy
to tell you them. This fellow here, the one
for whom the others gathered out of Hellas,
is known as Jason, son of Aeson, son
of Cretheus. And if he is indeed   470
of Cretheus' stock, he would be kinsman
to us on our father's side because
Cretheus and Athamas both were sons
of Aeolus, and Phrixus was the son
of Aeolid Athamas. Surely, king,   475
you've heard of Helius' son Augeas—
he's standing here—and this here's Telamon,
the son of famed Aeacus, son of Zeus.
Likewise the others traveling with them
are all the sons or grandsons of immortals."   480 (366)

So Argus sought to win Aeëtes over.
The king, however, when he heard this speech,

boiled with wrath. His heart shot up in anger.
He raged widely, but most against the sons of
Chalciope, because he thought they'd guided   485
the strangers there on purpose. In his fury
his eyes were flashing underneath his brows:

"Get from my sight, you scoundrels, right this minute!
Pack up your tricks and get out of my land
before someone starts ogling the fleece   490
and visits Phrixus in the Underworld!

I greatly doubt you fellows leagued together
and sailed from Hellas to retrieve the fleece—
no, you desire my realm and royal scepter.
If you had not first tasted of my table,   495 (377)
rest assured, I would have cut your tongues out,
lopped your hands off and dispatched you homeward
wearing your feet alone, so that you never
come back a second time. What blasphemy
you have pronounced against the blessed gods!"   500

Thus King Aeëtes raged and so incensed
Telamon's spirit that the latter burned
to utter deadly insults in reply.
Jason, however, cut him off by speaking
gentle words before the curses flew: 505

"Aeëtes, I beseech you, please be lenient
toward this expedition. By no means
are we here visiting your court in Cyta
with the intentions you impute to us.
What man would hazard of his own free will   510 (389)
voyaging over such high-swelling seas
to steal another man's possession? Fate,
rather, and an abominable tyrant's
heartless insistence have compelled this visit.

Bestow a favor on your suppliants,   515
and I shall speak of you as of a god

throughout the land of Hellas. Furthermore,
we are prepared to pay immediate
indemnity in battle, whether you
might wish us to subdue beneath your scepter   520
the Sauromatae or some other tribe."

So he proposed, with soft persuasion aiming
to sway Aeëtes. But the king was mulling
divided purposes within his chest:
whether to charge and slay them then and there   525 (398)
or test their mettle first. The latter course
seemed better in the end, and he responded:

"Stranger, why should you tell your whole tale through?
If you were truly sired by deities
and have arrived no weaker than I am   530
in strength for my possession, I shall give you
the fleece to carry home, if that's your wish,
but only if you pass my test. By no means
am I tightfisted with distinguished men,
not like that king in Greece you told me of.   535
The contest will be one of strength and mettle,
one I myself perform with my own hands,
life-threatening though it be.
                              I am the owner
of two bronze-footed oxen. As they graze
the plain of Ares, fire rather often   540 (410)
shoots from their mouths. Once I have yoked their necks,
I drive them over all four stubborn acres
of Ares' fallows. Yes, I cleave the plain
from end to end up to the riverbank,
casting into the furrows all the while   545
not seed to summon up Demeter's grain,
but fangs instead, fangs from a wondrous serpent.
They sprout up in the shape of armed and armored
soldiers and, when they charge in all around me,
I harvest them at once beneath my spear.   550
I yoke the bulls at daybreak and at dusk
rest from the reaping.

On the very day
that you complete these tasks as I do, you
may take the fleece back to that king of yours.
Until you do, though, you should not expect   555 (420)
I will bestow the golden prize upon you.
It's unbecoming for a gentleman
to yield to a man of lesser birth."

Such was his challenge. Jason fixed his eyes
before his feet in silence and remained   560
speechless and lost in the predicament.
He sat a long time wondering what to do,
but there was no way to accept the labor
with confidence—it seemed impossible.
He came out, in the end, with wary words: 565

"Aeëtes, your demand, though justified,
leaves me no choice, it seems. Therefore I, too,
shall risk the contest, daunting though it be,
and though it be my doom to die of it.
Nothing harder can befall a man   570 (430)
than dire necessity. Necessity
has driven me to you—a king's insistence."

So Jason answered, stricken with despair.
Seeing that he was paralyzed, Aeëtes
dismissed him with a still more heinous threat: 575

"Go now with your companions, since you are
so keen to try. But if you balk at yoking
the bulls or harvesting the deadly crop,
the consequences I have outlined here
will then befall you, so that in the future   580
base men will shrink from troubling their betters."

Such was his bluntness. Jason left his couch,
and Telamon arose, and then Augeas.
But, of the sons of Phrixus, only Argus
departed with their party—he had signaled   585 (441)
his brothers to remain behind at home.

They all strode from the hall, and Jason shone
brilliantly in his grace and beauty, gorgeous
above the others, and the maiden fixed
her eyes, sidelong, on him, appraising him   590
obliquely from behind her veil. Her heart
was smoldering in its distress. Her soul,
like a pursuing dream, went fluttering
about his footsteps as he walked. And so,
in great dismay, the heroes left the palace.   595

On guard against the anger of Aeëtes,
Chalciope retreated with her sons
swiftly into her room. Medea followed,
her heart obsessing over all the worries
love excites. The vision still appeared   600 (453)
before her eyes: what he himself was like,
what clothing he had worn, what he had said,
how he had sat upon his chair, and how
walked out the door. When she considered him,
she thought that she had never seen his equal.   605
His voice and luscious phrases sounded over
and over in her ears. She feared for him—
the oxen or invincible Aeëtes
would slay him, and she grieved and grieved as though
he were already dead. At her bereavement   610
round tears of earnest pity wet her cheeks.
So she was softly sobbing when she mourned:

"Why has this woe assailed me? I am ruined.
Whether he be the greatest of the heroes
who now is doomed to perish, or the weakest,   615 (465)
let him meet his fate. I would prefer, though,
that he escape uninjured. Hecate,
daughter of Perses, Holy Queen of Dread,
please help him to survive and sail for home.
But if his fate requires that he die   620
beneath the oxen, let him first know this—
his sad misfortune gives me no delight."

Such were the love cares torturing her heart.

While Argus and the heroes were proceeding
out of the city and its press of people   625
down the road they took in from the plain,
Argus offered Jason a suggestion:

"Son of Aeson, you may scorn the counsel
that I will give you now but, all the same,
though you are in a bind, it is unseemly   630 (476)
to shirk the trial. You have already heard me
talking about a girl, a witch who learned
black arts from Perses' daughter Hecate.
If we can find a way to win her over,
you need no longer fear Aeëtes' trial   635
will end with your demise. I am afraid, though,
very afraid, my mother will refuse
to help us in this matter. All the same,
I shall return and plead our case to her
because the same doom hangs above us all."   640

Thus in a friendly fashion he proposed,
and Jason said:
                    "Dear comrade, if this plan
seems prudent to you, I do not oppose it.
Go and beseech your mother, beg for help
with carefully selected words. But, mind you,   645 (487)
if we entrust our homecoming to women,
our hopes are very pitiful indeed."

So he responded, and they quickly reached
the river marsh. Their comrades in excitement
shouted out questions when they saw them coming,   650
but Jason gave a sorrowful response:

"My friends, inflexible Aeëtes wildly
rages against us in his heart of hearts.
No need for me to tell you all the details;
no need for you to question me about them.   655
In sum, he spoke of two bronze-footed bulls
that graze the plain of Ares, how they shoot
fire out of their mouths. He challenged me

to plow four fallow acres with the things.
He will provide, he said, the following seed: 660 (498)
fangs from a serpent's jaws, and from these fangs
armed men, earth-nurtured soldiers, will emerge.
The very hour they sprout I must destroy them.
Since I could not come up with something better,
I vowed to take the challenge on myself."   665

So he explained. The contest seemed a labor
none could accomplish, so they stood awhile
unspeaking, silent, eying one another.
Thoughts of catastrophe and then despair
oppressed them. Then at long last Peleus   670
spoke words of inspiration to his comrades:

"It's time to make a plan, though there is less
profit in talk, I think, than our own strength.
Heroic son of Aeson, if you truly
do intend to yoke the bulls, that is,   675 (508)
if you are passionate to win the contest,
keep your word and gird yourself for action.
But if your heart does not have perfect faith
in your ability, do not, yourself,
attempt it nor sit swiveling your eyes   680
in search of someone else to do the labor,
since I am not the sort that runs and hides.
The worst that I can suffer will be death."

So Peleus proclaimed, and Telamon
was moved as well to stand as a contestant.   685
The third to rise was haughty Idas, then
Tyndareus' sons stood up beside him
and, finally, the son of Oeneus,
who made the cut of foremost fighters, though
the down had not yet flowered on his cheeks,   690 (519)
because so great a battle lust inspired him.
The other men deferred to them in silence.
Argus, however, quickly spoke his mind
to all those who were keen to try the contest:

"Friends, yours would be an act of desperation.   695
It's likely that my mother will provide
crucial support, so, eager as you are,
remain here on the ship a little longer
just as before, since holding back is better
than rashly snatching up a dreadful doom.   700

There is a girl, a maiden. King Aeëtes
raised her here at court, and Hecate
has taught her to prepare with perfect skill
all the magic herbs that earth and water
nurture to growth. Armed with these tinctures, she   705 (531)
can blunt the fury of relentless fire,
check suddenly a roaring river's spate,
pause stars, and halt the holy moon's advance.
As we were coming back along the road
out of the court, I thought of her and thought   710
to ask my mother to persuade this girl,
her sister, to assist us in the contest.
If all of you agree to my proposal,
I shall return to King Aeëtes' palace
this very day and see what I can do.   715
With god's assistance my attempt will prosper."

So he submitted, and the gods provided
a sign to show their will: a timid dove
that happened to be fleeing from a hawk
dropped, in confusion, into Jason's lap,   720 (542)
and its assailant then impaled itself
upon the splintered stern post. Mopsus swiftly
interpreted the omen for his comrades:

"My friends, this auspice has appeared for you
with god's approval. There's no better way   725
to read the sign than that we should approach
the girl and win her over with persuasion.
She won't refuse, I think, if Phineus
has rightly prophesied that our return
lies with the goddess Cypris, since it was   730

her gentle bird that just escaped its doom.
And as the heart within me reads this omen,
so may it now be brought to pass. Come, friends,
first call on Cytherea to protect us,
then go and act on Argus' proposal."   735 (554)

So he interpreted, and all the heroes
took thought of Phineus' prophecy
and shouted in approval. Only Idas
the son of Aphareus started up
and grumbled an abominable reproach: 740

"My, my, have we come here as fellow crewmen
to women, now that we are asking Cypris
for help and not the mighty Enyalius?
Look at you—ogling hawks and doves and shirking
heroic labors. On your way, then, boys.   745
Neglect the work of soldiers; go and woo
fainthearted maidens over to our cause."

So growled he in a huff. Though many heroes
murmured words of muted disapproval,
none of them spoke against him, so he gruffly   750 (565)
sat down again, and Jason spoke his mind
to the assembly, rousing them to action:

"Now, since everyone agrees, let Argus
head to the palace. We ourselves should loosen
our cables from the riverbank and fix them   755
openly to the mainland. Lurking here
like coward ne'er-do-wells is unbecoming."

So he commanded and at once dispatched
Argus at full speed back toward town again
while all the others heeded Jason's orders,   760
weighed the anchor stone, and rowed the ship
ashore a short ways from the river flats.

Aeëtes, meanwhile, had convened the Colchians
far from the palace at the council place

where they had often met, and they were planning   765 (577)
atrocious schemes and torments for the Minyans.
Aeëtes vowed that, once the bulls had ravaged
the man who had agreed to undergo
the lethal labor, he would fell the oaks
atop the wooded banks and torch the ship   770
and all the men aboard it, so that they
might scream away their wicked insolence,
and all their wanton scheming come to nothing.

He never would have welcomed to his hearth
Phrixus the son of Aeolus, despite   775
the fact that he surpassed all other guests
in piety and kindness, and despite
his desperate need, had Zeus himself not sent
Hermes from heaven as a messenger
to make sure Phrixus found his host receptive.   780 (588)

So much the less, then, would the band of pirates
who had descended on his land abide there,
uninjured, long. Their only interest
was laying hands on other people's goods,
hatching dishonest plots, and plundering   785
the herdsmen's steadings in tumultuous raids.

He added that, beyond these penalties,
the sons of Phrixus personally should pay him
fitting indemnities for bringing home
impetuous marauders who were plotting   790
to drive him from his throne and royal power.
In fact, his father Helius had once
uttered a baleful prophecy that warned him
to be on guard against clandestine plots
and treachery within his family—   795 (601)
that was the reason he had sent the boys
out of the way to Hellas, though the trip
was what they wanted and their father's bidding.
He knew his daughters never could devise
infernal schemes, nor could his son Absyrtus.   800

No, he assumed Chalciope's sons only
would bring the prophecy to its fulfillment.

So in his rage he spoke of horrid deeds
among his subjects and with mighty threats
warned them to watch the ship and heroes closely   805
and make sure none of them escaped destruction.

Argus, meanwhile, had reached Aeëtes' palace
and with resourceful pleading urged his mother
to ask the girl for help. Chalciope
had thought of this already, but a fear   810 (612)
had gripped her heart, a fear that fate would stop her
or her appeals would come to naught because
the girl would dread their father's deadly anger
or, even if the girl agreed to help them,
their plan would be discovered and forestalled.   815

The girl herself was lying on her bed.
Deep sleep at first relieved her of her torment,
but soon beguiling, violent dreams assailed her,
as often happens with an anxious girl.

She dreamed the stranger undertook the trial   820
not from a need to bring the fleece to Hellas,
no, that was not why he had visited
Aeëtes' palace; rather, he had come
to take her back home as his wedded wife.
She dreamed that she herself had undertaken   825 (623)
the contest and performed the tasks with ease,
but that her parents backed out of the promise
since they had set the labor of the yoking
not for their daughter but the visitor
alone. And then a two-edged quarrel broke out   830
between her father and the visitors.
Both sides submitted to her arbitration
and bade her side with whom her heart preferred.
Straight off she chose the stranger and ignored
her parents. Infinite resentment gripped them.   835

They howled in rage and at their howling sleep
released her. She awoke in shock and shivered,
her wild eyes swiveling from wall to wall
around the room. She strained to pull her spirit
back down inside herself and said aloud: 840 (635)

"Oh, how these baneful dreams have frightened me.
I fear the coming of these heroes means
catastrophe. My thoughts keep fluttering
around that stranger. Let him go and woo
a Greek girl far away among his people.   845
Maidenhood and the palace of my parents
should be my lone concerns. And yet, my heart
made shameless as a bitch's, I no longer
shall stand aside but go feel out my sister
to see if she entreats me to assist   850
the trial, because she hopes to save her sons.
Yes, that would quell my heart's rebellious anguish."

So she resolved, then rose and left the chamber,
barefoot and covered only by a nightgown.
She was desperate to see her sister,   855 (646)
yet, when she crossed the threshold of the courtyard,
she lingered for a spell before her chamber,
checked by shame. She turned around, returned,
then stepped outside again, and then again
shrank back inside. Her feet conveyed her here,   860
there, nowhere, since, whenever she emerged,
the shame within her turned her steps around.
Whenever shame, though, turned her steps around,
fierce longing turned her back and urged her onward.
Three times she started and she stopped three times.   865
The fourth time, though, she whirled about, then tumbled
headlong onto her bed.
                              Think of a girl,
a bride, bewailing in the marriage chamber
the absence of the blooming youth on whom
her parents and her brothers had bestowed her—   870 (658)
how, out of shame and shyness, she does not

make conversation with his household's servants
but sits apart in grief. Some death has claimed him
before, as man and wife, they had the pleasure
of one another's charms. Her heart on fire,   875
she looks upon her freshly widowed bed
and sobs in silence, worrying that women
will mock and scorn her. So Medea wept.

Just then it chanced that, while she was lamenting,
one of the servants who attended her   880
approached and noticed her and right away
bustled next door to tell Chalciope,
who happened to be with her sons, debating
how she might win her sister to their cause.
Though busy planning, she did not ignore   885 (669)
the serving woman's unexpected news
but rushed in wonder straight out of her chamber
into the chamber where Medea lay
distraught, with two fresh scratches on her cheeks.
Chalciope could see her sister's eyes   890
were dim with weeping, so she started thus:

"Dear, dear Medea, why are you in tears?
What's wrong? What heavy grief has crushed your heart?
What, has some heaven-sent affliction wrapped
its coils around your body? Have you heard   895
some dire threat that father has pronounced
against my sons and me? If only I
were not now looking on our parents' palace
or even on this city but were living
off at the world's outskirts where the word   900 (680)
'Colchian' never, ever has been spoken."

So she exclaimed. The maiden's cheeks turned red,
and for a long time virgin modesty
restrained her, though she ached to tell her tale.
At one time words were rising to her tongue's tip   905
and at another sinking in her breast.
Time and again they reached her shapely lips

and strained to blossom forth, but no sound came.
When she at last could speak, she lied, because
the stubborn love gods still were pressing on her: 910

"Chalciope, my heart is all atremble
over your sons. I fear our father shortly
will cut them down together with the strangers.
Sleeping just now a fitful sleep, I saw
such ghastly nightmares. May a god make sure   915 (691)
they never come to pass. Yes, may you never
endure hard sorrow for your children's sake."

So she exclaimed to find out if her sister
would come out with a plea to save her sons.
The story overwhelmed Chalciope   920
with terror past all bearing. She disclosed:

"I, too, was worrying about this matter
and came to see if you, perhaps, might work
together with me to devise a plan.
First, you must swear by Heaven and Earth to seal   925
whatever I reveal inside your heart
and thus be my accomplice. In the names
of all the blessed gods, in your own name,
and those of father and mother, I implore you
not to sit by and watch an evil doom   930 (702)
viciously cut my children down or else,
when I have died beside my darling sons,
I shall return hereafter out of Hades
as an avenging Fury to torment you."

So she threatened, and a flood of tears   935
burst forth when she had finished. Then she knelt
and gripped Medea's knees with both her arms
and laid her head upon her sister's lap.
Each of them poured out piteous lamentation
over the other, and the sound of wailing   940
echoed faintly through the court. Grief-stricken
Medea was the first to speak again:

"How can I help you, sister, when you threaten
Furies and baneful curses? All I want is
to save your sons. I summon as my witness   945 (713)
the potent oath code of the Colchians
by which you have insisted that I swear.
I call as well on mighty Heaven and Earth,
the mother of the gods, to witness that,
as much as there is strength within my body,   950
you never shall be lacking in support,
provided what you ask is possible."

So vowed Medea, and her sister asked:

"To save my sons, Medea, could you please
conjure some trick to help the stranger win   955
the contest? He is desperate as well.
Argus, in fact, has just now come from him
and asked that I attempt to win your aid.
When I came out, I left him in my chamber."

So she explained. The heart within Medea   960 (724)
leapt up for joy. Her lovely cheeks went flush.
She melted with delight. A mist descended
over her liquid eyes, and she replied:

"Sister, I shall provide whatever aid
you and your sons would find most beneficial.   965
Never may dawn again light up my eyes,
nor may my mouth take in another breath,
if I place anything above your life
and that of all your sons. They are my brothers,
my dear protectors and my playmates. Yes,   970
I tell you that I am a sister to you
and daughter also, equal with your sons,
because you nursed me at your breast when I
was but an infant, as I've heard my mother
many times declare.
                    Go now, but bury   975 (736)
all that I shall perform for you in silence,

so that I can do what I must do
without my parents finding out. At daybreak
I shall be at the shrine of Hecate
with drugs to beat the bulls and so assist   980
the stranger who has started all this trouble."

With that, her sister strode out of the chamber
to tell her sons about Medea's plan.
Shame, though, and hateful terror gripped the maiden
when she was left alone. To help a stranger   985
by weaving schemes behind her father's back!

Now night was covering the earth in darkness,
and sailors from their ships were studying
the stars of Ursa Major and Orion.
Travelers and watchmen turned their thoughts
      toward sleep,   990 (746)
and deep, deep slumber was relieving even
those mothers who had lately lost their children.
No dogs were barking in the streets; no voices
echoed; silence held the blackening gloom.
Sweet sleep, however, never eased Medea—   995
no, worry and her love for Jason roused her.
She feared the bulls, the overwhelming force
beneath which he was all but sure to suffer
shameful destruction on the field of Ares.

Her heart was fitful, restless in the way   1000
a sunbeam, when reflected off the water
swirling out of a pail or pitcher, dances
upon the walls—yes, that was how her heart
was quivering. And tears of pity flowed
out of her eyes, and anguish burned her insides   1005 (759)
by smoldering into her skin and sinews,
even into the apex of her spine,
the point where torment peaks when the relentless
love gods have filled us up with agony.

Sometimes she said, yes, she would offer him   1010
the magic drug to charm the bulls; at others,

no, she would not and she would kill herself;
at others, she would neither take her life
nor offer him the magic, but remain
just as she had been, suffering, in silence.   1015

She sat down then and, wavering, exclaimed:

"Which of these woes am I to choose? My mind
is reeling. There's no respite from the pain.
It burns and burns. It burns. I wish the arrows
of Artemis had struck me dead before   1020 (774)
I saw that man, yes, long before the sons of
Chalciope had ever left for Greece.
Some god, some Fury shipped pains overflowing
with grief from there to here, right here, to me.
Let Jason perish in the competition,   1025
if he is doomed to perish. If I gave him
the drug, how could my parents fail to learn
what I had done? What reason could I give them?
What lie or ploy would be of any use?

If I see him alone, without his friends,   1030
will I acknowledge him? My lot is cruel.
I cannot hope that, even when he dies,
I will be free from anguish. He will be
a curse on me when he has lost his life.
So good-bye, modesty. Good-bye, fair name.   1035 (786)
Once I have saved him, let him go unharmed
wherever he desires while I, the day
that he completes the contest, leave this life
by dangling my body from a rafter
or taking drugs, the kind that kill the heart . . .   1040

but, when I'm dead, they all will stand there eyeing
my ruin. The entire town will pass
around the story of my fall, and all
the Colchian girls will bear me on their lips
everywhere, harshly savaging my name: 1045

She loved that foreigner so much it killed her.

By giving way to lust, she has disgraced
her house and home.
                      What shame will not be mine?
Ah, mad obsession! No, it would be better
to take my life here in my room tonight   1050 (799)
and by an inexplicable demise
escape such dreadful infamy before
I do this shameful and outrageous deed."

So she resolved and went to fetch the casket
in which her many drugs, some good, some baneful,   1055
were kept. She set it on her knees and wept.
Her nightgown's folds were wet so thoroughly
with tears that streams of grief were flowing from her.
Shrilly lamenting, keening her own death,
she wanted to reach out, select, and swallow   1060
poison to end her life. She was already
unfastening the hasps in her desire
to take it out, poor girl. Soon, though, a deathly
antipathy to baneful Hades vanquished
the urge. She was a long time held there, speechless.   1065 (811)
The heart-delighting joys of daylight sparkled
before her eyes, and she recalled the countless
pleasures the living relish and recalled
her darling playmates, as a maiden would.
So long as she kept going over all   1070
these pleasures one by one inside her mind,
the light of life was sweeter to behold
than it had been before. And so she took
the casket off her knees and set it down.
Hera had redirected her intentions.   1075
No longer did Medea waver, no,
she yearned for sunrise, burned to meet the stranger
face-to-face, and offer him the drug.
Over and over she undid the door bolt
and peeped out waiting for the glow of daybreak,   1080 (822)
and welcome were the rays that Dawn shot forth.
People throughout the city started stirring,
and Argus bade his brothers stay behind

to monitor the girl's resolve while he
slipped out and went before them to the ship.   1085

Soon as the maiden saw that Dawn had come,
she tied off with her hands the golden tresses
that had been hanging loose in disarray.
Once she had pinched her cheeks and doused her body
in fragrant oil, she put a brilliant robe on   1090
and pinned it with exquisite, spiral brooches.
Last of all, she donned a veil—it shone
like silver over her ambrosial features.
And so she pirouetted round her chamber,
oblivious to all the griefs before her   1095 (836)
and all those that would multiply with time.

Twelve handmaids, each her age, and each unmarried,
slept in the forecourt of her fragrant chamber.
She summoned them and bade them harness mules
beneath a cart to bring her to the goddess   1100
Hecate's handsome temple. When her handmaids
had gone to rig the cart, Medea opened
the hollow casket and removed a tincture,
a drug called Prometheon.
                                    If a man
should first appease the Lone-Begotten Virgin   1105
with nighttime sacrifice and then anoint
his body with this extract, he would be
invulnerable against all strokes of bronze,
unscorchable by blasts of blazing fire,
and greater for a day than any mortal   1110 (850)
in might and bravery.
                            The herb first sprouted
after the flesh-devouring eagle dripped
tortured Prometheus' bloody ichor
onto the rugged slopes of the Caucasus.
Twin stalks emerged and then, atop them, flowers   1115
closest in hue to the Corycian crocus.
Their taproots looked like freshly slaughtered flesh;
their resin, like a mountain oak's black sap.

Before the girl had used a Caspian seashell
to catch the resin and prepare the potion,   1120
she had bathed in ever-flowing waters
seven times and seven times invoked
Brimo the Youth Nurse, Brimo Dark Traverser
and Netherworldly Queen. The night was starless,
and the girl had donned a pitch-black mantle.   1125 (863)
When the Titanian root was severed, Earth
shook from her depths and raised a groan because
the son of Iapetus himself was groaning,
his soul twisted with pain. Such was the drug
she took and placed inside the fragrant band   1130
supporting her ambrosial breasts.
                                    She left
her room and climbed aboard the swift-wheeled cart.
When two handmaids had climbed aboard beside her,
she took the reins and braided whip in hand
and drove through town. The other handmaids gripped   1135
a basket at the wagon's rear and jogged
along the broad cart road, their gauzy skirts
hiked as high up as their shining thighs.

Just as when Leto's daughter Artemis,
after a bath in the Amnisus River   1140 (877)
or the Parthenius' tepid shallows,
ascends her golden car and rides through hills
behind a team of swift-hooved bucks to visit
steaming and fat-rich cattle sacrifices,
a retinue of nymphs beside her, some   1145
assembled from the source of the Amnisus,
others from groves and many-fountained summits
and, everywhere around her as she passes,
the wild creatures fawn and whimper—so
the young girls sped through town, and all the people   1150
gave way and shunned the royal maiden's gaze.

Once she had left the well-built city roads
and traveled through a plain, she reined the mules in
before the shrine, jumped from the smooth-wheeled
     wagon,

full of desire, and said to her attendants: 1155 (890)

"Goodness, my friends, what a mistake I made!
I never stopped to think it wasn't safe
with all those strangers roaming through our kingdom.
The whole city is wild with turmoil, so
none of the women who attend the temple   1160
have come today. Since we are here, however,
and no one else is coming, let's delight
our hearts with choral song. Once we have picked
these gorgeous flowers from the tender grass,
we shall return at our accustomed hour.   1165

And you will go home rich in gifts today
if you agree to do me one small favor:
Argus, you see, will not stop begging me to—
Chalciope as well—oh, but be sure
to keep the words I tell you to yourselves   1170 (903)
so that they never reach my father's ears—
well, it's about the stranger who agreed
to undertake the trial of the oxen—
you see, they asked me to accept his gifts
and keep him safe in that atrocious contest.   1175

Well, once the terms were set, I bade the stranger
come here alone, apart from his companions,
to meet me face-to-face, so that we girls
might share among ourselves whatever gifts
he brings us. We shall give him, in exchange,   1180
a very potent herbal tincture. Please, though,
stand at a distance when the man arrives."

So she requested, and her subtle words
persuaded all the maids.
                        As soon as Argus
learned from his brothers that the girl had left   1185 (913)
at daybreak for the shrine of Hecate,
he led the son of Aeson out alone,
apart from his companions, through the plain.
And with them went the offspring of Ampycus,

Mopsus, an expert at interpreting   1190
bird signs and guiding heroes on their quests.

Never among the men of long ago—
not among all those sired by Zeus himself,
nor among those the other gods begot—
had any man appeared as irresistible   1195
to speak with and adore as on that day
Jason appeared. Hera the wife of Zeus
had made him so. Even his comrades marveled
as they admired his radiant appeal,
and Mopsus swaggered as they walked because   1200 (925)
he knew already of the trip's success.

Beside the footpath through the plain there stands,
next to the shrine of Hecate, a poplar
that wears long hair, innumerable leaves.
Crows regularly sit and chatter in it,   1205
and one of them was way up toward the crown
flapping its wings as they were walking by.
At Hera's prompting it insulted Mopsus:

"You are a sorry sort of seer, too stupid
to recognize what even children know: 1210
a maiden never tells a gentleman
sweet words of love when others are around.
Get yourself gone, false prophet, bad adviser.
Neither Cypris nor the gentle love gods
breathe their seductive kindnesses your way."   1215 (937)

So spoke the crow in insult. Mopsus, though,
when he had heard the sacred bird's command,
smiled in reply and said:
                          "You go on, Jason,
go on and meet the maiden at the temple.
Her welcome will be very warm indeed   1220
thanks to the goddess Cypris, who will help you
complete the labor, just as Phineus
the son of Agenor predicted to you.

Argus and I will wait right here until
you finish. You alone must state your case   1225
and win her over with convincing phrases."

So he insisted, under good advisement,
and his companions gave assent at once.

Medea's heart, however much she sang,
could not escape from thoughts of Jason, Jason.   1230 (949)
None of the tunes she tried distracted her
for long. She broke them off in helplessness
and failed to hold her gaze steady and constant
upon her maids. Her head kept swiveling;
she kept on staring out along the roadways.   1235
Time and time again the heart convulsed
within her breast as she debated whether
a passing sound was footsteps or the wind.

Soon he appeared. Her longing eyes perceived him
rising from the horizon, as the Dog Star,   1240
Sirius, rises from the River Ocean—
mesmerizing, beautiful—to wreak
unspeakable destruction on the flocks.
In just such splendor did the son of Aeson
rise into view, and his arrival leveled   1245 (961)
still greater anguish at the lovesick girl.
Her heart dropped from her breast, her eyes were fog,
and hectic redness chafed her cheeks. She lost
the strength to lift her knees and move forward
or back. Her soles were rooted to the earth.   1250

Meanwhile the handmaids had withdrawn from them.
The two stood face-to-face, unspeaking, silent
like oaks or lofty pines that stand unrustled
beside each other on a windless day
atop a peak, until a gust of wind   1255
rouses them, and they rustle ceaselessly.
So both of them would soon have much to say
under the impact of the gusts of Eros.

Jason could tell the gods had sunk the girl
in madness, so he plied her gently:
                                        "Maiden,   1260 (975)
why are you scared to be alone with me?
I'm not like other men, a no-good boaster,
not now or back when I was in my homeland.
Therefore, though you are young, don't act so wildly
bashful before me that you shrink from saying   1265
what you desire, or anything at all.
Since we have come with goodwill toward each other
and meet on hallowed ground where harmful deeds
are sacrilege, speak freely, ask your questions.
But please don't lead me on by saying simply   1270
what I would like to hear, since from the outset
you have assured your sister you will give me
the strength-inspiring potion.
                                 I beseech you
both in your parents' names and in the names
of holy Hecate and Zeus Upholder   1275 (986)
of Suppliants and Strangers. I have come,
a suppliant and stranger, to embrace
your knees in desperation, since alone—
that is, without your favor—I shall never
return successful from this wretched contest.   1280

I am prepared to pay you future honor
for your assistance, all the honor due
between two people living far apart,
by glorifying both your name and virtues.
After my comrades have returned to Greece,   1285
they, too, will spread your fame, as will their mothers
and wives, who right now possibly are sitting
and wailing on the shore. You, you could scatter
their cruel flock of worries on the winds.

Minos' maiden daughter Ariadne   1290 (998)
once rescued Theseus from a deadly trial—
yes, Helius' daughter Pasiphae,
the sister of your father, was her mother.
Once Minos had recovered from his anger,

the girl embarked upon the hero's ship   1295
and left her fatherland. Even the gods
adored this girl, and a memento of her,
a garland known as Ariadne's Crown,
revolves among the heavenly constellations
at night. The gods will give you thanks as well   1300
if you assist so mighty an assembly
of heroes. Judging from your beauty, you
should be supreme in gentle kindnesses."

So he addressed her, playing to her pride.
She dropped her gaze but, as she did, a smile   1305 (1008)
as sweet as nectar spread across her face.
Her heart had thawed beneath his flattery.
When she looked up at him again, she failed
to find words fit to start with, since she was
so keen to tell him everything at once.   1310

All modesty behind her, she removed
the vial of resin from her fragrant bodice,
and he was quick to wrap his hands around it.
He seemed so very pleased. She would have tugged
the soul out of her breast and happily   1315
bestowed it on this man who needed her.
Eros had kindled a miraculous
and winning fire on Jason's golden hair,
and he was ravishing her gaze. Her eyes
were glinting, and her heart grew warm and melted   1320 (1020)
like dew on roses in the dawn's first light.

Each of them awkwardly admired the ground
at times and then at times kept firing glances
at one another, shooting forth desire
from underneath their brows. A good while later,   1325
under extreme duress, the girl brought out:

"Please listen. I shall give you some instructions:
Once my father has bestowed upon you
the serpent's deadly fangs to sow the field,
wait for the darkest hour of the night,   1330

then wash your body in a rushing river,
don an all-black mantle, and retire
somewhere alone, apart from your companions,
and dig a wide round hole. Once you have slit
an ewe's throat, drained the blood into the pit,   1335 (1033)
and laid the carcass, whole, upon a fire
that you have duly built up round the edges,
call upon Hecate, the only child
of Perses, while decanting from a goblet
the comb-begotten labor of the bees.   1340
Then, after you have dutifully sought
Hecate's favor, turn and leave. Make certain
neither the sound of footsteps nor the baying
of dogs moves you to turn and look behind you,
or you will cancel all that you have done   1345
and fail to come back ready to your comrades.

At daybreak steep the drug I have provided
in pure spring water, strip off all your clothes,
and rub your body with it as with oil.
There will be awesome power and boundless valor   1350 (1044)
within it. You will find your strength a match
not for mere mortals but the deathless gods.
Sprinkle your shield, sword, and spear with it.
The weapons of the earthborn men will never
injure you then, nor the unbearable fire   1355
that shoots out of the deadly bulls. Not long
will you be so enhanced, just one day only.
Be sure, then, not to shrink before the challenge.

And I shall grace you with a second favor:
once you have yoked the mighty bulls and swiftly   1360
with might and main plowed up the stubborn fallows,
then, as the earthborn men are sprouting skyward
out of the snake's fangs planted in the furrows,
cast a stone into their midst, a large one.
Make certain no one sees you. They will slaughter   1365 (1057)
each other over it, like wild dogs
contending over scraps of food. Make sure
that you yourself then rush into the fray.

Because of your successes you will carry
the fleece back into Hellas, to some place   1370
far from Aea. Go, though, all the same,
wherever you desire, wherever you
insist on going once you spread your sail."

With that, she fixed her eyes before her feet
in silence and suffused her gleaming cheeks   1375
with sultry tears, bereft because he soon
would sail the sea far, far away from her.
She took his hand and gazed upon his face.
Modesty left her eyes, and yet again
in agony she spoke to him:

                               "Remember   1380 (1069)
the name Medea if, by chance, you live
to come back home. When you are far away
I shall remember yours as well. Please, though,
kindly inform me where your home might be.
Where will you go when you go sailing off   1385
across the sea? Will you approach luxurious
Orchomenus or skirt Aeaea Island?
And please do tell me more about that girl,
the one you named, you know, the famous daughter
of Pasiphae, who is my father's sister."   1390

Such were her inquiries, and devastating
affection crept up over him, because
she was a maiden, crying. So he answered:

"Never, day or night, shall I forget you—
that is, so long as I escape my death   1395 (1080)
and do return uninjured to Achaea,
and if Aeëtes doesn't force still worse
trials upon us. If you wish to know
about my homeland, I will tell you of it.
My heart as well commands I do as much: 1400
there is a broad plain ringed by lofty mountains,
a sheep land rich in pasture. It was there
Prometheus, the son of Iapetus,
begat the excellent Deucalion

who was the first to draw up plans for cities   1405
and raise temples to the immortal gods.
He also was the first to serve as king.
My people call this land Haemonia.
My city Iolcus stands in it, and in it
stand a hundred other cities where   1410 (1092)
the name Aea never has been heard.
And, yes, a legend states that Minyas,
a son of Aeolus, once left this land
to build the city of Orchomenus
on the Cadmeians' eastern border. Why, though,   1415
do I keep rambling on about my home
and Minos' most reverend daughter
Ariadne? (That's the famous name
the lovely maiden you have asked about
once called her own.) I pray that, just as Minos   1420
eventually accepted Theseus,
your father may be joined to us in friendship."

So he responded, stroking her with soothing
utterances. Most distressing worries, though,
kept troubling her heart, and she was sad   1425 (1104)
when she addressed these throbbing words to him:

"Although in Hellas it may be considered
noble to keep one's word, Aeëtes differs
greatly in that regard from Minos, husband
of Pasiphae—that man you mentioned to me.   1430
Nor do I rank myself with Ariadne.
Say nothing, therefore, of a fond guest-friendship.
But think of me when you return to Iolcus,
and I shall think of you in spite of all
my parents say. May news or bird of omen   1435
bring us together, when we live apart.
Yet, if I slip your mind, may sudden storm winds
snatch me aloft and carry me to Iolcus,
so that I may confront you face-to-face,
reproaching you, reminding you that you   1440 (1115)
escaped this land alive by my assistance.

Yes, may I then appear out of the blue
and haunt you right beside your palace hearth."

So she proclaimed, with liquid sorrow streaming
down her cheeks. After a while he answered: 1445

"Sad maiden, let your storm winds rove
in vain and all your birds and rumors, too.
You're talking nonsense. If you come to Greece
and any of those places you have mentioned,
men and women will esteem and love you,   1450
yes, they will venerate you like a goddess,
some because your counsel helped their sons
come home alive, others because you saved
their brothers, relatives, and valiant husbands
from such great trouble. In our wedding chamber   1455 (1127)
you shall enjoy the marriage bed with me,
and nothing shall divide us from our love
until our predetermined end enshrouds us."

So he explained. The heart within her melted
to hear it, but she shuddered as it did,   1460
imagining the crime she would commit.
Poor maiden, she would not long shrink from living
in Hellas. Hera had already ruled
Medea of Aea would forsake
her fatherland and come to holy Iolcus   1465
to ruin Pelias.
                    Meanwhile the handmaids
watching them in silence from afar
grew agitated: daylight was expiring;
Medea should be home beside her mother.
The girl herself had not yet thought of leaving,   1470 (1140)
since she was so bewitched by Jason's beauty
and winning words. It was the son of Aeson
who sensed the hour and said to her at last:

"It's time for us to go, or else the sun
will set before you reach the court, and someone   1475

will note your absence and discover all.
But we will come back here and meet again."

They tested one another with endearments
so far, then turned and went their separate ways,
Jason departing to his crew and ship   1480
in an exultant mood, she to her handmaids.
They all went out to meet her, but she hardly
noticed them gathering around her, no,
her soul was flying through the clouds. Her feet
all on their own conveyed her to the wagon.   1485 (1152)
One hand reached out to take the reins, the other
the intricately braided whip, and off
the mules went toward the city and the palace.

When they returned, Chalciope of course
asked questions, since she hoped to save her sons.   1490
The girl, though, spun by swiftly shifting thoughts,
heard nothing and was not disposed to answer.
She settled on a stool beside her bed,
cheek resting flat upon her clenched left hand,
and worried, teary-eyed, about the plot   1495
she had devised, how traitorous it was.

When Jason joined his comrades at the spot
where he had left them to approach Medea,
he set out with them toward their shore-side camp,
recounting what she'd said along the way.   1500 (1165)
They reached the ship together. When the heroes
caught sight of Aeson's son, they greeted him
with questions, and he told them all about
the maiden's scheme and showed the potent drug.
Though Idas sat apart from his companions   1505
and gnawed his anger, all the rest were joyful
and, when the lateness of the hour compelled them,
cheerfully went about their chores.
                                        At daybreak
they sent a pair of soldiers to Aeëtes
to fetch the seed—Telamon, dear to Ares,   1510

and Hermes' famous son Aethalides.
Nor did this embassy set out in vain:
when they arrived haughty Aeëtes gave them
the dire fangs of the Aonian serpent
they needed for the contest.
                    While in Hellas   1515 (1178)
searching for Europa, Cadmus found
this serpent watching over Ares' spring
in ancient Thebes. He slew it there and founded
a town at the direction of the heifer
that gave him guidance, as the Lord Apollo   1520
had prophesied. Tritonian Athena
knocked the fangs out of the serpent's jaws
and gave half to Aeëtes, half to Cadmus
the son of Agenor, the monster's slayer,
who planted them in the Aonian plain   1525
and took as citizens those earthborn men
left over after Ares harvested
the others with his spear.
               Aeëtes gave them
the serpent's fangs to carry to the ship
and did so gladly since he never thought   1530 (1189)
Jason would actually complete the labor,
even if he somehow yoked the oxen.

The sun god Helius was gliding under
the twilit earth beyond the farthest summits
of Aethiopia, and Night was yoking   1535
her mares, and all the men had made their beds
beside the *Argo*'s cables—all but Jason.
Once the Greater Bear, the constellation
Helica, had descended, and the air
had gone completely still beneath the heavens,   1540
he slipped off like some calculating thief
to a deserted spot with the supplies
he needed. He had spent the whole day fretting
over the details. Argus had already
brought in an ewe and fresh milk from the sheepfold,   1545 (1199)
and Jason fetched the rest out of the *Argo*.

When he had found a spot out of the way
and free of traffic, a deserted heath
beneath an open sky, he duly bathed
his supple body in a sacred stream,   1550
then wrapped around his limbs a pure-black mantle,
the one that Lemnian Hypsipyle
had given him as a memento of
innumerable vehement caresses.

He dug a pit, a cubit wide and deep,   1555
placed logs and sticks therein, and lit a bonfire,
then slit a sheep's throat over it and duly
laid on the victim. Once the fire was burning
solidly upward from the woodpile's base,
he poured a mix of liquid offerings   1560 (1210)
upon it, begging Brimo Hecate
please to assist him in the coming trial.
After the prayer, he backed up without turning.
The awesome goddess heard him and ascended
through deep moist caverns to accept his gifts,   1565
and horrid serpents crowned her head, with oak leaves
mixed in among them, and the glow of torches
gleamed far and wide, and hellhounds howled keenly
around her, and the swampy meadow trembled
beneath her footsteps. All the moorland nymphs,   1570
the ones who traipse in rings around the flats
of Amaranthian Phasis, trilled and shrieked.
Though awe instantly gripped the son of Aeson,
he never once turned round and looked behind him,
and so his feet returned him to his comrades.   1575 (1222)
The Early-Rising Dawn, by then, had climbed
over the snowcapped peaks of the Caucasus.

Aeëtes, meanwhile, round his torso bound
a hard breastplate, a special gift from Ares.
The god, in fact, had worn this very armor   1580
when he had cut Phlegraean Mimas down.
Then King Aeëtes put his helmet on,
a four-plumed marvel, golden and as bright as

sunlight emerging from the River Ocean.
Next he took up a buckler thick with bull hide   1585
and formidable spear. None of the heroes
could have withstood it, no, not since the hero
Heracles left the roster. He alone
could have opposed that mighty shaft in battle.

Phaëthon was waiting near at hand   1590 (1235)
holding a tight-knit chariot and team
of fleet-foot stallions for the king to mount.
Aeëtes soon got in, received the reins,
and took the broad cart road out of the city
to reach the field of contest. Countless rushing   1595
citizens thronged around him. Think of how
the god Poseidon travels in his war car
to Isthmia to watch the sacred games,
or Lerna's spring, Taenarus or the holy
greenery of Hyantian Onchestus   1600
before proceeding to Calaurea,
Haemonian Petra, forested Geraestus—
that's how Aeëtes looked, the Colchian chieftain,
riding behind a team of chargers.
                                    Jason,
meanwhile, obeyed the precepts of Medea,   1605 (1246)
steeped the magic herbs and laved his shield,
sword, and sturdy spear with the concoction.
When his companions pounded on the spear
to test its fortitude, they failed to blemish
the metal even a little—it emerged   1610
fresh and undented from their mighty blows.
When Idas son of Aphareus wildly
hacked at the spear butt with his giant broadsword,
the blade rebounded, and the clang resembled
that of a hammer that has struck an anvil,   1615
and all the heroes whooped with ecstasy
before the trial.
                  As soon as Jason rubbed
his body with the salve, he felt divine
and boundless vigor welling up within him.

His hands were tingling, quivering with vim.   1620 (1258)
Think of a warhorse eager for a fight,
the way it neighs and stamps the ground, the way
it rears its neck and pricks its ears, exulting—
that's how the son of Aeson looked, exulting
in the excitement of his newfound strength.   1625
The way he ran around, kicked up his heels,
and waved his ash-wood spear and big bronze shield,
you would have thought of winter lightning flashing
against a pitch-black sky, the bright forks shooting
from clouds that bring a thunderstorm in tow.   1630

No longer wary of the trial, the heroes
took their places at the rowing benches
and fought the stream. The plain of Ares lay
upriver on the far side of the city
as distant from them as a chariot   1635 (1272)
must travel from the starting line to reach
the turning post, when a deceased king's kinsmen
put on games for charioteers and sprinters
to do him honor. When the heroes landed,
they found the Colchians sitting at the foot   1640
of the Caucasus while Aeëtes wheeled
his chariot along the riverbank.

Soon as his shipmates bound the hawsers, Jason
vaulted ashore and swaggered to the lists,
on one arm shield and spear and in the other   1645
the burnished bowl of a bronze helmet, brimful
of jagged fangs. Save for these armaments,
he was all nude, like Ares, some would say,
or Lord Apollo of the golden sword.

His sweeping survey of the fallows found   1650 (1284)
a bronze yoke and a plow compact as iron,
its haft and harrow hewn out of one trunk.
Nimbly he jogged out to the plow and yoke,
planted the spear butt in the soil, propped the
helm up against the shaft. Then, stripping down   1655

to shield alone, he backtracked through a haze
of exhalation countless cloven hoofprints
until he struck on something like a burrow
or buried stall. Thence the bulls burst abruptly,
muzzle and nostril of a sudden scorching   1660
the air around him. Soldiers on the sidelines
recoiled in terror, but not Jason, no—
he spread his feet for leverage and fought them,
taking the shock as a rock headland greets
the big waves rising from a sudden squall.   1665 (1295)
Roaring, they stabbed and slashed with brutish horns,
ramming his buckler with their brows, but Jason
never retreated, never gave an inch.

Think of a blacksmith's bull-hide bellows, now
shooting a spire of cinders through a vent   1670
while stirring up the deadly blaze, now wheezing,
now still, and all the while infernal hiss
and flicker issue from the furnace grate—
panting and heaving thus, the bulls snuffed thrice
and bellowed, and a brimstone blast consumed him,   1675
calamitous but for the maiden's salve.

He gripped the tip of a right horn and yanked
masterfully, muscles taut, until the neck
had met the yoke. A quick kick followed after,
foot against brazen fetlock, and the beast   1680 (1308)
was hunkered on its knees. A second kick
crumpled the other. Casting shield aside,
he bore, head-on, a swirling ball of flame
by gripping earth more widely with his feet,
his left hand and his right holding the bulls   1685
bent over both on buckled knees.
                                    Meanwhile
Aeëtes gaped at Jason's fortitude
and Castor and his brother Polydeuces
played their part and dragged the yoke afield.
Soon as the bulls' hump necks were harnessed, Jason   1690
fed the bronze brace beam between the team

and drove its beveled end into the yoke loop.
The brothers shrank back from the flames, but Jason
took up his buckler, slung it over his shoulder,
and cradled in his arm the helm brimful   1695 (1321)
of jagged fangs. Like a Pelasgic farmer,
he pricked the oxen's haunches with his spear
and steered the stubborn plow unbreakable.

The bulls still mettlesome, still spitting out
eddies of frustrate flame, a roaring sounded   1700
loud as the lightning-frazzled gusts that warn
old tars to reef the mainsail. Soon enough
they lumbered forward at the spear's insistence;
soon enough the hoof-drawn harrow cleft
boulders and left them crumbled in its wake.   1705
Clods with the girth of soldiers loudly ruptured
and turned to tilth. Feet planted on the draw bar,
he sledded after, and each backward toss
sent fangs some distance from him, lest the rows
of earthborn soldiers rush him unprepared.   1710 (1338)
And still the bulls leaned on their brazen hooves
and lumbered forward.
                          At the hour when elsewhere
the third part of a workday still remained
and plodding plowmen prayed aloud that soon
the sweet hour of unyoking would arrive,   1715
here was a field already tilled and sown,
and Jason shooed a tame team back to pasture.

Since he could see no earthborn soldiers sprouting
out of the soil, he paused to catch his breath
and walked back to the *Argo* where his mates   1720
gathered around him, whistling and whooping.
He scooped the river with his helm, drank deeply,
and slaked his thirst. Stretching from side to side
to keep his muscles' suppleness, he puffed
his chest with lust for battle—rippling, ready,   1725 (1350)
keen as a boar that whets its tusks on oak
while slaver dribbles earthward from its snout.

Now in the god of slaughter's garden sprang
an army nursed in earth—all rounded shields
and tufted spears and crested helmets bristling;   1730
and from the soil through middle air the glint
shot to the gods. As, when a heavy snowfall
has covered all the fields, fresh gusts will scatter
the clouds in patches from a moonless night,
and crowds of congregated constellations   1735
light up the darkness from both sky and snow—
so rose the soldiers from the furrows, sparkling.

Jason obeyed the mandates of the maiden,
the clever one. He lifted from the field
a great round rock, the war god's shot to toss,   1740 (1365)
a mass four strapping laborers would struggle
to budge in vain. Raising it without strain,
he spun round and around and cast it far
into their midst, then under his buckler crouched,
valiant, in hiding. The Colchians went wild,   1745
roaring as hoarsely as the sea swell roars
on jagged cliffs. Aeëtes stood there dumbstruck,
dreading what would come. The earthborn soldiers
like famished mongrels snapping for a morsel
mangled each other round the boulder, falling   1750
to Mother Earth beneath each other's spears
like oaks or pines a leveling wind lays low.

Then, as a fiery meteor shoots from heaven
trailing a wake of light (a signal always
ominous to the men who see its brilliance   1755 (1379)
separate the night), the son of Aeson
dashed on the earthborn ones with naked sword,
slashed here and there and harvested them all—
the seedlings grown as far as chest and back,
the waist-high, the knee-deep, those freshly afoot   1760
and rushing to the fray—all fell beneath him.

As, when a border war has broken out,
a man who fears that foes will torch his yield

seizes upon a freshly whetted scythe
and runs to reap the too-green grain before   1765
the proper time has parched it to perfection,
Jason mowed the growth of soldiers. Blood
flowed in the furrows like torrential flooding,
and still they fell—some, stumbling forward, bit
the fine-ground, fang-fomenting dirt, some backward   1770 (1393)
tumbled or wallowed on an arm or flank
like beached sea beasts; a hundred more, hamstrung
before they first took steps upon the earth,
slumped over just as far with drooping head
as they had sprouted into air.

                    Such ruin,   1775
one can imagine, pelting Zeus would wreak
upon a vineyard—nurslings sprawling, stalks
snapped at the root, and so much labor wasted,
a crushing heartbreak and dejection pressing
the vintner who had set the slips himself.   1780
In such wise, heavy grief of mind came over
Aeëtes, and he turned homeward to Colchis
together with his Colchians contriving
how he might best contest the strangers' claim.
The sun went down, and Jason's work was done.   1785

BOOK 4

Now Zeus' daughter, deathless Muse, describe
for me the Colchian maiden's wiles and worries.
The mind within me spins in speechlessness,
wondering whether I should call the impulse
that drove her to forsake the Colchian people   5
a wild obsession's lovesick injury
or headlong panic running from disgrace.

Up in the palace all night long Aeëtes
worked with his council on a foolproof plan
to catch the heroes. He was vengeance-hearted,   10
wildly incensed about the painful contest,
but never for a moment thought his daughters
had worked to bring about the stranger's triumph.

Hera, meanwhile, had pierced Medea's heart
with poignant dread. The girl was shaking like   15 (12)
a nimble fawn that baying hounds have trapped,
trembling, in a densely wooded thicket.
All in a flash she sensed the aid she gave
the foreigners had not escaped her father;
her cup of woe would soon be overflowing;   20
surely her handmaids would divulge the crime.

Her eyes were full of fire, her ears abuzz
with trepidation. Time and time again
she gripped her throat, time and again pulled out
her hair, and moaned in sorry misery.   25
She would have drained a vial of poison, died

right then and there before her proper time,
and ruined all of Hera's plans, had not
the goddess driven her to run away,
in utter terror, with the sons of Phrixus.   30 (22)
Once her fluttering heart had calmed, she poured
the potions from her lap into the casket.
She kissed her bed good-bye and kissed the frame
around the double doors and stroked the walls.
She clipped a lock and left it for her mother   35
as a memento of her maidenhood,
then, sobbing, brought out heartfelt lamentation:

"I'm going, Mother, but have left this tress
to take my place when I am gone—farewell.
Farewell, Chalciope. Farewell, old home.   40
Stranger, I wish the sea had torn you up
before you ever reached the land of Colchis."

So she spoke, and from her eyelids tears
came pouring down. Picture a girl that fate
has torn out of a wealthy home and homeland,   45 (35)
how, since she is unused to heavy labor
and ignorant of what slaves do and suffer,
she goes abroad to serve a mistress'
relentless whims in terror—that's the way
lovely Medea crept out of the palace.   50
The latches on the doors undid themselves
all on their own before her muttered spells.
Barefoot, she scampered down the narrow alleys,
her left hand pressed against her brow and draping
a veil that cloaked her eyes and radiant cheeks,   55
her right hand holding up her dress's hem.

So, frantic and in fear, she made her way
by covert routes outside the battlements
of broadly paved Aea. No watchmen
observed her, no, she hastened past unseen.   60 (49)
Safely outside, she contemplated deep
within herself how best to reach the temple.

She was quite familiar with the roads
since she had traveled on them many times
in search of corpses and the earth's worst herbs,   65
the kinds that witches use. Convulsive terror
fluttered her spirit.
              The Titanian Moon
had just then risen over the horizon.
She saw the maiden straying far from home
in misery and cackled to herself: 70

"Well, well, I'm not the only one, it seems,
to slip away into a Latmian grotto,
no, not the only one to burn with love
for an adorable Endymion.
You bitch! How often you have woven magic   75 (59)
to drive me from the sky in search of love
so that, in total darkness, you could work
your sorcery at ease, your precious spells.
Now you are subject to the same obsession
I suffered. Yes, the god of lust has given   80
Jason to you—a grievous blow. Go on,
suffer, for all your ingenuity,
a heavy sentence fraught with misery."

So Moon was thinking, as the maiden's feet
carried her, swiftly, on. The riverbank   85
was steep but welcome to her, since she saw,
on the opposing bank, the vivid bonfires
the heroes had been stoking all night long
to celebrate the victory. A sound
out of the night, she called across the stream   90 (72)
to Phrontis, youngest son of Phrixus. He,
his brothers, even Jason recognized
her voice, and all the heroes stared in silence.
They knew, of course, just what was happening.
She shouted "Phrontis" thrice, and Phrontis thrice   95
responded, at the crew's encouragement.
The ship, meanwhile, was swiftly heading toward her
under oar. Before they threw the cables

onto the facing bank, the son of Aeson
had vaulted from the deck. Phrontis and Argus,   100
two sons of Phrixus, jumped ashore behind him.
Clasping their legs with either hand, she pleaded:

"I'm helpless. Save me, friends, from King Aeëtes,
and save yourselves. My deeds have come to light.
Danger is everywhere around me now.   105 (85)
Let us escape by ship before he mounts
his eager chargers. I myself will win you
the fleece by putting its protector serpent
to sleep. First, though, in front of your companions,
you, stranger man, must call the gods to witness   110
the oath you gave—that you shall never leave me
contemptible, despised, without protection,
once I have traveled far away from home."

Though she had uttered anguish, Jason's heart
greatly rejoiced. He hurried over to her   115
and eased her up from where she had collapsed
around her brothers' knees. His words were soothing:

"Sad maiden, may Olympian Zeus himself
and Hera, Wife of Zeus and Queen of Marriage,
attest that I shall take you to my palace   120 (97)
to be my wedded wife, once we have made
our journey home to Greece."
                                                Such was his pledge,
and he was quick to clasp her hand in his.
She ordered them to row the swift ship nearer
the sacred grove, so that they could acquire   125
the fleece against the wishes of Aeëtes
and sail off under cover of the night.
Their haste was such that word and deed were one.
They took the girl aboard and shoved off quickly,
and loud, then, were the grunts of heroes straining   130
to work the oars. Medea ran astern
and reached her hands out sadly toward her homeland,
but Jason soothed her fears with heartening words

and held her in his arms.
                          It was the hour
when huntsmen shake the slumber from their eyes   135 (109)
(because they want the most out of their dogs,
they never sleep the full night, no, they start
before the potent light of dawn effaces
the quarry's signs and scents). Such was the hour
when Jason and Medea disembarked   140
onto a grassy meadow that is called
"The Manger of the Ram" because the ram
first bent its knees in utter weariness
upon it, after bearing on his back
Minyan Phrixus, offspring of Athamas.   145
There was a soot-stained course of stones nearby,
the bottom of the shrine that Aeolid Phrixus
set up for Zeus the God of Fugitives.
That was the spot where Phrixus sacrificed
the gilded miracle at Hermes' bidding   150 (120)
(the god had kindly met him on the way).
At Argus' behest, the heroes landed
Jason and Medea near this altar.
They took a footpath, reached the sacred grove,
and found the huge oak tree from which the fleece   155
was hanging, brilliant as a cloud that glows
red in the rays of fiery dawn.
                               The serpent
lying before it reared his endless neck.
The sleepless slits had been alert and caught them
approaching, and his hiss was loud and monstrous.   160
The whole grove, then the riverbanks resounded.
Many Colchians heard it, though they lived
as far off as Titanian Aea,
way out beside the sources of the Lycus
which, as it leaves the loud, sacred Araxes,   165 (132)
joins with the river Phasis, and they swirl
together down to the Caucasian Sea.
Young mothers started up in trepidation
and squeezed the newborns cradled in their arms.
Their little limbs were quivering.

                                        Imagine   170
spirals, innumerable coils of smoke,
swirling above a pile of smoldering wood,
one billow coming swiftly on another,
each of them rising in a hazy wreath—
that's how the serpent rode on countless coils   175
covered with hard dry scales.
                              Soon, though, the maiden
fixed the writhing creature with her gaze
and summoned with a sweet voice Sleep the Helper,
the highest of the gods, to charm the serpent.
She also asked the Netherworldly Queen,   180 (147)
the Late-Night Wanderer, to support the venture.
Jason, terrified, came on behind her.

The song, though, had already charmed the snake.
Loosing the tension of his coils, he settled
upon his countless spirals like a dark wave   185
settling soft and soundless on a sluggish sea.
Still, though, his crested head was lifted, still
he burned to grip them in his deadly jaws,
and so the maiden dipped a fresh-cut sprig
of juniper into a magic potion   190
and drizzled it into his open eyes,
warbling all the while a lullaby,
as the aroma of its potency
spread sleep. The monster laid his head down then,
and his innumerable convolutions   195 (160)
lay flat among the undergrowth behind him.

Then, at the maiden's bidding, Jason took
the golden fleece down from the topmost boughs.
She stayed right where she had been, raining slumber
upon the serpent's head, till Jason told her   200
the time had come to head back to the Argo.
So they left the leaf-dark grove of Ares.

Just as a maiden catches in a gauzy gown
the shimmer of the full moon as it rises

above her lofty chamber, and her heart   205
rejoices as she looks upon the light,
so, then, did Jason hold the great fleece up.
A sheepfold's worth of wool gave forth a gleam
like flame that flushed his comely cheeks and brow.
Wide as a yearling ox's hide or that of   210 (174)
the stag that huntsmen call the "moose," the fleece
was golden on the surface, heavy, dense,
and thick with wool. The path that Jason followed
glimmered before him every step he took.
He started with the fleece around his neck   215
dangling from his shoulder to his ankles,
then rolled it up and stroked it, fearing greatly
some man or god would come and take it from him.

Dawn was already spreading through the world
when they arrived at camp. The heroes marveled   220
at the colossal fleece, jumped up and down,
giddy to touch it, take it in their hands,
but Jason held them back and threw across it
a freshly woven robe. He scooped the girl up,
set her down astern, and spoke as follows: 225 (189)

"No longer, friends, restrain yourselves from turning
homeward. By this maiden's means the prize
for which we undertook our grievous voyage
and toiled in misery has been attained.
And I shall take her home to be my wife   230
since she desires that it be so. Because
she has so nobly saved both you yourselves
and all Achaea, you must keep her safe.
Quite soon, I think, Aeëtes will descend
with all his men around him to prevent us   235
from sailing from the river to the sea.
Therefore, let every other man among you
sit and attend to rowing while the rest
hold up their ox-hide shields to make a strong
bulwark against the arrows of our foe,   240 (201)
and so safeguard our voyage home. We hold

parents and children, our entire homeland,
here in our hands. On our persistence hangs
the glory or the infamy of Greece."

Such were his words. He donned his battle armor,   245
and they replied with raucous cheers, and so
he drew his broadsword from the sheath and severed
the hawsers. Fully armed beside the maiden,
he stood up near the new steersman, Ancaeus,
and soon the ship went speeding under oar,   250
with all his comrades heaving, passionately,
to clear the river's mouth.
                              But by that time
news of Medea's love and treachery
had spread through town and reached the Colchians
and King Aeëtes. Armed from head to foot,   255 (214)
they started swarming toward the Council House
as thickly as the dead leaves tumble earthward
out of a tree with many boughs in autumn
—who could count them? So they all came swarming,
mad with clamor, down the riverbank.   260
Aeëtes was preeminent among them
because he rode upon a war car drawn
by wind-swift stallions, gifts of Helius.
His left hand waved a big round shield, his right
a giant pine-wood torch, while at his side   265
a six-foot throwing spear was pointing forward.
His son Absyrtus held the stallions' reins.

The *Argo* was already off, however,
riding the river's seaward current under
its oarsmen's power. Throwing up his hands   270 (228)
in wild frustration, King Aeëtes summoned
Zeus and Helius as witnesses
to all that he had suffered. Furthermore,
he leveled horrid threats against his people:

Unless they should by their own hands arrest   275
the maiden there on land or on the waves

of open ocean and return her to him
so that he could satisfy his rage
by punishing the girl for her misdeeds,
they all would learn, through summary beheadings,   280
what it was like to know his wrath and vengeance.

So he proclaimed, and when the Colchian sailors
dragged out their warships, loaded tackle in them,
and took to water, you would not have thought
so vast a gathering was an armada,   285 (239)
no, rather, an innumerable flock
of seabirds clamoring across the swell.

The winds were blowing strong to aid the heroes,
as Hera had devised, so that Medea
might leave Aea, reach Pelasgia,   290
and prove a bane to Pelias' house
as soon as possible. Three mornings later
they reached the coast of Paphlagonia
and tied the Argo's hawsers to the shore
right at the Halys River's mouth. Medea,   295
you see, insisted that they disembark
and honor Hecate with sacrifices.
Holy dread prevents me from divulging
all that she did to carry out the rites—
no man should know them; let my mind cease straining   300 (249)
to name them. But the shrine the heroes built
to honor Hecate remains today
for later generations to admire.

Jason and all the others then remembered
Phineus had informed them that their route   305
out of Aea would be different,
but what that route would be remained unknown
to all of them, so they were quick to listen
when Argus spoke his mind about their course:

"We four were sailing to Orchomenus   310
the way the faithful seer you met en route

had forecast to you. We already knew
there is another route to Greece. The priests
who serve the powers born of Triton's daughter
Theba recorded its discovery: 315 (261)

Not yet had all the stars that circle heaven
come into being, nor is any record
available, however much one searches,
about the sacred race of the Danaans.
Back then Arcadians alone existed,   320
the Apidanian Arcadians,
that is, Arcadians who, legends tell us,
lived in the mountains eating acorn mash
before the moon was born. Way back before
Pelasgia was under the illustrious   325
sons of Deucalion, the land of Egypt,
mother of all the men of old, was called
the fecund 'Misty Land,' and River Ocean
went by the name of ever-flowing 'Triton.'
This river was required to irrigate   330 (270)
the Misty Land because the showers of Zeus
had never graced its soil. (The annual flooding
is what brings up the ample harvests there.)

From there, they say, a certain king, relying
upon his soldiers' courage, might, and vigor,   335
pushed through all of Europe, all of Asia,
founding settlements along the way.
Some of the cities have survived, some not.

Though many ages have expired since then,
Aea has remained right where it was,   340
along with the descendants of the men
this king had settled there. The priests, you see,
preserved this ancient knowledge by inscribing
pillars with markers. You can trace around them
all the courses of the land and sea   345 (281)
from the perspective of a navigator.

The River Ocean's north-most arc is broad
and deep enough for vessels to traverse.
They label it the Ister on the pillar
and mark its whole course off. For quite a ways   350
it runs through an interminable plain
in one great rush because its sources rumble
and burst forth up in the Rhipaean mountains,
yes, up among the blasts of Boreas.
However, when this mighty river enters   355
the country of the Scythians and Thracians,
it splits in two. Half of the water drains
right there into the Eastern Sea; the rest
reaches a deep and navigable gulf,
a bay of the Trinacrian Sea, which borders   360 (291)
your homeland—that is, if the Acheloös
does, in fact, run seaward out of Hellas."

So he submitted, and the goddess sent
a clear and timely portent. When they saw it,
the heroes voiced approval of the route   365
he had described—a comet had appeared
before them, and its tail delineated
the heading they should follow.
                            Giddy, then,
they dropped off Dascylus the son of Lycus
and in a hopeful mood put out to sea   370
with bellied sails. The Paphlagonian mountains
were what they steered by, but they never rounded
Carambis, since a gale and gleams of fire
from heaven haunted them until they reached
the Ister's mighty spate.
                            As for the Colchians,   375 (303)
one squadron sailed beyond the Clashing Rocks
out of the Pontus on a useless search.
Absyrtus turned the rest of the armada
upriver at the Ister through the inlet
known as "the Handsome Mouth." Thus they went past   380
the neck of land and reached the farthest gulf
of the Ionian Sea before the heroes.

There is an island in the Ister's mouth,
a large three-sided island known as Peuca.
While its base looks outward toward the coastline,   385
its apex points upriver and divides
the outflow into two. The upper entrance
is called the Narex and the lower one
the Handsome Mouth. Whereas Absyrtus sailed
his Colchian sailors swiftly through the latter,   390 (314)
the heroes had already sailed around
the former.

        All along the river flats
shepherds abandoned their abundant flocks
because they saw the ships as sea beasts rising
out of the monster-generating depths.   395
None of these peoples ever had observed
seagoing vessels—not the Scythians
(who breed with Thracian tribes), not the Sigynni,
not even the Graucenni or the Sindi
(who at the time inhabited the vast   400
Laurian flatlands).

        Once the Colchians
had skirted Mount Angurum and, beyond it,
Mount Cauliacus where the Ister splits
and drains into the sea from two directions,
they passed, at last, the Laurian flatlands, sailed   405 (326)
into the Gulf of Cronus, and blockaded
the exits everywhere so that their foes
by no means ever could escape them. Meanwhile
the heroes moved downstream and reached the two
Brygian Isles of Artemis nearby.   410
One of them hosts a temple sacred to her,
but the heroes landed on the other
and thus escaped the soldiers of Absyrtus.
The Colchians, you see, had left those islands,
alone of all the islands there, untouched   415
because they venerated Zeus' daughter.
But they had occupied the other ones
and blocked all access to the sea. What's more,
Absyrtus had dispatched a host of soldiers

to posts along the neighboring coasts as far   420 (336)
as the Salangon River and Nesteia.

Outnumbered as they were, the Minyans
would have been worsted in an ugly battle
right then and there and so they cut a treaty
to put off all-out war. The treaty stated   425
the heroes could retain the golden fleece,
whether they had acquired it by guile
or simply stole it in the king's despite,
since he himself had promised it to them
once they had proved their mettle in the contest.   430
Medea, though, because her case was pending,
would be released to Leto's daughter's temple
and kept apart, until one of the local
scepter-bearing kings decided whether
she should return to King Aeëtes' palace   435 (348)
or travel with the Minyans to Greece.

Now, when the maiden learned about the treaty,
a wave of anguish rumbled through her body.
She rushed to Aeson's son, pulled him away
from his companions to a private spot,   440
and voiced her grievance to him, face-to-face:

"Jason, what is this plot you have conceived
concerning me? Have your successes launched you
into forgetfulness, so that you take back
all you said when you were gripped by need?   445
Where are the honeyed vows you made to me
with Zeus Savior of Suppliants as witness?
I ran off in contempt of all convention,
yes, with appalling urgency I left
the country of my birth, a glorious palace,   450 (361)
even my parents—all that I held dear—
and now alone, alone at sea, I travel
among the miserable kingfishers,
and all because of you and your concerns.
It was because of me that you survived   455

the trial of the bulls and earthborn men,
and then, when our misdeeds were widely known,
I foolishly procured the fleece for you
and called down horrid shame upon my sex.
Now, since I am your daughter, wife, and sister,   460
I say that I shall sail with you to Greece.

Kindly protect me, then, in every way.
Stand at my side, no matter what transpires,
and, when you meet the magistrates, do not
desert me, but be faithful to my cause.   465 (372)
Either let Justice and the Vow we sealed
between us stick steadfast within your breast
or draw your sword and slit my throat to pay me
fit retribution for my lust.
                                 You wretch!
If the authority to whom you handed   470
this stony-hearted arbitration rules
I am my brother's chattel, how can I
endure my father's glare? Ah, reputation.
What rancor, what harsh blows will I endure
to pay for all the awful things I've done?   475
And all the while will you be off somewhere
winning your heart-delighting passage home?
Never may Zeus' wife, the mighty queen
of whom you boast, allow you to complete it.

Remember me someday when agony   480 (383)
is squeezing you, and may the fleece then flutter,
dreamlike, into the depths of Erebus
and yield no good to you. Yes, may the Furies
drive you upon arrival from your homeland
because of all I suffered through your cruelty.   485

Themis will not allow my execrations
to tumble unfulfilled onto the earth—
because you swore an oath to me and broke it,
you traitor-hearted man. Not long, however,
will you and your companions sit at ease   490
and laugh at me, no, not for all your treaties."

So she threatened, and her bitter rage
boiled over—how she longed to torch the ship,
ignite the whole wide world, and hurl her body
into the blaze! Dreading what she might do,   495 (394)
Jason appeased her fears with honeyed words:

"Calm down, strange maiden. I don't like this, either,
but we are seeking means to stave off war.
A thunderhead of foes is flashing round us
because of you. The men who hold this land   500
are keen to help Absyrtus bring you home
because they think that you were kidnapped. Now,
if we engaged them hand to hand, we all
would suffer most abominable deaths,
and still more bitter, then, would be your grief   505
if we, by dying, left you as their prize.

This parley, though, is just an artful pretext
to draw Absyrtus out to his destruction.
Once their lord, your guardian and brother,
is dead, the locals will be far less keen   510 (405)
to take his side in this dispute about you.
Then I, for one, would hardly shrink from fighting
the Colchians, if they obstruct our passage."

So Jason said in an attempt to calm her,
but her reply was still more devastating: 515

"You listen now. Our shameless actions drive us
to still more shameless actions. It was I
who took the first false step. Once I was duped
by my obsession, higher powers forced me
to execute the evil scheme I plotted.   520

Tonight your comrades' part will be to fend off
Colchian spears in battle. Mine will be
to place Absyrtus safely in your hands.
I see, yes, you must welcome him to parley
with splendid gifts, so that I can persuade   525 (417)

the heralds heading back to him to make him
come all alone to listen to my plan.
Then, if the deed is pleasing to you, kill him
and start a battle with the Colchian soldiers.
I don't care."
                    So they together wove   530
a mighty web of ruin for Absyrtus.
They sent him many friendship-gifts, including
the sacred raiment of Hypsipyle,
a crimson gown. The Graces had themselves
made it by their own hands for Dionysus   535
on Dia. He bestowed it on his son,
Thoas, and he in turn upon his daughter,
Hypsipyle, who offered it to Jason
to take away, a finely woven guest-gift,
along with many other treasures. Neither   540 (428)
by ogling nor fondling this garment
could you fulfill your sweet desire for it.
The fabric still exhaled ambrosia essence
from the night when the Nysaean king,
tipsy with wine and nectar, lay upon it   545
to fondle Ariadne's gorgeous breasts—
this is the girl whom Theseus abandoned
on seagirt Dia after she eloped
from Knossos with him.
                    Once the plan was set,
Medea issued orders to the heralds—   550
they were to tell Absyrtus to arrive
after she reached the temple of the goddess
in keeping with the treaty and as soon as
the deepest darkness of the night had come,
so that they could devise a scheme by which   555 (438)
she would retrieve the mighty golden fleece
and bring it home to King Aeëtes' palace
(she had alleged it was the sons of Phrixus
who dragged her off and gave her to the strangers
as spoils of war). Making such false excuses,   560
she scattered on the airy breezes drugs
potent enough to lure a savage creature

down a precipitous cliff, even a creature
that happened to be very far away.

Wretched Eros, great abomination,   565
great bane of humankind, from you arise
murderous feuds and groans and lamentations
and countless other miseries besides.
Great god, may you arise and shoot your arrows
against the offspring of my enemies   570 (448)
just as you shot Medea's insides full
of cursed spite. How cruelly did she slaughter
Absyrtus, her own brother, when he came
to meet her? That's the next part of my song.

After the heroes put the girl ashore,   575
according to the treaty, on the Isle
of Artemis, the parties separated
and beached their vessels on opposing shores,
and Jason chose an ambush to await
Absyrtus first and his companions later.   580

The fatal promises deceived Absyrtus,
and he went sailing right away across the river
and landed in the darkest hour of night
upon the sacred isle. He started forth,
without a guard, to learn his sister's mind   585 (459)
through conversation, as a little boy
dares sailing on a runoff-swollen torrent
not even adults would attempt. He hoped
that she would plot with him against the strangers.

As they were settling the details, Jason   590
vaulted out of the leafy ambuscade,
a naked sword-blade hefted in his hand.
The girl was quick to turn her eyes away
and veil them, so that she would not behold
the coming deathblow and her brother's blood.   595

Think of a butcher slaughtering a bull,
a giant, big-horned bull—yes, that's the way

that Jason struck the man. He had been lurking
beside the temple that the Brygians
who live upon the mainland opposite   600 (470)
had built for Artemis. Knees buckling,
Absyrtus crumpled in the temple's forecourt.
A hero gasping out his life, he caught,
in both his hands, the crimson geyser streaming
out of the wound and smeared his sister's mantle   605
and silver veil as she recoiled from him.
A dauntless Fury watched it all, sidelong
and without sympathy—a putrid deed.

The son of Aeson, then, the hero, hacked off
the corpse's limbs, three times imbibed its blood   610
and spat the taint out through his teeth three times,
as is the proper way for murderers
to purge perfidious assassination.
He stashed the sagging carcass in the earth,
and to this day the bones are lying there   615 (481)
among a people known as the "Absyrtians."

As soon as his companions saw before them
the glimmer of the torch the girl had raised
to signal them to come, they rowed the *Argo*
up alongside the Colchian ship and started   620
massacring all the men aboard it
as hawks descend upon a flock of doves,
or savage lions, when they reach the fold,
pounce on a teeming flock of huddled sheep.
They overwhelmed them like a conflagration,   625
slaughtered them—none of them escaped destruction.
Jason returned at last to join the battle,
but his companions needed no assistance;
rather, they had been worrying for him.

When they were done, they all sat down to form   630 (492)
some prudent plan about their journey home.
Medea joined in the deliberations,
but Peleus was first to speak his mind:

"I say that right now while the night remains
we climb aboard and row in the direction   635
opposite to the one that they are watching.
At dawn, when they discover what has happened,
I doubt that anyone among them urging
further pursuit of us will win support.
Like any people orphaned of a leader,   640
they will be rent by nasty factions. Then,
after their forces are divided, we shall find
safe passage when we come back later on."

So he proposed, and all the young men cheered
the words of Peleus. They leapt aboard   645 (503)
without delay and labored at the oars
relentlessly until they reached the farthest
island in the chain, divine Electris,
right next to the Eridanus' mouth.

Soon as the Colchians saw their leader dead,   650
they swore to hunt the *Argo* and the Minyans
across the whole wide Cronian Sea. But Hera
checked them with horrifying lightning flashes.
Finally, then, since they had come to loathe
their homes in the Cytaean land and dread   655
Aeëtes' savage temper, they divided
and sailed to settlements by separate routes.
Some landed on the very islands where
the heroes had been beached. They live there yet
under the name they took from Prince Absyrtus.   660 (515)
Others settled near the deep and brackish
Illyrian River, where Harmonia
and old King Cadmus share a common tomb.
(Thus they were neighbors to the Encheleians.)
Still others settled in the mountain chain   665
known as "Ceraunian" (or "Thundering"),
because the thunderbolts of Cronian Zeus
frightened them from the island opposite.

Once their homeward journey seemed secure,
the heroes coasted back and bound the hawsers   670

to the Hyllaean land. The islands here
are packed in tight and jut so from the mainland
that it is hard for helmsmen to avoid them.
The local tribesmen, though, were kind. They helped
the heroes navigate the strait and earned   675 (528)
a tripod of Apollo in return.

You see, when Jason went to holy Pytho
to ask about the quest, Apollo gave him
two tripods to be kept aboard the ship
throughout the journey he would undergo.   680
According to the oracle, no hostile
forces would ever occupy a land
that kept one of these sacred tripods in it.
Thus, even to this day, the tripod stands
close to the friendly citadel of Hyllus,   685
but underground, so that it will remain
forever out of sight.
                        The heroes, though,
did not find Hyllus still among the living—
Hyllus, whom shapely Melita had borne
to Heracles among the Phaeacians.   690 (539)
Heracles, you see, had come to visit
Nausithoös' court and Macris, nurse
of Dionysus, to expunge the ghastly
murder of his own children from his hands.
And there it was he coveted and conquered   695
the daughter of the river god Aegaeus,
the water spirit Melita, who bore
Hyllus the Strong.
                    When Hyllus came of age,
he chafed beneath Nausithoös' rule
and wished no longer to reside beneath it.   700
So, after gathering from among the natives
a crew of Phaeacian journeymen,
he sailed into the Cronian Sea. (In fact,
the hero-king Nausithoös had helped him
outfit the voyage.) Hyllus settled here,   705 (550)
and the Mentores killed him as he fought
to keep a grazing herd of cattle from them.

Come, tell me, goddesses, how is it that,
beyond the Adriatic Sea, off near
Ausonia and the Ligystian islands   710
known as the Stoechades, such mighty
proof of the *Argo*'s route can still be found?
What great necessity, what wants and needs,
drove them so far abroad? What winds conveyed them?

After the brutal slaughter of Absyrtus,   715
Zeus himself, the King of the Immortals,
succumbed to wrath against the perpetrators.
He ruled that they must purge themselves of bloodguilt
under the guidance of Aeaean Circe
and then endure ten thousand miseries   720 (561)
before returning home. None of the heroes
knew of this verdict, no, they simply left
Hyllaea and went speeding on their way.

Soon they had left all the Liburnian islands,
one by one, behind them in their wake,   725
Issa, Dysceladus, fair Pityeia—
islands that lately had been full of Colchians.
Then they passed Corcyra where Poseidon
settled the fair-haired daughter of Asopus,
Corcyra, far, far from the land of Phlius   730
from which the god had snatched her up in love.
Sailors who see it from the sea, all wooded
and somber, call it Dark Corcyra.
                              Next,
cheered by a balmy breeze, they passed Melita,
sheer Cerossus, then, much farther on,   735 (573)
Nymphaea where the queen Calypso lived,
Atlas' daughter. They would soon have seen
the misty mountains of Ceraunia,
but Hera turned her thoughts toward Zeus' verdict
and heavy penalty. To force the heroes   740
onto the necessary course, she roused
storm winds, which fastened on the ship and pushed it
back to the rocky island of Electris.
Next thing they knew, as they were dashing backward,

one of the *Argo*'s beams, the one Athena   745
had chopped out of an oak tree in Dodona
and fitted as the *Argo*'s keel, emitted
a human voice, a warning. Holy dread
possessed them when they heard the voice proclaiming
Zeus' terms—to wit, that they would never   750 (585)
survive the long sea paths and fierce sea squalls
unless the goddess Circe washed away
their cruel assassination of Absyrtus.
What's more, it told the brothers Polydeuces
and Castor to beseech the gods to grant   755
safe passage into the Ausonian Sea
where they must stop and visit Circe, daughter
of Helius and Persa. So the *Argo*
cried through the night. Tyndareus' sons
arose and raised their hands to the immortals,   760
praying, *Please, may all this come to pass,*
though grief had gripped the other Minyan heroes.

The ship dashed onward under sail and reached
the halfway point on the Eridanus
where Phaëthon, chest smitten by a flashing   765 (598)
lightning bolt, fell, half-incinerated,
out of the chariot of Helius
into the river muck, and to this day
foul vapors rising from the smoldering wound
bubble out of the brackish slick. No bird   770
can pass on flapping wings above that fen,
no, they all catch fire and drop midflight.

Hidden in lofty poplars there, sad maidens,
the Heliades, raise sorrowful laments
and from their eyelids gleaming drops of amber   775
fall to the sand. The sunlight dries them there.
Then, when a strong wind heaves the current over
its banks, the flood tide rolls them, hardened balls
of amber, into the Eridanus.

The Celts, who give a variant of the story,   780 (611)
claim that the tears the rapids sweep along

are really those that Leto's son Apollo
shed many years before, when Zeus was angry
over the boy that beautiful Coronis
bore to Apollo, next to the Amyrus,   785
on gleaming Lacereia. Riled in turn,
Apollo spurned the sky and stayed awhile
among the holy Hyperborean tribes.
Such is the story told among the Celts.

The heroes felt no thirst or hunger there,   790
nor did their minds think happy thoughts. No, rather,
all day burdened with the noxious stench,
they tired and sickened. The Eridanus
and all its streams were boiling off the vapors
of Phaëthon's still smoldering corpse—   795 (623)
unbearable. All night the heroes heard
the Heliades lamenting his demise,
weeping and weeping, and their tears went drifting
downstream like little drops of oil.
                                        From there
they crossed into the deeply flowing Rhône.   800
Here, where it marries the Eridanus,
enemy roars contend. The Rhône, you see,
starts at the farthest outskirts of the earth
where Night's portcullis and embankments stand.
Part of it flows into the River Ocean,   805
part empties into the Ionian Sea,
and part goes rushing out through seven mouths
into a large bay off Sardinia.

While on the Rhône, they crossed into a chain
of stormy lakes that pock the vast, unmeasured   810 (635)
plains of the Celts. They almost met with shameful
destruction there because a tributary
was trending off into the Gulf of Ocean,
and they, in ignorance, resolved to take it.
They never would have gotten out alive.   815
But Hera leapt from heaven just in time
and shrieked *turn back!* from a Hercynian peak,
and all the heroes trembled at the cry,

so ominously did the vast sky echo.
So, with divine assistance, they reversed   820
their course and found a route to take them home.

A good long slog, and they had reached at last
a beach and ocean breakers, after passing,
unchallenged, through a thousand tribes of Celts
and Ligyans, and all because of Hera—   825 (647)
she poured impenetrable mist around them
all the days they traveled on the river.

They coasted out the fourth mouth of the seven
and beached safely amid the Stoechades,
thanks to the sons of Zeus—this is the reason   830
altars and rites were founded here to honor
the two of them forever. They were not
to serve as saviors only on that voyage,
but Zeus bestowed on them the privilege
of saving future sailors' vessels, too.   835

Once past the Stoechades, the heroes reached
the island of Aethalia and there,
exhausted, scrubbed away their scum of sweat
with pebbles, and the pebbles on that beach
are fleshy colored to this very day.   840 (657)
Their discuses of stone and marvelous tackle
are still there also, and the site is named
The *Argo*'s Anchorage because of them.

From there they sailed swiftly through the heaving
Ausonian Sea with the Tyrrhenian coast   845
in view beside them. After they arrived
at the illustrious harbor of Aeaea,
they tied the lines up at the nearest shore.
And there was Circe in the sea spray washing
her hair because a dream had troubled her.   850

During the night it seemed that all the walls
and chambers of her house were dripping blood,

and flames were eating up the cache of drugs
with which she had, up to that time, bewitched
whoever came to visit. She herself   855 (668)
had quenched the flames with sacrificial blood
and so recovered from her horrid fright.

And that was why she rose at dawn and went
to wash her hair and clothing in the surf.
And there were beasts around her that resembled   860
neither carnivorous animals nor humans
in any normal way but some mélange
of limbs from each. These creatures followed Circe,
as flocks of sheep in countless numbers follow
their shepherd from the fold.
                              Long, long ago,   865
before dry weather had solidified
the soil, before, as well, it had received
moisture enough beneath the arid sun,
Earth made this sort of thing all on her own,
a kind with mixed-up limbs, out of the slime.   870 (680)
And Time, then, sorted out and reassembled
the animals at long last into species.
Crossed like those ancient creatures, the amorphous
monsters of Circe followed in her train.
Boundless amazement overcame the heroes,   875
and when they gazed on Circe's skin and eyes,
they knew at once she was Aeëtes' sister.

When she had cleansed the terror of her nightmares,
she turned homeward and bade the heroes follow
by slyly stroking them as she went by.   880
The crew, however, at a nod from Jason,
remained behind, and he alone escorted
the Colchian maiden, and the two of them
followed the path until they reached the palace.
Though Circe was disturbed by their arrival,   885 (692)
she bade them rest at ease on polished chairs.
They sprinted to the hearth, though, without speaking
and sat there, in accordance with the customs

that rule the rueful rites of supplication.
Medea hid her beauty in her hands,   890
and Jason plunged straight down into the floor
the sword with which he killed Aeëtes' son,
and they did not lift up their eyes and look
upon the goddess. Thus she knew, straight off,
their lot was exile and their crime kin-murder.   895

So, in accordance with the rites of Zeus
the God of Suppliants who, on the one hand,
mightily despises murderers
and, on the other, mightily defends them,
she made the sacrifice required to cleanse   900 (702)
the suppliants sitting, tainted, at her hearth:

First, to expunge the deed's contamination,
Circe picked out and held above their heads
the offspring of a swollen-uddered sow.
Then, opening the piglet's throat, she lathered   905
Jason's and Medea's hands with blood.
A second time with different libations
she made an offering to Zeus Purgation,
the last defense of suppliant homicides.
The Naiad slaves who served her every need   910
then whisked the toxic stuff out of the palace.
Circe herself beside the hearth fire offered
wineless libations and devotional cakes
as gifts to soothe the dogged Furies' rage
and soften Zeus to leniency, regardless   915 (715)
of whether they implored his grace with hands
tainted by foreign or familial blood.

When she had finished with the expurgation,
she told them they could rise, then seated them
on polished chairs and took a seat before them.   920
She was the first to speak, inquiring all
about their quest, its purpose and the place
from which they came to seek her land and palace,
and why they had collapsed beside her hearth.
The troubling specifics of her nightmare   925

recurred to her as she assessed the couple.
What's more, she had been eager to discover
their language ever since the maiden first
lifted her gaze up from the ground. You see,
all of the sun god Helius' descendants   930 (727)
are easy to identify because
their radiant eyes emit a light like gold.

All earnestness, Aeëtes' daughter answered
each of her questions in the Colchian tongue.
She told her of the heroes' quest and travels,   935
how they had toiled in the awful contest,
how she had erred by heeding her distracted
sister, and how, among the sons of Phrixus,
she had escaped her father's dreadful threats.
She left the murder of Absyrtus out   940
but Circe, all the same, surmised the crime,
pitied her sobbing niece and said:
                                        "Poor wretch!
Look what a scandalous, obscene elopement
you have devised. No, I do not expect
you will escape Aeëtes' brutal rage   945 (740)
for long. He shortly will be hunting even
the citizens of Hellas to avenge
his son's assassination. It was you
who perpetrated those appalling crimes.

Still, since you are my niece and at my knees,   950
I shall refrain, now that you're here, from making
further trouble for you. Go on, now.
Please leave my home and take this stranger with you—
whoever he might be that you have taken,
against your father's wishes, as your own.   955
Don't bother sitting at my hearth again
and supplicating me for help, because
your reckless schemes and impudent elopement
are things of which I never shall approve."

So Circe scolded, and insufferable   960 (749)
agony gripped the girl. She pulled a robe

over her eyes and poured forth liquid grief
until the hero took her by the hand
and led her, quivering, across the threshold.
And so they made their way from Circe's palace.   965

Cronian Zeus' wife had not been left
unbriefed of their departure. Iris saw them
leave the palace and informed her mistress,
Hera, who had commanded her to note
when they departed for the ship, and Hera   970
gave Iris fresh instructions:
                              "Iris darling,
if ever in the past you have performed
my bidding, set out on your rapid wings
and summon Thetis up out of the sea
to join me here. I have a need of her.   975 (759)
Next, travel to the shores where heavy hammers
pound the big bronze anvils of Hephaestus.
Tell him to pacify his fiery forges
until the heroes' ship has passed them. Next,
find Aeolus, who regulates the gales,   980
those naughty children of the upper air,
and give him my instructions: he must temper
all the winds of heaven so that not
the slightest breeze disturbs the sea, except
a kind west wind, until the heroes reach   985
Alcinoös' Phaeacian kingdom."

So she commanded. Iris flew at once
down from Olympus on extended wings,
tapered and glided into the Aegean
just over Nereus' deep-sea palace.   990 (772)
To execute the first of her three tasks
she swam in search of Thetis and delivered
the message, just as Hera had instructed,
to call the sea nymph up to talk with her.
Next, Iris paid a visit to Hephaestus   995
and told him to desist forthwith from swinging
his iron hammer. Then at last she reached

Aeolus, famous son of Hippotas.
While she was giving him the news and resting
her swift knees from her travels, Thetis left   1000
Nereus and her sisters, swam, then flew
up to Olympus and the goddess Hera,
and Hera offered her a seat and said:

"Hear, goddess Thetis, what I want to tell you.
You know how highly Jason and his comrades   1005 (784)
rate in my love. You know I pushed them safely
through the Clashing Rocks, when forks of fire
were violently thundering above them
and waves were boiling round the jagged headlands.
Now their journey leads them past imposing   1010
Cape Scylla and Charybdis' eruptions.
But listen. Ever since you were an infant,
I myself have nursed and cherished you
more than the other ocean goddesses
because you never dared to go to bed   1015
with Zeus, though he was sorely yearning for it—
yes, he has always had his love affairs
with mortals and immortals, too. But you
were fearful in your thoughts because you so . . .
esteemed me.
             Though he swore a mighty oath: 1020 (798)
Never would you be called the wife of god,
he never did abstain from leering at you—
against your will, of course—no, not until
venerable Themis told him what would happen,
how it was fated you would bear a son   1025
mightier than his father. So at last
he gave you up, for all of his desire,
so that no one would be his match and rule
the gods in lieu of him, but he would keep
his empery forever.
                      So I gave you   1030
the finest of the mortals for a husband
so that you might enjoy a heartfelt wedding
and bear a child. I summoned all the gods

down for the wedding feast, and I myself
held up the bridal torch in my own hands   1035 (809)
to pay you for the kind esteem you gave me.

Now let me tell the truth about the future:
your son—the one the Naiads now are nursing
in Centaur Cheiron's cave, the one who wants
his mother's milk—that very son of yours   1040
will come one day to the Elysian Fields,
and it is fated that he wed Medea,
Aeëtes' daughter, there. Mother-in-law,
therefore, protect your son's betrothed-to-be,
along with Peleus. Why do you hold   1045
so fixed a grudge against him? He was foolish,
but folly sometimes blinds immortals, too.

I am quite confident that on my orders
Hephaestus will desist awhile from stoking
his forges to a rage, and Aeolus   1050 (820)
the son of Hippotas will check the gusts
of rushing winds, that is, except for Zephyr,
until they reach the Phaeacian harbor.
You must guarantee the men safe passage.

My worst fears are the rocks and toppling waves,   1055
but you can foil them with your sisters' help.
Prevent my friends from plunging, through ineptness,
into Charybdis—she would suck them down
and keep them there. Also be sure they skirt
the loathsome lair of Ausonian Scylla,   1060
fell Scylla, whom the prowling goddess known
sometimes as Hecate, sometimes Crataeis,
conceived from Phorcys. Mind their course or else
this fiend will swoop down with her horrid maws
and gobble up the finest of my heroes.   1065 (831)
Yes, guide the *Argo* so that they escape,
if only by a hairsbreadth, their demise."

Such were the queen's commands, and Thetis answered:

"If all the gales and furious lightning flashes
do, in fact, relent, then I assure you   1070
I will be bold and push the ship through safely,
even if waves arise to check its progress,
so long as Zephyr keeps on stiffly blowing.

It's time for me to go and make my long,
long, indescribable journey through the sea   1075
to ask my sisters' help. Then I shall swim
to where the ship's stern cables have been fastened
so that the heroes at the break of dawn
will turn their thoughts again toward sailing home."

With that, the goddess plummeted from heaven   1080 (842)
and splashed into the churning dark-blue waves
to summon all her sister Nereids.
They heard and, when they were assembled, Thetis
delivered Hera's orders and at once
deployed them all to the Ausonian Sea.   1085
Then she herself, more rapid than a glint
of light or sunbeam clearing the horizon,
shot through the depths until she reached Aeaea
on the Tyrrhenian coast. She found the heroes
beside the *Argo,* playing skip-the-stone   1090
and shooting arrows. Thetis on the sly
came close and squeezed the hand of Peleus
son of Aeacus, since he was her husband.
None of the others could perceive her, no,
she showed herself to him alone. She told him: 1095 (855)

"No longer rest on the Tyrrhenian coast
but loose the cables of your speedy ship
at dawn—thus you will be obeying Hera,
your helper, since it is at her command
the maiden Nereids have all assembled   1100
to guard your ship and guide it safely through
the rocks they call the Ever-Floating Islands,
because that is your fated route. But you—
when you perceive me coming with my sisters,

do not divulge my presence to your comrades,   1105
no, keep it quiet or you will enrage me
still more than when your reckless shout enraged me."

So she explained and plunged into the depths,
and withering sorrow seized on him because
his wife had never paid a visit to him   1110 (867)
since she had first bereaved his bed and bedroom—
their son, the great Achilles, then an infant,
had been the reason for her anger.
                                    Thetis,
you see, was burning off his mortal nature
each night within the hearth fire and by day   1115
rubbing his tender body with ambrosia
to make him an immortal and prevent
grotesque old age from ravaging his body.
Peleus, though, leapt out of bed one night,
spotted his dear son writhing in the flames   1120
and raised a frightening cry—the fool.
                                    When Thetis
heard him, she snatched the baby up and hurled him,
screaming, onto the ground, and she herself,
her body like a breeze or dream, went swiftly
out of the palace, jumped into the sea,   1125 (878)
and never came back home to him. That's why
mute helplessness had bound and gagged his thoughts.
Nevertheless, he brought himself to tell
all Thetis' instructions to his comrades.

They stopped at once and set aside their games.   1130
Then, after building fires and strewing leaf beds
along the beach, they dined and slept the night
as usual.
            When day-reviving Dawn
had lightened heaven's rim, a swift west wind
arose with her, and they embarked and mounted   1135
the rowing benches. Quickly, then, they weighed
the anchor stone and set the gear in order.
Once under sail, they used the sheets to pull

the canvas taut, and stiff winds drove the *Argo*
onward.
         Soon they spotted Anthemousa,   1140 (892)
the gorgeous island where the clear-voiced Sirens,
daughters of Acheloös, sang sweet songs
to lure in and ruin every sailor
who passed their shores. Shapely Terpsichore,
a Muse, once bedded down with Acheloös   1145
and bore them to him. Ages back, the Sirens
had waited on Demeter's noble daughter
and sang their odes to her while she was still
unmarried. Now, though, they appeared part bird,
part maiden to the eyes.
            Always on lookout   1150
from their attractive-harbored roost, they often
seduced seamen from honeyed homecomings
by withering them with languidness. And so,
without delay, and this time to the heroes,
the Sirens hurled lilylike contraltos   1155 (903)
out of their mouths. The heroes would already
have run aground if Orpheus of Thrace,
son of Oeagrus, hadn't taken up
his lyre, set his fingers to the strings,
and strummed the rhythm of a lively march   1160
so that their ears were buzzing with a rival
and upbeat song. And so the lyre's vibrations
overpowered all those virgin voices.

Zephyr and the resounding ocean waves
rose up astern and swept the vessel onward,   1165
and soon the Sirens' song was less distinct.
Nevertheless, alone of his companions,
Boutes the noble son of Teleon
leapt from his sanded bench into the sea
because the Sirens' clear-toned notes had melted   1170 (914)
his spirit, and he swam through somber surges,
unlucky soul, toward shore. They would have snatched
his homecoming away right then and there
if Cypris the Erycian Queen had not,

in pity, picked him up out of the eddies   1175
and swept him safely to her seaside haven
at Lilybaeum.
              So, with great regret,
the heroes left the Sirens. Other dangers
awaited them, however—ship-destroying
menaces at the crossroads of the seas: 1180
Scylla appeared atop her sea-washed headland
on one side; on the other hoarse Charybdis
was gurgling and coughing water up.

Not far from them, the Ever-Floating Islands
were booming as the mighty sea swell struck them.   1185 (925)
Not long before, their summits had been venting
blazes of fire above the liquid rock,
and smoke so choked the atmosphere that one
could not have spotted daylight. Then, although
Hephaestus had retired from the forge,   1190
the sea was still emitting bursts of steam.
The Nereids assembled at this spot
from all directions to assist the heroes,
and then the goddess Thetis gripped the *Argo*
and steered it through the Ever-Floating Islands.   1195

As dolphins during tranquil weather rise
out of the depths and swim about a ship,
starboard, astern, larboard, and at the prow,
a joy for sailors, so the Nereids
emerged and synchronized their circulations   1200 (937)
while Thetis steered the course. Then, when the men
were just about to hit the Floating Islands,
Nereus' daughters hiked their skirts
above their gleaming knees, clambered atop
the rocks protruding from the froth of surf,   1205
and stood in two lines, one on either side.
The current rocked the ship starboard and larboard,
and all around the heroes ruthless breakers
were vaulting and exploding on the rocks,
which were like cliff walls towering above them.   1210

Now would the ship have broken up and sunk
to the abysmal bottom of the sea,
and rough waves soon would have been churning fathoms
above the wreck.
               Imagine maidens standing
upon a sandy shoreline, how they roll   1215 (948)
their gowns up to their waists, pick up a ball,
toss it around or high into the air
so that it never hits the ground—that's how
the Nereids passed the ship to one another,
keeping it in the air, above the breakers,   1220
always above the rocks, and all the while
sea spray kept shooting up around the heroes.

Mighty Hephaestus stood atop a cape
of sea-scoured stone, his brawny shoulder leaning
against a hammer's haft, to watch them. Hera   1225
stood there in radiant heaven watching them
and even threw her arms around Athena,
so wrenching was the frightful sight she saw.
So long as springtime stretches out the day,
the sea nymphs worked at portaging the *Argo*   1230 (962)
over the roaring rocks until its sail
picked up the wind and pulled the heroes onward.

Once they had reached the meadows of Thrinacria
where Helius' cattle graze and grow,
the Nereids like sea mews plunged asunder   1235
because they had fulfilled the will of Hera.
Then, through the mist, the bleats of sheep arose,
and lows, the lows of cattle, struck their ears.
There she was—Helius' youngest daughter
Phaethousa strolling round a dewy meadow,   1240
a shepherdess attending to her sheep
with silver staff in hand, while Lampeteia,
her cowherd sister, kept a drove in line
by brandishing a copper prod. The heroes
could see the cattle feeding on the lowlands   1245 (975)
and flats beside the river—none of them

were darkly colored, no, they all were white
as milk and glorying in golden horns.

They passed the island in the daylight hours
and cleaved the billows in a cheerful mood   1250
all night, till Dawn the Early Riser cast
her beams athwart their course. There is an island,
a curved one, facing the Ionian strait
in the Ceraunian Sea, its topsoil thick
and bountiful. Beneath the island lies   1255
the sickle that, as ancient legends tell us—
Muses, forgive me since I tell this story
out of necessity—the Titan Cronus
ruthlessly hacked his father's privates off.
Others have claimed it is the scythe that served   1260 (987)
Demeter, goddess of the Underworld,
who lived upon the island once and taught
the Titans how to harvest ears of grain.
The island, therefore, has been called Drepana
or "Scythe," the nursemaid of the Phaeacians,   1265
and all of its inhabitants are sprung
from Ouranus' blood.
                 The heroes rode
a gale wind in from the Thrinacrian Sea
and landed there, constrained by great exhaustion.
Alcinoös and all his people greeted   1270
their coming warmly and with sacrifices.
The whole town reveled, and you would have thought
that they were toasting their own sons' return.
The heroes felt as happy meeting them
as if they had regained Haemonia.   1275 (1000)
Soon, though, they drew their swords and raised the
   war cry—
in ranks before them stood a countless host
of Colchians who had passed the Pontic mouth
and Clashing Rocks to apprehend the heroes.
They swore that they would either seize the girl   1280
immediately or raise the battle cry
and fight to win their claim both then and there
and in the future once their king arrived.

But King Alcinoös restrained their zeal
to start a battle. He preferred to settle   1285
the troublesome dispute without both sides
embracing war. All in a killing fear,
the maiden pleaded time and time again
with Jason and his men and grasped the knees
of King Alcinoös' wife Arete: 1290 (1013)

"Queen, I beseech you, please have pity on me.
Do not surrender me unto the Colchians
to carry to my father. Please do not
be one among the race of humankind
whose minds by minor errors tumble rashly   1295
into disaster—so my mind went tumbling . . .
but no, no, it was not because of lust.
Let Helius' sacrosanct resplendence
and the unspoken rites of Perses' daughter,
the Nighttime Walker, vouch for the duress   1300
under which I eloped with all these men.
Fear, it was dreadful fear that made me think
of running off when I had gone astray.
No way around elopement could be found.

My virgin belt remains as innocent   1305 (1024)
and undefiled as in my father's palace.
Pity me, lady, and convince your husband.
So may the gods bestow on you a perfect
life, and renown, and children, and the glory
of an eternally unconquered city."   1310

So with a flood of tears she begged Arete
and then approached, in turn, her friends the heroes:

"Because of you, O mightiest men of all,
because of your affairs, I now am sunk
in desperation. It was with my help   1315
you yoked the bulls and reaped the fatal crop
of earthborn soldiers. Thanks to me, you shortly
will sail away to bring the golden fleece
back to Haemonia. And here I am,

bereft of country, parents, home, and all   1320 (1036)
life's pleasures, while I have restored to you
your homes and homeland, and your honeyed eyes
will gaze again upon your parents. No,
some grievous god has ripped those pleasures from me,
and I am wandering the sea with strangers,   1325
a derelict. Beware your oaths and vows;
beware the Fury who avenges suppliants;
beware the gods' resentment when I tumble
into Aeëtes' hands and perish piecemeal
under unending agony and torture.   1330

There stand before me in defense no temples,
no guardian towers, no battlements, but you,
just you alone, men ruthless in their coldness,
wretches who suffer not a hint of shame
on seeing me, a helpless little girl,   1335 (1048)
embrace the knees of an exotic queen.

When you were burning to acquire the fleece,
you would have rushed to join your spears in battle
against the Colchians and proud Aeëtes.
Now you forget your courage, though these men   1340
are all alone and far from reinforcements."

So she exclaimed and begged, and every man
she supplicated tried to hearten her
and soothe her misery. They drew their swords,
brandished their sharply whetted spears, and swore   1345
that they would not hold back from saving her
if she should meet with an unlucky judgment.

Night, though, the rest from labors, soon subdued
the weary men and stilled the whole wide world.
Slumber, however, never reached the girl,   1350 (1060)
but anguish churned her heart, as when a poor,
hardworking woman twirls and twirls her spindle
all night long, and all around her wail

the children orphaned since her husband died,
and tears drip down her cheeks as she considers   1355
the miserable lot she has been given.
Like hers, Medea's cheeks were wet with weeping
and her heart kept spinning, spinning, spun
by agonizing pangs.
                        Back in the city
Alcinoös and his respected wife   1360
Arete lay in bed within the palace,
talking about the maiden late at night.
As women do when managing their husbands,
she addressed him intimately:
                        "Darling,
please do something for me. Please preserve   1365 (1073)
this girl of many worries from the Colchians
and do, thereby, the Minyans a favor.

Argos and the people of Haemonia
live closer to our island, and Aeëtes
does not at all live near. In fact, we know   1370
nothing of this Aeëtes, only hearsay.
The maiden, though, has undergone harsh trials;
her pleas have split my heart in two. Therefore,
do not, my lord, release her to the Colchians
to drag away back to her father's palace.   1375
Yes, she was mad with folly when she gave
Jason the magic drug to beat the oxen.
Yes, she fled her ruthless father's wrath,
trying to cure one error with another,
as people often do with a mistake.   1380 (1082)
Still, I have heard that Jason since that time
has taken mighty oaths to marry her
in proper legal fashion at his palace.

My love, do not then stubbornly compel
Jason to break his oath, nor let the father   1385
inflict unending torture on his daughter,
if you can stop it. Parents can oppress
their children overmuch. Consider what

Nycteus did to fair Antiope
and what afflictions Danaë endured   1390
at sea through her own father's wickedness.
In fact, not long ago or far away,
that wicked king Echetus jabbed bronze brooches
into his daughter's eyeballs. Now she labors
under a grievous fate, forever grinding   1395 (1095)
grains of bronze in an unlighted dungeon."

So she pleaded, and the king's heart softened
under his wife's persuasion. He replied:

"Arete, I could have my soldiers scatter
the Colchians as a favor to the heroes,   1400
and all for that girl's sake, but I am loath
to disrespect the stringent laws of Zeus.
Nor is it wise to disregard Aeëtes,
as you propose. No one alive is more
kingly than King Aeëtes. If he wanted,   1405
he could bring war down on Hellas, even
from far away. Therefore, I must deliver
a judgment that will seem disinterested
in all men's eyes. But I will not conceal it
from you: I shall command the Colchians   1410 (1106)
to bring the girl back home if she is still
a virgin. But if she is not a virgin,
I shall not divide her from her husband
nor shall I yield unto her enemies
the child she may be bearing in her womb."   1415

So he disclosed and went to sleep at once.
His wife, though, stored his wisdom in her heart,
rose from her bed, and hurried through the palace,
and all her serving ladies rushed together
to wait on her. She whispered for a herald   1420
and sent a message, prudently advising
the son of Aeson to deflower the girl
and not risk pleading with Alcinoös.
And she revealed her husband would deliver

the following judgment to the Colchians: 1425 (1117)
that, *If Medea has remained a virgin,*
he will dispatch her to her father's home;
but if she has been sleeping with a husband,
he will not divide connubial love.

So she reported, and the herald's feet   1430
whisked him out of the palace to deliver
Arete's favorable news to Jason,
along with good Alcinoös' verdict.
The messenger directly found the heroes
sitting under arms and keeping watch   1435
beside the city in the port of Hyllus.
He told them everything, and his report
so pleased them that their spirits grew ecstatic.

Frantically, then, they mixed wine in a bowl
to offer the immortals, as is proper,   1440 (1129)
and duly dragged sheep to the sacred altar.
Yes, that very night they made the maiden
a bridal bed within the sacred cave
where Macris once had lived.
                                        She was the daughter
of Aristeaus, lord of honey. He   1445
it was who first invented apiculture
and olive pressing, after much hard work.
Off in Abantian Euboea, Macris,
his daughter, was the first nursemaid to hold
Zeus' Nysaean son up to her bosom.   1450
She also wet his holy lips with honey
once Hermes had retrieved him from the flames.
Hera had seen her, though, and out of spite
exiled her from the island. Macris, then,
went off and settled in this sacred cave   1455 (1140)
and gave the Phaeacians great abundance.

They laid a mighty mattress in the cave
and spread the glinting golden fleece upon it
so that the wedding would be more distinctive

and memorable in song. The nymphs collected   1460
colorful flowers and brought them in protruding
from their resplendent bosoms. Over them
a glimmer as of fire was flickering,
so scintillating was the light that issued
out of the golden wool. It sparked sweet yearning   1465
in all their eyes, but modesty restrained
each of the nymphs, in spite of her desire,
from reaching out and fondling the fleece.

The nymphs had come from various places: some were
daughters of the Aegaeus River, others   1470 (1149)
were dwellers on the peak of Melita,
and others wood nymphs from the tablelands.
Hera herself, the wedded wife of Zeus,
had summoned them to pay respects to Jason,
and to this day the grotto where the nymphs   1475
laid out the sweetly fragrant sheets and married
Jason and Medea bears the name
Medea's Cave.
            Meanwhile the heroes took
their spears in hand in case some gang of foemen
dashed upon them unforeseen. They also   1480
garlanded their heads with leafy sprigs
and to the thrum of Orpheus' lyre
melodiously sang the wedding hymn
outside the entrance to the bridal chamber.
Alcinoös' realm was not the place   1485 (1161)
where Jason son of Aeson had desired
to consummate the marriage, no, he rather
had hoped to do it in his father's palace
once he returned. The girl had hoped so, too.
Necessity, however, had compelled them   1490
to make love then and there.
                            The truth is, we
the members of the woe-struck tribes of mortals
never tread the pathways to delight
with confidence. Some bitter anguish always
shambles along beside our happiness.   1495

Thus, after Jason and Medea's souls
dissolved in sweet lovemaking, terror gripped them:
Would King Alcinoös, in fact, deliver
the verdict Queen Arete had described?

Dawn had returned, and her ambrosial beams   1500 (1170)
scattered the dusky darkness from the sky.
The island beaches laughed, the dew-drenched pathways
laughed as they ran in from the distant plains,
and there was movement in the streets, the townsfolk
were stirring, and the Colchians were stirring   1505
out on the farthest spit of Macris Island.

Alcinoös, in keeping with his promise,
went out to them at once to speak his mind
about Medea. In his hand he held
a golden staff, the staff of law, with which   1510
he rendered rightful judgments to the people
throughout the city. Phaeacian nobles
marched behind him in their battle armor,
and women swarmed out of the city gate
to see the heroes. Country folk as well   1515 (1183)
came in to hear Alcinoös because
Hera had made sure news was sent abroad.
One of them picked the best ram in his flock
and drove him there; another led a heifer
that had not yet been broken to the yoke;   1520
still others set up mixing bowls for wine,
and the aroma wafted far and wide.

Women presented garments they had woven,
as women will, along with gifts of gold
and every sort of splendor customary   1525
for newlyweds. They stood awhile admiring
the builds and faces of the famous heroes
and there among them Orpheus, tapping out
a merry tempo with a purple sandal
while strumming something gorgeous on his lyre.   1530 (1195)
And when the heroes sang the wedding hymn

the Naiads sang as well, sometimes in answer,
sometimes a wholly separate part, while dancing
a cyclic dance, and in your honor, Hera,
because you were the one who put the thought   1535
into Arete's mind to warn the couple
about Alcinoös' wise decision.

Once he had given his momentous verdict,
Alcinoös upheld it to the letter.
By then the consummation of the marriage   1540
was widely known, but neither King Aeëtes'
grudging anger nor the fear of battle
swayed his mind, since he had bound both parties
by steadfast oaths to reverence his ruling.
So, when the Colchians perceived appeals   1545 (1206)
were useless, and Alcinoös insisted
they either heed his word or keep their ships
far from his harbors, they were all so frightened
of King Aeëtes' threats that they entreated
Alcinoös to welcome them as allies.   1550
They lived awhile among the Phaeacians
until some tribesmen from Ephyra called
the Bacchidae arrived and settled there
among them. So the Colchian soldiers picked up
and settled on the island opposite.   1555
From there they moved, at destiny's behest,
to the Ceraunian hills of the Abantes
and then to Oricum and the Nesteians,
but all this happened many ages later.

The shrines Medea founded in the precinct   1560 (1217)
of Nomian Apollo still receive
annual sacrifices to the Moirae
and nymphs. Alcinoös bestowed rich gifts
upon the Minyans at their departure,
and Queen Arete did the same. What's more,   1565
she gave the girl twelve Phaeacian handmaids
out of the palace store to wait upon her.

They left Drepana on the seventh day.
A stiff, favorable wind arose from Zeus

that morning, and the ship was speeding onward   1570
before the gale. Still, it was not their fate
to rest their feet upon Achaean land,
no, not until they suffered further, farther
away in distant Libya. Soon the heroes
had left astern the Ambracian Gulf,   1575 (1228)
soon they had skirted, with their sails spread wide,
the Curetes' dominion and a string
of islands, the Echinades among them.

But, at the very moment when the land
of Pelops had arisen into view,   1580
a dismal gust of wind out of the north
seized them midcourse and carried them away
across the Libyan Sea for nine whole nights
and nine whole days until they coasted deep
into the Syrtes. Any ship that hits them   1585
never can sail back out to sea again.
Shallows are everywhere, and everywhere
tangles of bracken washed out of the depths.
The sea scurf passes over them in silence.
The sand extends to the horizon. Nothing   1590 (1240)
that walks or flies is ever stirring there.

Over and over flood tides leave the mainland
and then come rushing back to drag salt water
across the sand. One of these tides abruptly
dropped the *Argo* so far up the beach   1595
that little of the keel was still in water.
So all the heroes jumped out of the ship,
and sorrow struck them when they saw the sky
and the expanse of endless land extending,
just like the sky, into the endless distance.   1600
No path, no herdsman's shelter, no oasis
appeared. A dead calm haunted everything.
They said to one another in despair:

"Where have the storm winds landed us? Where are we?
If only we had laughed at deadly fear   1605 (1251)
and risked retreating back out through the Rocks

the way we came. It surely had been better
if we had gone against the will of Zeus
and died attempting something glorious.
Now if the winds compel us to remain here   1610
even a short time, what are we to do?
The coast of this vast land is too, too barren."

So each of them exclaimed. Ancaeus even,
their helmsman, helpless to relieve their troubles,
addressed them bleakly as they sat there grieving: 1615

"I'm sorry—we must die a shameful death.
There's no escaping this catastrophe.
Even if gale winds blow in from the land,
we've foundered on a desert. All the worst
a mortal can endure is now before us.   1620 (1264)
However far I stare into the distance,
I see more ocean shallows, brackish water
ceaselessly washing over dull gray sand.
This holy vessel would have roughly foundered
far from the beach, except the surf itself   1625
swept it at high tide inland from the bay.
Now that the tide has drained back out again,
only a surf too thin for sailing laps
about us, lightly covering the sand.
That's why I say all hope of sailing home   1630
is severed from us. Let some other man
display his skill. He's welcome to sit down
and take the tiller if he wants to save us,
but Zeus, it seems, has no desire whatever
to land us at our port of embarkation   1635 (1276)
in Hellas, even after all our efforts."

So Ancaeus spoke and broke down weeping.
The men with nautical experience
agreed with his despair. All hearts were ice,
all cheeks surrendering to sallowness.   1640
Just as when people wander through a city
like breathless ghosts, awaiting their destruction

by war or plague or some relentless flood
that will erase the oxen's work afield,
and all because odd omens have been witnessed—   1645
statues spontaneously sweating blood,
roars sounding, mouthless, from the holy groves—
and high noon only means more night in heaven,
and stars do not stop shining all day long,
so did the heroes wander without purpose   1650 (1288)
along the endless shore.
           A somber dusk
too soon came over them and, sadly, then,
they wrapped their arms around each other, wept,
and said good-bye, so that they each could then
go off alone, fall in the sand, and die.   1655
They staggered off, each farther than the last,
to pick their final resting places. Heads
shrouded by their cloaks, they lay unnourished,
weakening, all night long, all day, awaiting
the most horrendous death imaginable.   1660

The handmaids shuffled to a place apart
and clustered, wailing, round Aeëtes' daughter.
As unfledged nestlings chirrup desperately
when they have tumbled from a cliff-side nest,
or swans release their dying proclamations   1665 (1301)
from banks along the gorgeous Pactolus,
and dew-drenched glades are echoing around them,
and, echoing, the river's handsome current,
so did the maidens loose their long blond hair,
drape it along the dust, and wail all night   1670
a pitiful lament.
           And now these men,
these heroes, would have left their lives behind
and no names, no renown for later men
to study, and their mission would have failed.
But, as they withered there in helplessness,   1675
the local nymphs, the guardians of Libya,
took pity on them. Once upon a time,
these goddesses had come to tend Athena

after she leapt out of her father's head
sublimely armed. These were the goddesses   1680 (1311)
who bathed her in the tide of Triton Lake.

The hour was noon. The sun's most cruel rays
were scorching Libya. These powers gathered
around the son of Aeson, and their fingers
gently tugged the mantle from his head.   1685
He dropped his gaze out of respect for them,
but they were bright before him and addressed him,
terrified as he was, with soothing words:

"Unlucky fellow, why has feebleness
afflicted you? We know about your journey,   1690
how you were questing for the golden fleece.
We know your labors, too, the mighty deeds
you have performed while wandering across
the land and sea. We are the Lonely Ones,
daughters and guardians of Libya,   1695 (1323)
fluent in human utterance. Stand up now.
Stop grumbling and carrying on like this.
Go rouse your men. As soon as Amphitrite
unyokes Poseidon's smooth-wheeled chariot,
you and your comrades must repay your mother   1700
for all the pain she suffered bearing you
so long inside her womb, and you may yet
come to the holy country of Achaea."

So they spoke and vanished in a flash
from where they had been standing, and their voices   1705
faded away. But Jason started upright,
looked everywhere around him, and implored:

"Be kind, you noble powers of the dunes,
though I confess the meaning of your words
about our journey home eluded me.   1710 (1334)
Still, I shall rouse my friends and tell them all
you told me in the hope that we can find
some sign to guide us out of this morass.
In counsel many men outdistance one."

So he implored and leapt up, cloaked in dust   1715
from head to foot. He shouted to his comrades
far into the distance, as a lion
wandering through a forest roars to summon
his mate, and even distant mountain valleys
tremble at the sound, and all the herdsmen   1720
and oxen shake with fear. (But Jason's cry
was not at all upsetting to his men
because it was the bellow of a friend
calling to friends.) The heroes gathered round him,
their heads all hanging. Still, despite their sorrow,   1725 (1345)
he got the crew to sit beside the ship,
the women, too. He spoke among them, then,
telling them all that he had witnessed:
                                        "Listen,
my friends: as I was lying in despair,
three goddesses appeared to me, like maidens,   1730
but clad in wild goatskin from neck to waist.
They gathered round my head, pulled off my cloak
with no unfriendly tug, and bade me rise
all on my own and wake you up to pay
due recompense for all our mother suffered   1735
while bearing us inside her womb so long.
This should be done whenever Amphitrite
unyokes Poseidon's smooth-wheeled chariot.

I don't quite grasp the holy mandate's meaning.
They said they were, in fact, divinities,   1740 (1358)
daughters and guardians of Libya.
What's more, they claimed they had a thorough
    knowledge
of what we have endured by land and sea.
Suddenly I could see them there no longer—
some mist or cloud, it seemed, had hidden them   1745
right in the middle of their apparition."

So he explained, and they were all amazed.
Suddenly an extraordinary omen
appeared before the Minyans—a stallion,

gigantic, monstrous, leapt from sea to land,   1750
the mane golden and blowing round his neck.
After he shook the sea spray from his flanks,
he galloped off, his hoofbeats like the wind,
and Peleus exulted in the vision
and cried into the crowd of his companions: 1755 (1369)

"I hereby do proclaim Poseidon's wife
has just now loosed his chariot with her hands.
What's more, our mother is the ship herself
because, indeed, she bears us in her womb
and constantly endures the pains of labor.   1760
Come, let us lift her with a hearty heave,
place her upon our unrelenting shoulders,
and lug her inland through the sand-choked waste
along the course the sprinting horse has shown us.
For surely he will not go plunging under   1765
the earth. No, rather, I suspect his hoofprints
will point us toward a gulf that feeds the sea."

So he proposed and everyone agreed
to heed his plan.
                    The Muses own this story.
I sing at the Pierides' command   1770 (1382)
and now shall tell precisely what they told me—
that you, by far the mightiest sons of kings,
with strength and courage heaved the *Argo* up
onto your shoulders, also everything
the ship had in it, and you lugged that burden   1775
over the arid dunes of Libya
for twelve whole days and twelve whole nights. But who
could narrate all the pain and misery
they suffered at their task? Let no one doubt
they were descended from immortal gods,   1780
so weighty was the chore they undertook
out of necessity. They felt as much joy
lugging that tonnage down the salty bank
to Triton Lake as they did reaching brine
and easing *Argo* from their sturdy shoulders.   1785 (1392)

Then like wild dogs they all ran off
scavenging for a spring. Persistent thirst
weighed on them, many aches and sufferings.
Nor was their search in vain. They soon discovered
a sacred plain where only yesterday   1790
the earthborn serpent Ladon had been guarding
pure-golden apples in the realm of Atlas
while the Hesperides, the local nymphs,
murmured delightful hymns to ease his watch.
But, by the time the heroes reached the spot,   1795
Heracles had already shot the serpent.
There beneath the apple tree it sprawled.
Only its tapered tip was still in motion—
everything from the coils to the head
lay lifeless. Flies had melted round the wounds   1800 (1405)
because the arrows had injected poison,
the acid taint of the Lernaean Hydra,
into its innards. The Hesperides
were nearby, with their silver hands held up
before their golden faces, wildly keening   1805
over the carcass.
                    When the heroes gathered
around the nymphs, they withered in an instant
and turned to dust. Orpheus recognized
the sacred sign and for his comrades' sake
tried to appease the nymphs with winning words: 1810

"Beautiful, gracious queens, divinities—
whether you rate among the goddesses
who live in heaven, dwell beneath the earth,
or bear the name of solitary nymphs,
be kind to us and come, O powers, appear   1815 (1414)
before our longing eyes and point us, please,
either to where a spring escapes from rock
or where some freshet rises from the ground.
Please, please show us something to relieve
the fiery torture of our thirst. I vow   1820
that, if we ever make it home to Greece,
we shall reward you there as we reward

the foremost goddesses, with countless gifts,
feasts, and libations."
                          So he prayed to them,
using a plaintive and beseeching voice.   1825
They stood nearby invisibly and pitied
the heroes. First of all they made some grass
sprout from the sand and then, above the grass,
tall stalks arose and saplings soon enough
stood where there had been dunes: Hespera turned   1830 (1427)
into a poplar, Erytheis an elm,
Aegla a venerable willow's trunk.
Then they emerged out of the trees and looked
just as they had before—prodigious wonders!
Aegla addressed the men with gentle words   1835
in answer to their looks of desperation:

"A mighty boon to you in your afflictions
already passed through here—a most rude man,
who soon deprived our guardian snake of life,
picked all the goddess' pure-golden apples,   1840
and went and left us here in grief and horror.
Yes, a man came yesterday, a man
most murderous in arrogance and bulk.
Eyes glowering beneath a savage brow,
he was a brute without a trace of pity.   1845 (1437)
He wore around his bulk the raw, untreated
hide of a lion, held a sturdy bow
of olive wood and used it to dispatch
this creature here.
                          The fellow had arrived
on foot and, like the other guests we've seen,   1850
ablaze with thirst. He dashed about at random
in search of water, which, to tell the truth,
he wouldn't have discovered in the dunes . . .
save for that bedrock outcrop over there
beside Lake Triton. Either on his own   1855
or at some god's suggestion, he decided
to kick its base, and water gushed, full force,
out of the rupture. Leaning on his hands,

with chest pressed to the ground, he swilled colossal
volumes out of the riven rock until,   1860 (1448)
bent forward like a grazing beast afield,
he had appeased his superhuman belly."

Such was the tale she told them, and they all
burst into joy and ran like mad until
they reached the place where she had pointed out   1865
the spring. Imagine ants, earth excavators,
a dense gathering of them, how they swarm
around a narrow crack, or flies perhaps,
how they collect en masse around a sweet
droplet of honey with voracious lust—   1870
that's how the heroes pushed in tight around
the spring they found there gushing from a rock.
Without a doubt someone among them, lips
dribbling, shouted joyously:
                            "Amazing!
Even from far off, Heracles has saved   1875 (1459)
his friends when they were withering with thirst.
If only we could chance upon his footprints
while we are traveling across this land."

So they were saying, and the men best suited
to find their absent comrade rose in answer   1880
and headed off in separate directions
because the nighttime winds had stirred the sand
and wiped out Heracles' deep impressions.
Calaïs, Zetes—Boreas' sons—
took to their wings and sought him from the air.   1885
Euphemus sprinted off on speed-blurred feet.
Lynceus set out fourth—he had the gift
of long-range sight. As for the fifth man, Canthus,
bravery and the gods' commandments urged him
to learn, firsthand, where Heracles had last seen   1890 (1469)
Polyphemus offspring of Eilatus.
Yes, Canthus burned to ask what happened to him,
but Polyphemus had already founded
a glorious town among the Mysians

and later, longing for his home return,   1895
set out across the continent to find
the *Argo*. When he reached the Chalybes
who live beside the sea, fate beat him down.
A monument was raised for him beneath
a tall white poplar, very near the sea.   1900

The day the heroes searched for Heracles
Lynceus thought that he had maybe caught
sight of him, all alone and far away
on that interminable continent.
Lynceus glimpsed him in the way one sees   1905 (1479)
(or thinks he sees) the moon behind the clouds.
So, once he had returned to his companions,
he broke the news that no one any longer
could hope of overtaking Heracles.
The others came back, too—swift-foot Euphemus   1910
and both the sons of Thracian Boreas.
The hunt had come to nothing.

                                    Then, O Canthus!,
the doom of death took hold of you in Libya.
After you stumbled on a flock at pasture,
the shepherd who was tending it could only   1915
fight to defend the sheep you tried to steal
for your emaciated comrades. Yes,
he struck you with a stone and knocked you dead.
At least the man was not a slave but noble
Caphaurus, grandson of Lycorian Phoebus   1920 (1490)
and the respected maiden Acacallis.
Minos packed this maiden off to Libya,
his own daughter though she was, because
she had conceived a child by Apollo.
Their splendid offspring, known as Amphithemis   1925
and also Garamas, then bedded down
with a Tritonian nymph, who bore him sons:
Nasamon and intractable Caphaurus
who beat down Canthus to protect his flock.

Soon as the heroes found the corpse, Caphaurus   1930
did not escape harsh vengeance at their hands.

Then they took up their fallen comrade's body,
trundled it back, and laid it in the earth
with sighs and tears. They also took the sheep.

Then on the selfsame day relentless fate   1935 (1502)
claimed Mopsus, too, the scion of Ampycus.
No, he could not evade harsh destiny
for all of his prophetic prescience.
A person's death is fixed and unavoidable.
There it was, lying in a sand dune, shunning   1940
the midday heat—the lethal sort of asp.
Too sluggish on its own to sink its fangs
in accidental passersby, this breed
would never launch itself against a person
who spotted it in time and backed away.   1945
However, once it has injected black
poison into any of the breathing
creatures the life-supporting earth sustains,
the path to Hades is a cubit long.
Yes, even if Apollo plied his drugs—   1950 (1512)
and may it not be sacrilege to say it—
death would still be certain once those fangs
had pumped their venom. When the godlike Perseus
(known to his mother as Eurymedon)
flew over Libya to bring a king   1955
the Gorgon's freshly severed head, the drops
of red-black blood that fell onto the ground
sprouted into this noxious breed of snake.

And Mopsus, well—he set his left foot down
firmly upon the taper of its tail,   1960
and it coiled up around his calf and shin
and tore some skin out of him when it bit.
Medea and her handmaids scampered off
in fear, but he, a hero, bravely stroked
the open wound—the bite did not distress him   1965 (1523)
much at all, poor man. Already, though,
Slumber the Loosener of Limbs was spreading
beneath his skin. Deep darkness doused his vision.
Soon he had strewn his heavy arms and legs

along the ground and grown cold helplessly.   1970
Jason and his companions gathered round
and stood there gaping at his grim demise.
Not even for a short time after death
could he be left out in the sun because
the toxin right away had started rotting   1975
the flesh within him, and the hair all over
his body thawed and dribbled off the skin.
They hurried with their bronze-wrought spades to dig
a deep grave for the corpse, and everyone,
females and males alike, tore out their hair   1980 (1534)
and mourned the man, the sorry way he died.
Then, after they had marched three times around
the body, and it had received full honors,
they raised a funerary mound above it.

They boarded ship again and, with a wind   1985
out of the south blowing across the sea,
sailed off to find a path out of the lake.
Hour after hour they lacked a course and drifted
idly the whole day through. As when a serpent
wriggles, hissing, on its crooked way   1990
to slip from under a ferocious noon
and squints all round, its slits aglint with flickers
like little streaks of fire, until it finds
a crack and glides into a burrow—so
the *Argo* wandered for a long time seeking   1995 (1546)
a navigable outlet from the lake.
Orpheus then suggested they should lug
the tripod of Apollo off the ship
and set it on the shore, to leave a gift
for any local power that might guide   2000
their homeward journey. So they beached the ship
and placed Apollo's tripod on the sand,
and Triton, god of the unbounded ocean,
walked over, masquerading as a youth.
He scooped a bit of mud up, formed a ball,   2005
and gave it to them as a guest-gift, saying:

"Take this, my friends, since I don't have on hand
any appropriate gift to offer you.

Now, if you happen to be seeking outlets
into the sea (as sailors often are   2010 (1557)
when traveling in lakes), I can direct you.
Poseidon is my father, and he schooled me
thoroughly in the pathways of the sea,
and I am regent of the beaches. Maybe,
even in your own country far away,   2015
you've heard about Eurypylus, a man
brought up in Libya, home of wild beasts."

Such was his greeting, and Euphemus held
his hands out gratefully and gave this answer:

"If you, friend hero, are acquainted somewhat   2020
with Apis and the Sea of Minos, please
help us by giving us an honest answer.
We wound up here by chance. After the northern
storm winds marooned us on this desert coast,
we picked our vessel up, a heavy burden,   2025 (1568)
and lugged it overland until we reached
this giant lake, and we have no idea
where there is passage to the sea, so that
we may sail homeward round the land of Pelops."

So he explained, and Triton stretched his hand out,   2030
pointed toward a deep-blue estuary,
an outlet from the lake, and gave directions:

"There where the lake is calm and dark with depth,
a passage leads out to the sea. White breakers
are churning there on one side and the other,   2035
and there's a narrow channel set between them.
The effervescent sea beyond it stretches
past Crete to the exalted land of Pelops.
When you emerge among the open rollers,
cleave to port and skirt the coast so long   2040 (1580)
as it is trending to the north. As soon as
the coast retreats and slopes the other way,
cut seaward, and your journey will be safe.
Proceed in joy. As for the work involved,

there should be no complaints when limbs endowed   2045
with youthfulness are toiling at a task."

So, in a friendly way, he gave directions,
and they embarked at once, giddy to row
out of the lake at last. As they were speeding
eagerly onward, Triton seized the tripod   2050
and seemed to disappear into the lake,
so swiftly did he vanish with the gift.
Their hearts exulted at the hopeful omen—
a blessed god had stopped to aid their journey.
So all the men urged Jason to select   2055 (1593)
the finest of the flock and sacrifice it
and thus propitiate the god. He picked out
a sheep at once, held it above the stern,
and slaughtered it, proclaiming:
                              "Helpful god,
whichever power it was that has appeared   2060
upon this shorefront, whether holy Triton
Soothsayer of the Sea or Nereus
or Phorcys (as your ocean-dwelling daughters
address you), please be favorable and grant us
a heartwarming conclusion to our journey."   2065

While he prayed, he slit the throat and dropped
the victim from the stern into the lake.
Triton in answer surfaced, undisguised
and in his sacred person, from the depths.
As when a trainer who has led a stallion   2070 (1604)
onto the broad arena of the games
takes bushy mane in hand and jogs beside him,
and the horse obeys his master, head
upreared with mettle, and the foam-flecked bit
clinks as he champs it side to side, so Triton   2075
took hold of hollow *Argo*'s sturdy stern post
and pushed her toward the sea.
                              His upper parts—
head, back, and torso—perfectly resembled
the gorgeous bodies of the blessed gods,

but from the abdomen on down extended   2080
the forking tail of an aquatic creature.
He slapped the surface of the lake with fins
that, farther out, divided into spines
curved like the tapers of a crescent moon.
He pushed the ship a good long ways, launched her   2085 (1617)
across the surface, then abruptly plunged
into the depths. As they beheld, up close,
this awesome miracle, the heroes broke
into a cheer.
          There is a stretch of coast
known as the *Argo*'s Harbor to this day.   2090
Signs of the ship are there, as well as shrines
set up to honor Triton and Poseidon
because the heroes rested there that day.
At dawn, a healthy Zephyr in their sails,
they cruised along, keeping the desert coastline   2095
off to their right. Next morning they discerned
a jutting headland and the gulf that stretches
beyond it. All at once the Zephyr died.
A stiff south wind had risen, and their hearts
rallied before it. Once the sun had set   2100 (1628)
and Hesperus the herdsman's star had risen
(the one that brings tired plowmen home from work),
then, when the evening breezes died away,
they furled the sails, stepped the tall mast down,
and heaved upon the sanded oars all night   2105
and through the day and still were rowing, rowing
when daylight came around again.
                    From there
the distant, rugged island of Carpathus
received them and from there they had intended
to cross to Crete, which is of greater size   2110
than all the other islands in the sea.
Talus, however, stood there on the shore—
a giant wholly made of bronze. He broke
sharp rocks from jagged cliffs and held them up
as threats to keep the Minyans from mooring   2115 (1640)
once they had sailed into the bay of Dicte.

Long, long ago ash trees had given birth
to men of bronze, and Talus was the last
still living in the age of demigods.
The son of Cronus gave him to Europa   2120
to guard the island. Three times every day
he strode the coastline on his brazen feet.
All of his limbs and body were of bronze
impenetrable, all except the vein
that carried blood down through the ankle tendon.   2125
The tender film across it meant the limit
of life and death for him. The heroes, though,
subdued already by their own exhaustion,
quickly rowed the ship away from land
in terror. And they would have fled from Crete   2130 (1651)
in a distress of thirst and agony
had not Medea said as they were leaving:

"Listen. I think that I can kill that man
all by myself, whoever he might be,
yes, even if his body is entirely   2135
made out of bronze, so long as he is not
invulnerable. Come, then, friends, and hold
the *Argo* steady here outside his range
until he yields and tumbles down before me."

So said Medea, and they worked the oars   2140
to hold the ship steady outside his range,
and everyone was eager to discover
what sort of spell she would employ. She draped
a doubled purple veil before her face
and mounted to the deck with Jason holding   2145 (1664)
her hand and guiding her between the benches.

Once there, she sang hypnotic lullabies,
praising the heart-devouring Fates of Death,
Hades' intrepid monster hounds, who range
abroad in air to hunt the living down.   2150
In her entreaty she pronounced their titles
thrice in incantation, thrice in prayer.

Then, putting on a wicked cast of mind,
she hypnotized the eyes of brazen Talus
and held him helpless in her hostile glare.   2155
Grinding her teeth in earnest anger, then,
she hurled homicidal ghosts his way.

Father Zeus, profound astonishment
has stormed my mind—to think that death can come
not only through disease and injury,   2160 (1674)
but people can undo us from afar,
just as that man, though made of bronze, surrendered
and fell down underneath the far-flung onslaught
of that ingenious conjurer, Medea.

Just as he heaved a stone to block the heroes   2165
from reaching anchorage, he scraped his ankle
across a jagged rock, and all the ichor
drained from him in a rush like molten lead.
No, he did not long stand astride the outcrop
but like a massive tree atop a mountain,   2170
a Cretan pine that woodcutters had only
cut half through with their axes and abandoned
when they started back down through the forest,
and then the breezes shake it in the night
and then it snaps off at the trunk and comes   2175 (1686)
rumbling earthward, so did Talus totter
this way and that way on his stubborn legs
and then at last lost balance, toppled sideways,
and landed with a crash as loud as thunder.

So in the end they spent the night on Crete.   2180
When daylight came again, they built a shrine
in honor of Athena the Minoan,
drew water, and embarked, eager to row
quickly beyond the Salmonian cape.
But as they crossed the spacious Cretan Sea,   2185
a deep and nightlike darkness called the "Shroud"
swept down and frightened them. No constellations,
no moonbeams penetrate its deathlike blackness.

No, it was like the depths fell from the sky
or an abyss had risen from the depths,   2190 (1698)
and they themselves no longer knew if they
were on the waves or down in Hades' hall.
Left without options, they could only trust
the sea, wherever it might steer their course.

So Jason raised his palms and cried *Apollo!*   2195
Apollo! summoning the god to aid them,
and tears were falling from him in his grief.
He vowed to offer many gifts at Pytho,
more at Ortygia, and at Amyclae
countless gifts. And you, O son of Leto,   2200
ready of ear, came swiftly down from heaven
and settled on the Melanteian rocks
that crop out of the ocean. Perched upon
one of the pair of summits there, you brandished
in your right hand a golden bow from which   2205 (1709)
a dazzling light shot out in all directions.

A tiny island then appeared to them,
one of the Sporades beside the small
Isle of Hippuris. There they dropped anchor
and waited for the light of dawn. At daybreak   2210
they cordoned off a plot of land as sacred
in honor of the god and built a shrine
under the shade of trees. They also coined
a title there, Apollo God of Radiance,
because his beams were radiant, and they named   2215
that barren isle Epiphany because
the god revealed it to them, like a vision,
when they were sunk in fear.
                              The men could only
offer the god the paltry sorts of things
sailors marooned on desert shores could offer,   2220 (1720)
so, when Medea's Phaeacian handmaids
saw them decanting liquid offerings
of water on the blazing altar fire,
they couldn't keep the laughter in their chests

since they had only ever seen expensive   2225
ox offerings at Alcinoös' palace.
Delighted by their taunts, the men responded
with crude suggestions, and delightful insults
and sweet harassment sparkled back and forth
among them. So, because of all this humor,   2230
the women on that island to this day
fling naughty innuendos at their men
whenever in their holy sacrifices
they toast Apollo God of Radiance
and Guardian of the Isle Epiphany.   2235 (1730)

When they had loosed the cables, and the weather
was fair, Euphemus happened to recall
a dream that he had dreamed one night, a dream
sent down to him by Maia's famous son:
it seemed that he was clutching to his breast   2240
a clod of earth, a sacred gift, and white
droplets of milk were somehow nursing it,
and from the clod, small as it was, emerged
what seemed a maiden. Ravenous desire
took hold of him, and he made love to it   2245
but afterward cried out in lamentation—
he felt as if he had deflowered the daughter
he had been nourishing with his own milk.
Soon, though, the figure said to reassure him:

"Dear friend, I am the child of Triton, nurse   2250 (1741)
of all your heirs-to-be, and not your daughter,
no, Libya and Triton are my parents.
Please hand me over to the Nereids
beside the island of Epiphany.
I later shall emerge into the sunlight   2255
and be the grounds for all of your descendants."

Euphemus had retained this night encounter
within his memory and now divulged it
to Jason. Jason thought the dream resembled
an utterance of the Archer-King Apollo,   2260
and he himself proclaimed the prophecy:

"Dear friend, a glorious destiny awaits you.
Once you have thrown this clod into the sea,
the gods will make an island out of it,
and there your children's children shall reside.   2265 (1752)
The sea god Triton graced you with the earth,
a piece of Libya, as a parting gift—
it was none other of the deathless gods
than he who gave it to you when he met us."

So Jason read the omen, and Euphemus   2270
did not invalidate his friend's prediction.
No, giddy with the prophecy, he flung
the clod of earth into the sea and from it
emerged the sacred island of Callista,
the nursemaid of Euphemus' descendants.   2275
In former days they lived on Sintian Lemnos
but, driven thence, they settled down in Sparta
as hearth friends. Then, once they had moved from
    Sparta,
Theras, Autesion's distinguished son,
guided them to this island of Callista   2280 (1763)
and named it Thera after his own name.
But all this happened generations after
Euphemus.
                    After this they swiftly left
the great expanse of sea astern and landed
on Aegina. At once they set about   2285
a friendly contest over fetching water
to find out who could draw it and return it
first to the *Argo*, since the stiff tailwind
and hope for home were urgent. To this day
the Myrmidons compete with big jugs full   2290
of water on their shoulders, sprinting round
a track, light-footed, seeking victory.

O heroes, offspring of the blessed gods,
look warmly on this work, and may my song
grow sweeter year by year for men to sing.   2295 (1774)
No further trials befell you once you sailed

from Aegina, no other gales opposed you,
so I have now arrived at your adventure's
glorious conclusion. After gladly passing
the land of Cecrops, Aulis in Euboea,   2300
and the Opuntian cities of the Locrians,
you landed on the beach of Pagasae.

Notes

ABBREVIATIONS

fr. fragment

frr. fragments

Gr. Greek

Pf. R. Pfeiffer, ed. *Callimachus.* 2 vols. Oxford: Clarendon Press, 1949–53.

PMG D. L. Page, ed. *Poetae Melici Graeci.* Oxford: Clarendon Press, 1962.

V. E.-M. Voigt, ed. *Sappho et Alcaeus: Fragmenta.* Amsterdam: Plak and Van Gennep, 1971.

W. M. L. West, ed. *Iambi et Elegi Graeci.* 2 vols. 2nd ed. Oxford: Clarendon Press, 1992.

BOOK 1

1 1.1 *from you, Phoebus Apollo:* The *Argonautica* begins and ends (*Argonautica* 4.2293–2302) with poetic gestures that mark it as a traditional Greek hymn, one of the many indications of generic complexity of the poem.

1 1.7–8 *Pelias had received / a prophecy:* The background to the poem is given as a very short summary, set between parts of the proem: a feature of Hellenistic poetry is variation of emphasis.

2 1.28 *Past poets:* Interestingly, we do not have any evidence about whom the poet refers to here, whether individual poets, poems, or a larger poetic tradition.

2 1.34 *surrogates of my song:* One of the most enigmatic and debated phrases in the poem. It is clear, however, that the poet is in some way repositioning himself in relation to the Muses, traditionally figured as the direct source of the poet's artistic inspiration, as the opening lines of Homer's *Iliad* and *Odyssey* both demonstrate.

2 1.35 *Orpheus is the first:* Catalog is a traditional feature of the epic genre. Whereas the Catalog of Ships in Homer's *Iliad* assembles mul-

tiple leaders and peoples, Apollonius' catalog of heroes figures individuals who man *one* ship, the *Argo*.

2 1.36 *Calliope:* The Muse frequently figured as the patron of poetic song, Calliope appears here in the context of the epic narrative as the mother of Orpheus, often thought to be the first poet.

2 1.43 *still today:* A standard feature of Hellenistic poetry is the *aetion,* or "origin" of, among other things, contemporary natural phenomena, animal behavior, and cult practices. Apollonius' contemporary Callimachus composed a four-book poem, his *Aetia,* that interweaves a series of individual etiological narratives. There are many *aetia* in Apollonius' poem.

3 1.90 *he sank into the earth:* One of many fantastical moments in the poem. The *Argonautica* is something of a combination of the heroic and the fantastical (rather like the narrative of Odysseus in the *Odyssey*).

3 1.95 *the sacred signs exhibited by birds:* Augury through reading the flight or sounds of birds was a standard practice in Greco-Roman antiquity. A recently discovered papyrus roll of short poems attributed to Apollonius' near-contemporary poet Posidippus includes a section of poems on bird omens.

4 1.121–22 *Libya, a land / as far from Colchis:* A possible learned double entendre, as the Colchians were sometimes thought to be originally Egyptian (Herodotus 2). The image may be a subtle allusion to the extent of the Ptolemaic Empire at the time of Ptolemy II.

5 1.135 *Peleus:* The father of Achilles, hero of the *Iliad.* An ongoing leitmotif of the poem is that the legend of the *Argonautica* occurs chronologically *before* the Trojan War, while Apollonius' poem is composed many generations later than the *Iliad.*

5 1.165 *the* Argo *was the most remarkable:* The construction of the *Argo,* the story *not* told in the opening of the poem, is invoked repeatedly in the course of the hexameter narrative.

6 1.190 *Hylas:* The hero's attendant is to be the cause of Heracles' separation from the expedition. The reference here, juxtaposed to that of Heracles' taskmaster Eurystheus, creates an ironic foreboding of what is to happen later in *Argonautica* 1.

9 1.288 *offspring of Hephaestus:* Hephaestus' hobbled feet are the source of laughter among the gods at the conclusion of the first book of the *Iliad.* Hephaestus' hobbled feet are a sign of his parents' wrath, those of Palaemonius rather one of the distinction of a divine father.

10 1.312 *a wonder to behold:* The Argonauts include among their number both the heroic and the fantastical, as befits a ship that has the power of speech.

10 1.319 *Argus:* With the shipwright of Athena, we return to the launch-

ing point of the catalog, the note that the poet would not sing of the ship's building, but of its heroes.

10 1.323 *"Minyans"*: Apollonius attempts here to clarify a problem in ancient genealogy regarding early southern Thessaly and northern Boeotia, to which he returns twice later in the poem, giving two other explanations. We do not know that all three of these explanations carried equal weight for the poem's audience. This one, that most of the heroes are descended from the shadowy figure Minyas, seems exaggerated (some certainly are: that Alcimide was descended from Minyas is found in Stesichorus).

12 1.378 *As a lonely maiden*: Apollonian similes are a fascinating enhanced development of Homeric ones, often with unusual implications within the surrounding narrative. Alcimede, through the possible loss of her son, risks being left a helpless and mistreated dependent.

13 1.425 *Think of Apollo*: The simile influences Virgil's description of Aeneas as Apollo at *Aeneid* 4.143–50. Apollo thus informs the poem as patron god of song, figure of comparison, and through his own two appearances as himself. The comparison of Jason to Apollo, and of Medea to Artemis in *Argonautica* 3, lends a particularly complex character to their eventual union.

14 1.456 *the course he thought most prudent*: One of many moments that mark Jason as cautious, a potentially ambivalent value in a traditionally heroic setting.

14 1.468 *mighty Heracles*: The heroes first choose Heracles as their leader, a moment that problematizes Jason's position among the assembled men and is indicative of a contrast of heroic types: managing details and alliances are not Heracles' standard attributes.

15 1.498 *the tasks at hand*: While eschewing to narrate the building of the *Argo*, the poet gives a detailed description of embarking the ship. A primary model for the scene is Odysseus' building of the raft in *Odyssey* 5.

16 1.540–41 *divvying / the benches*: Apollonius' response to an oft-repeated Homeric "set scene." Such scenes of eating, dressing, sleeping, and rising are a standard feature of Homer, and a characteristic of oral poetry.

18 1.625 *like a man in sorrow*: Jason's thoughtful, often reflective nature is at odds with the behavior of many an epic hero, as Idas' challenge here illustrates.

20 1.663 *forecast with your prophet's art*: A main model for this scene is Eurymachus' mistreatment of the seer Halitherses at *Odyssey* 2.178–80.

20 1.675 *He sang of how the earth*: Orpheus' cosmogony ("origin of the

world") is a reflection of earlier cosmogonic hexameter poetry. Orpheus was himself thought by many to have been the first poet.

22 1.742 *the gods looked down from heaven:* Another Apollonian response to a repeated Homeric scene, where the gods' major pastime in the *Iliad* is as spectators of the events on the battlefield. This is the only such scene in the *Argonautica.*

22 1.754 *infant Achilles:* The moment is emblematic of the poem's relationship to the Homeric epics. The Argonautica saga is of an earlier generation than the Trojan War, while Apollonius' poem is composed after, and in light of, the Homeric epics.

23 1.774 *Fish both big and small:* A fragment of the lyric poet Simonides (*PMG 567*) tells of Orpheus charming the birds and fish with his song, and suggests that Apollonius may well have had Simonides in mind here.

24 1.837 *Hipsipyle:* Earlier treatments of Hipsipyle and the Lemnian women include Aeschlyus and Euripides. Considerable fragments of the latter's play are extant. Callimachus (fr. 226 Pf.) also treated this story.

24 1.843 *Oenoa:* This unusual *aetion* plays, in chiastic form, with the possibilities of etiological transformation: Oenoa becomes Sicinus, Oenoa bears Sicinus.

25 1.874 *why have I digressed so widely:* One of several moments where the poet marks that his is not a continuous, linear treatment.

28 1.971 *Over either shoulder:* The description of Jason's cloak is a remarkable *ecphrasis,* a description of a work of art, or of a natural phenomenon in the manner of a work of art, in ancient Greek poetry. Over his shoulders Jason places seven scenes of Greek mythology; the final one blends into the *Argonautica* narrative—Phrixus is the father of the four Colchians whom the Argonauts encounter in Book 2.

29 1.998 *the shield of Ares in her hand:* Throughout the poem Apollonius plays on the reader's familiarity with the narrative told in *Odyssey* 8 of the love affair of Ares and Aphrodite, and Hephaestus' punishment of the errant couple. Aphrodite gazing at her own reflection is a standard theme of Hellenistic art.

30 1.1024 *Phrixus:* Son of the Boeotian king Athamas (who is Jason's great-uncle), Phrixus is driven, together with his sister Helle, by a cruel stepmother to flee on the back of a golden ram. Helle falls from the ram's back, thus giving her name to the Hellespont. Phrixus arrives in Colchis, where the golden ram is sacrificed, its fleece left to be guarded by a dragon. It is this fleece that Jason and the other Argonauts are sent to obtain.

30 1.1039 *like the star:* The first comparison of Jason to a celestial body. These similes highlight both Jason as the object of the (particularly female) gaze and the potentially destructive power of Eros (Love).

31 1.1076 *a vicious plot of Cypris:* This episode, while part of a tradi-
    tional myth, may have had particular resonance at the Ptolemaic
    court, where love and bloodshed were a feature of the lives of the
    reigning family.

33 1.1153 *Cypris Queen of Love:* An apparent but false ending to the he-
    roes' quest, a traditional feature of epic poetry.

33 1.1156 *had Heracles not called them:* The isolation from Heracles is a
    theme that gains ground throughout *Argonautica* 1, leading to his
    final separation from the Argonauts at the end of the book.

34 1.1178 *As bees swarm:* While the simile has Homeric models, it is espe-
    cially apt here in the context of the Lemnian women. Apollonian simi-
    les often have complex associations with the surrounding narrative.

35 1.1213 *and you have borne a son:* A passage Virgil may have had in
    mind in composing Dido's tragic lament at *Aeneid* 4.327–30 that Ae-
    neas has not left her the succor of a child.

36 1.1233 *of which it is forbidden me to sing:* A type of religious *praeter-
    itio* that allows just a hint of what cannot be told. Cf. Callimachus fr.
    75.4–7 for a similar first-person injunction that breaks into a sur-
    rounding narrative.

36 1.1259 *savage Earthborn Giants:* The reference to the Earthborn Gi-
    ants at once marks the island as primordial (so almost part of pre-
    heroic cosmogonic narrative) and underlines the early place of the
    Argonautica saga in Greek mythology.

37 1.1275 *the stone that served as anchor loose:* Another of many *aetia*
    in the poem, this one was also treated by Callimachus toward the end
    of his four-book *Aetia* (frr. 108–9 Pf.).

37 1.1299 *like Jason's:* Apollonius figures Cyzicus as something of a
    tragic double to Jason, hence the particular irony that Jason kills his
    young host—Jason's moment of epic heroism in the first book of the
    poem turns out to be one of unwitting manslaughter.

38 1.1322 *Jason's Way:* An *aetion* that marks the importance of mytho-
    history in Greek thinking about the past.

40 1.1380 *Just as he joined:* Cyzicus is killed at the moment of beginning
    a career as a heroic warrior, just as Jason's first act as a heroic warrior
    is to slay his host.

41 1.1425 *fastening a noose around her neck:* Cleite, in the manner of
    many female characters in Greek tragedy, hangs herself. On the
    tragic convention of women hanging themselves, see Loraux 1987.

42 1.1460 *Mother of the Blessed Gods:* The role of the Mother of the
    Gods (often figured as Rhea, or Cybele, or a combination of the two
    divinities) prefigures her role in *Aeneid* 9.

45 1.1559 *broke his oar:* Heracles' superhuman strength is ill-adapted to
    a cooperative effort like rowing—again his nature as a solitary figure
    sets him apart from the other heroes.

46 1.1600 *after dire Orion:* The simile is a particularly fitting one, since Orion, the solitary hunter, is cast apart from humanity (as a constellation), just as Heracles will shortly be separated from the Argonauts, and his solitary journey will appear around the periphery of the poem.

46 1.1607 *Hylas:* This figure appears in treatments by Apollonius' contemporaries Theocritus (*Idyll* 13) and Callimachus (*Aetia* frr. 24–25 Pf.), as well as the Roman poets Propertius (1.22) and Valerius Flaccus. In Apollonius' treatment, unlike Theocritus', the relationship of Heracles and Hylas is not specifically an erotic one.

47 1.1637 *how flush with beauty:* A recurrent feature in Apollonius' poem is the female erotic gaze, here of the water nymph on first catching sight of Hylas. Apollonius has a marked interest in the female psyche, which he develops to the greatest extent in his treatment of Medea in the third and fourth books of the poem.

47 1.1648 *so her right hand tugged:* A scene, oft repeated in Western art, of transference between two worlds, a motif with which Ovid was to excel in the *Metamorphoses.* The initial mirror scene in *Alice Through the Looking-Glass* would be a well-known modern parallel.

48 1.1686 *goaded by a gadfly:* The gadfly (Gr. *myops*) image recurs in the appearance of Eros at Aeëtes' palace in *Argonautica* 3. The simile here in *Argonautica* 1 is thus a very subtle suggestion on the poet's part of the relationship of Heracles and Hylas.

50 1.1746 *Glaucus:* This part-wondrous figure appears to "interpret" the gods' will to the heroes of the *Argo;* the Greek term *hypophetes,* "interpreter," recalls the poet's address to the Muses in the opening of the poem, and creates an understated moment of almost ring composition.

52 1.1818 *they rowed ashore:* Although there is no proem to the second book of the *Argonautica* (unlike Books 3 and 4), Jason's moment of landing forms a metapoetic closure to the first book. The second book likewise concludes with such a moment of disembarking.

BOOK 2

53 2.1 *Haughty Amycus:* The savage Bebrycian king is the antithesis of the correct host, and so takes on something of the role of the Cyclops Polyphemus in *Odyssey* 9. Apollonius' contemporary poet Theocritus also narrates the boxing match of Amycus and Polydeuces in *Idyll* 22 (see Introduction).

53 2.13 *who they might be:* Inquiring of a guest's origin and purpose is

one of the standard features of correct *xenia,* or guest-friendship, a
central social relationship in ancient mythology (and one that ensures
safe travel). Cyzicus is, tragically, a correct host: Amycus is the oppo-
site. Both come to terrible ends, the latter deservedly.

54 2.27 *Polydeuces:* Polydeuces is the immortal brother and twin of Cas-
tor (their sisters are Helen and Clytemnestra, the wife of Agamem-
non). He answers to the call to engage in a brutal athletic combat,
rather than Jason, another moment where the narrative problema-
tizes Jason's role as leader of the Argonauts.

54 2.46 *they had found a spot:* Boxing is an ancient sport for which there
were contests at Pan-Hellenic games, and which was celebrated in
ancient art and literature. Here, however, "civilized" athletic compe-
tition is turned into mortal combat.

54 2.55 *like the star of heaven:* Heroic comparisons to celestial bodies, a
standard feature of heroic vocabulary, usually refer to Jason in the
Argonautica. The comparison of Polydeuces, as the subsequent de-
scription of his youthful appearance, again casts him in a role of
something of a substitute for Jason.

55 2.90 *On a choppy sea:* This simile, which compares the forceful com-
bat of the two fighters to the struggle of a ship and a powerful wave,
is particularly effective given the surrounding narrative of the *Argo*
and its struggle with forces of nature.

56 2.129 *Castor was first:* The combat between superheroes being over,
Polydeuces' mortal brother, Castor, then enters the limelight. Castor
and Polydeuces, the *Dioscuri,* are important gods in Alexandria,
and they figure prominently in the promotion of Ptolemaic cult ico-
nography.

57 2.164 *And as when beekeepers:* A remarkable juxtaposition of simi-
les, one from herding, one from beekeeping, that have earlier epic an-
tecedents but also reflect a vivid Hellenistic interest in didactic poetry,
of which some lost examples include Nicander's *Georgics.*

58 2.184 *if Zeus had somehow left us Heracles:* Once Heracles has left
the *Argo*'s enterprise, he will reappear in a variety of ways on the pe-
riphery of the narrative, in comparisons, missed sightings, and future
references. Heracles' constantly present absence is one of the most
striking features of Apollonius' "modern" epic.

58 2.203 *sang a victory ode:* A reference at once to the performed poetic
art of *epinician* (poems sung in celebration of athletic victory) and to
Hellenistic inheritance of the genre as both performed art and text;
among the extant models of the *Argonautica* is Pindar's fourth *Py-
thian Ode,* composed in honor of Archesilaus IV, king of Cyrene.

59 2.225 *Phineus the son of Agenor:* The story of Phineus, his commis-
sion of sacrilege and his blinding, bears strong resemblances to that

of the Theban seer Tiresias. As in *Odyssey* 11, the seer's revelation, here of the course of the *Argo* through the Black Sea to Colchis, follows upon his being nourished, here by the Argonauts driving off the Harpies. There are also marked parallels with Callimachus *Hymn* 5, which tells of the blinding of Tiresias.

59   2.237 *Harpies:* These make a vivid reappearance in the third book of Virgil's *Aeneid,* where Virgil figures them specifically (lines 212–13) in their post-Phinean (and so post-Apollonian) existence.

61   2.312 *As soon as Zetes:* A fragment of the lyric poet Simonides (fr. 3 W.) may suggest (the text is very fragmentary) that Simonides treated of the brothers Zetes and Calais in his *Plataea Elegy.* This receives some support from a *scholion* (ancient commentary note) to Apollonius 1.211–15 (on Zetes and Calais) that notes that Simonides narrated the birth of the two heroes in his (now lost) *Sea Battle.*

63   2.364 *when their muzzles near the quarry's haunches:* The simile recalls something of the description of the golden brooch that the real (but disguised) Odysseus tells Penelope that he once saw Odysseus wearing (*Odyssey* 19.226–31).

63   2.372–73 *had not / swift Iris seen them:* In general, divine intervention in the *Argonautica* is rare, and markedly different from divine intervention in Homer (where gods appear to mortals in disguised form). Iris, the divine version of the rainbow, is something of an exception here, although again her appearance is rare.

64   2.398 *as people do in dreams:* One of several moments in the poem where Apollonius reflects a contemporary interest in the psychology of dreams.

64   2.406 *but what they do permit I shall reveal:* Phineus in his most Tiresias-like role. However, Tiresias foretells to Odysseus the future only *upon* his successfully reaching the island where the cattle of the Sun are pastured. The journey up to that point, beginning with the Sirens and the Clashing Rocks, is revealed rather by Circe at the opening of *Odyssey* 12, including her reference to the successful passage of the *Argo* (lines 70–72).

65   2.450 *into the Pontic Sea:* The geography of the Black Sea reflects Ptolemaic imperial interests in the area, and is dependent on a wide variety of models, among them Xenophon's *Anabasis.*

67   2.510 *everything from start to finish:* One of many moments of "Callimachean" metapoetics in the *Argonautica.* The poet, or here his spokesman Phineus, eschews a purely linear narrative in favor of an episodic one, with more attention to particular episodes.

68   2.543 *a second endless journey:* By this subtle sleight of hand, Apollonius introduces the possibility that the return journey will be by a different route than the outward one.

68 **2.554** *the goddess Cypris:* Cypris (Aphrodite) plays a major role in bringing about the action of the third and fourth books of the *Argonautica,* but particularly the third. The reference to a second journey, and to Aphrodite's role in the fulfillment of the quest, thus introduces the themes of the third and fourth books, interestingly, in reverse order.

69 **2.576–77** *if only light could shine / again:* It is worth noting that Jason's wish, as Phineus observes in his response, invokes an impossibility, what is often referred to as a poetic *adynaton.* This is another surprisingly awkward moment in Jason's portrayal.

69 **2.596** *Paraebius:* The narrative (on first reading seemingly superfluous) of the figure Paraebius effects a remarkable parallel with Apollonius' contemporary poet Callimachus. Paraebius' father sacrilegiously cuts down a tree in which a nymph dwelt, as does Erysichthon, the mortal sinner of Callimachus *Hymn 6* (to Demeter). The juxtaposition of Phineus and Paraebius reflects the heroes of Callimachus *Hymns 5* and *6,* and suggests that Apollonius knew these hymns in that order. See further in the Introduction.

70 **2.619** *he had been paying:* In Greek religious thought, *miasma* (pollution, sin) can be inherited as well as earned. Agamemnon in Aeschylus' play of that name is a classic example of a figure who both inherits the pollution of others and also brings about pollution by his own actions.

71 **2.652** *the Etesian Winds arose:* The Etesian Winds figure in Callimachus' *Aetia* (fr. 75), as does a mythographical history of the island of Ceos; the rape of Cyrene figures in Callimachus' *Hymn 2.* Cyrene will also appear at the end of *Argonautica 4.* Apollonius seems to be framing the Medea/Jason episode in a variety of ways.

72 **2.678** *Dog Star Sirius:* On his approach to Medea at *Argonautica* 3.1239–1243, Jason is compared to this destructive image. This is one of several moments of intratextual recall in the poem.

72 **2.705** *Euphemus was the one:* Euphemus recurs at the end of *Argonautica 4,* where again he holds a crucial element of future discovery in his hand, in the latter case a clod of earth from Libya that will transform into the island of Thera.

72 **2.708** *Nor did Athena fail:* One of the rare moments of divine intervention in the poem, mirrored by the action of the nymphs in *Argonautica 4.* Here, as will be true later in the book when the heroes catch sight of Apollo, the god appears in divine form.

75 **2.791** *just as the gods had fated:* An *aetion* that places the episode within a larger canvass of divine Fate. There is a striking parallel for this in the Phaeacians becoming stone on returning from delivering Odysseus safely to Ithaca in *Odyssey 13.*

75 2.813 *with subtle words and sidelong purpose:* Modeled in part on Agamemnon in *Iliad* 2, the passage is one of several in the *Argonautica* that highlights political astuteness and diplomacy as desirable qualities in a leader.

77 2.863 *Imagine oxen laboring to furrow:* One of many moments in Book 2 that prefigures what is to come later in the poem—here, the fire-breathing bulls that Jason will yoke as a feat of heroism in Book 3.

77 2.874 *"the morning twilight":* An hour that Callimachus evokes in a vivid description in one of the few longer fragments of his *Heacle* (fr. 74) as the "predawn."

77 2.877 *The son of Leto:* A truly remarkable moment in the poem, in which the Argonauts catch sight of the god Apollo as himself. A similar moment of revelation occurs when Apollo causes light to shine for the Argonauts toward the end of *Argonautica* 4.

78 2.914 *a choral dance:* The Argonauts perform a *paean,* a choral dance in honor of Apollo. There is a close parallel with this passage in Callimachus *Hymn* 2 (to Apollo), including the ritual cry *Hie, hie.* In both cases the poets have transposed a lyric poetic form into a hexameter narrative.

79 2.954 *a cave that leads to Hades:* These lines both echo the shadowy opening of *Odyssey* 11 and prefigure the site of Aeneas' descent into the Underworld in *Aeneid* 6. There is, however, a crucial difference: in Apollonius the expected journey downward (Gr. *katabasis*) does not occur; rather, this is replaced by the ingress to the river Phasis and the land of the Colchians.

80 2.984 *Jason named the names:* An unusual moment of catalog poetry (a much-beloved art form in the Hellenistic world) where the narrative of the poem up to now becomes the material of the catalog. There is a striking and controversial parallel in *Odyssey* 23, where Odysseus recounts the adventures of the earlier poem to Penelope.

82 2.1048 *Tyndareus' sons:* An *aetion* that also prefigures Polydeuces and Castor becoming the *Dioscuri,* twin gods (to the Romans Castor and Pollux) associated particularly with sailing, and of great significance in Ptolemaic cult.

82 2.1059 *Idmon son of Abas:* The deaths of the two seers, Idmon here and Mopsus in Libya in Book 4, frame the Jason and Medea narrative.

83 2.1092–93 *Because / I heed the Muses' will:* Here Apollonius varies the outline of the poet's relationship with the Muses that he suggests in the last line of the poem's proem (Book 1 line 22). This variation on the traditional phrasing of the rapport poet-Muse is a recurrent motif in the *Argonautica*.

84 2.1112 *they collapsed:* The first of two scenes that find the heroes given up to despair; the second occurs toward the end of the fourth book in the Libyan desert. In both cases the heroes are roused back to action by female divinities, here by Hera, in Book 4 by the Libyan maidens. While Apollonius generally does not use the type of repeated scene that is a standard motif in Homer (e.g., particularly scenes of dressing, eating, going to sleep), his repetition of larger thematic structures is one of the striking compositional features of the poem.

85 2.1170 *the Nysaean son of Zeus:* These lines briefly encompass the passage of the cult of Dionysus from India to the Mediterranean, one of the defining cultural evolutions of the ancient world.

87 2.1237–38 *their comrade / Heracles:* Again Heracles appears on the periphery of the poem's narrative. One of the models of this scene is Telemachus taking on the refugee seer Theoclymenus in *Odyssey* 16.

89 2.1304 *when a woman is with child:* On the anthropological phenomenon of male imitation of pregnancy and childbirth in antiquity, see Leitao 2012.

89 2.1312 *Odd laws and customs:* These lines are almost a short poetic rendition of Herodotus on the everyday life and practices of the Egyptians as opposite to those of the Greeks (esp. Herodotus 2.35). This is particularly striking at this point in the *Argonautica,* as Herodotus tells us that the Colchians were originally Egyptian (2.104–15), a narrative that in turn makes the cultural engagement of Greek and Colchian in Apollonius' poem particularly relevant for the Greek rulers of Egypt. Another text implicated here is Xenophon's *Anabasis* 5.4.26–34 on the Mossynoeci, an important source for Apollonius' Black Sea narrative.

90 2.1323 *Their ruler sits inside the highest tower:* Xenophon's *Anabasis* 5.4.26 on the king of the Mossynoeci is one text that clearly influences Apollonius here.

90 2.1355–56 *Not even / Heracles:* Not only does Heracles continue to figure around the margins of the poem, but so do past narratives about him, as here.

91 2.1365 *let's all set on our heads:* The stratagem to overcome the dangerous birds in part recalls Odysseus' plot to prevail over the Sirens in *Odyssey* 12, even though the Sirens and the contest with them will appear again in *Argonautica* 4. Each incident, differently and in part, recalls the Homeric original.

91 2.1383 *so half the heroes locked their shields together:* This reflects an actual military practice to avoid onslaught of missiles, in the Roman army known as the *testudo,* or "tortoise."

92 2.1405 *The sons of Phrixus:* The encounter with the sons of Phrixus brings two parts of the narrative together, with outward journeys

from Thessaly and from Colchis. The description of the shipwrecked Colchians recalls the shipwrecked Odysseus at the end of *Odyssey* 5, on the eve of the Phaeacian episode there, and its recasting in Apollonius' poem.

93 2.1449 *and give us clothes*: The act of supplication, and request for clothing, recalls Odysseus' entreaty to Nausicaa in *Odyssey* 6, and here suggests that a reworking of that episode is about to occur.

94 2.1471 *The ram, you see, could talk*: These lines evoke the last scene on Jason's cloak in *Argonautica* 1, where the ram appears to speak to Phrixus (1.1025–27).

96 2.1548 *The man could rival Ares*: The comparison is especially effective, as Ares, the god of war to whom Argus compares Aeëtes, is the god at whose altar the new friends have just offered sacrifice. At the same time the comparison heightens the fearful prospect of interaction with the Colchian king.

97 2.1585 *and infant Zeus*: Zeus as infant returns in the description of the ball at the opening of *Argonautica* 3, another example of Apollonius' frequent doubling motifs.

98 2.1606 *Prometheus*: As the Argonauts earlier saw the god Apollo himself walking across the landscape, so here they pass by earlier Greek mythology, the punishment of the Titan who gave fire to man. As in *Argonautica* 4 they will pass by the still smoldering Phaëthon, the Argonauts effectively enact their own place in Greek mythology.

99 2.1645 *or whether other means*: Epic choices are usually presented (as the one opening *Argonautica* 4) as two options, of which the latter is the one taken. While that is also true here, the option is not yet spelled out, as the "means," Medea's infatuation for Jason, has not yet happened.

99 2.1650 *and so they spent the night*: Apollonius recalls Odysseus at the end of *Odyssey* 5, when the shipwrecked hero is finally able to sleep on land, thus creating a pause to one line of narrative as another is about to open.

BOOK 3

100 3.1 *Erato*: Erato is one of the nine Muses (Hesiod, *Theogony* 75–79), who comes to be associated with love poetry (this passage is an important moment in that development). Apollonius opens his third book with an etymology of the Muse's name. This third book has markedly lyric overtones, and there is a distinct change of narrative direction, which will change yet again at the opening of *Argonautica*

4. Virgil imitates the division of the poem into two halves with the invocation to Erato at *Aeneid* 7.37.

100 3.2 *Medea, Jason:* Whereas the Argonauts appear as a group in the proem of the first book, here the focus moves to Medea's love for Jason, and his success because of that love. The final two books center much more on these two figures, with Medea in many ways in the role of an epic hero. Among the highlights of the third book are the careful details of her thought processes.

100 3.9–10 *Athena / and Hera:* The action of the two goddesses recalls their combined plotting and martial enterprise at *Iliad* 8.350–96. Another important Homeric passage recalled here is Hera's approach to Aphrodite in *Iliad* 14 to borrow her erotic "zone," or "girdle."

101 3.50 *Hephaestus:* The absence of Hephaestus, and the description of Aphrodite alone in her bedchamber, lead the reader to suspect the possible presence of Ares, who is, however, not here (in spite of the image of Aphrodite and Ares' shield on Jason's cloak). The fatherhood of Eros was a notorious problem in ancient mythology, and one Hellenistic poets enjoyed playing upon.

102 3.69 *Before today:* Aphrodite's address recalls that of Charis to Thetis at *Iliad* 18.385–86, when Thetis comes to Hephaestus (here husband to Charis) to ask for new armor for Achilles.

102 3.87 *Jason proved his worth:* Hera's short narrative here fills in a gap in the brief parenthetical background passage at *Argonautica* 1.5–17, and underlines the opening of Book 3 as a new beginning.

103 3.121 *little Eros:* In pre-Hellenistic Greek literature, Eros is often depicted as young, but not as a little boy. The Hellenistic period, however, shows a marked interest in children and their portrayal.

104 3.159–60 *Little Eros / stood clutching:* This image recalls a passage of the poet Anacreon (*PMG* 398), a poet whose images of Eros as competitor had much appeal for the Alexandrians.

105 3.174 *A nice bright ball!:* This is one of the remarkable *ecphrases* in Apollonius' poem, and it has a variety of scientific, poetic, and philosophical implications (particularly of the pre-Socratic philosopher Empedocles). Apollonius' contemporary Eratosthenes of Cyrene (276–194 BCE) is credited with inventing the armillary sphere or globe. Aratus' *Phaenomena* 525–36 is a close parallel to this passage.

106 3.208–9 *Thence / opens the downward path:* Eros' descent in some ways parallels that of Hermes to Calypso in *Odyssey* 6, where Hermes is also on a divine mission. In a moment of Apollonian variation, the expected simile (e.g., to a gull in descent) is absent.

107 3.262 *Circe's Plain:* Burial customs are a common feature of ancient ethnography, the one here a sign of the otherworldly realm the Argonauts are entering.

108 3.275 *Hera helped:* The model here is the mist Athena casts around
      Odysseus at the opening of *Odyssey* 7, so that he may enter the pal-
      ace of Alcinoös undisturbed. Virgil uses the same feature at *Aeneid*
      1.411–14.

108 3.286 *They softly crossed the threshold:* The description of the palace
      of Aeëtes is based in part on that of the palace of Alcinoös at *Odys-
      sey* 7.81–132, with some striking enhancements. Whereas Hephaes-
      tus fashioned gold and silver dogs for Alcinoös, for Aeëtes these are
      fire-breathing bulls, which prefigure the plowing scene later in *Argo-
      nautica* 3.

109 3.318 *"Phaëthon":* Phaëthon is the name of the son of Helios, and his
      smoldering corpse figures in the Italian part of the Argonauts' return
      in Book 4. That Absyrtus is called "Phaëthon" allows for the poet's
      etymology of the name here, but also introduces a somewhat sinister
      undertone suggestive of the boy's tragic fate later in the poem.

109 3.331 *she shrieked:* Medea's first utterance in the poem is one of
      alarm. The passage evokes Andromache hearing the tumult over the
      dead Hector. Here the immediate recognition, Chalciope seeing her
      sons safely returned, is one of joy, but the passage's tone bodes ill for
      the future.

110 3.359 *And Eros was descending:* This remarkable opening is a varia-
      tion on the Homeric poetic feature known as ring composition. We
      return to the descent of Eros at 217. At the same time there is a transi-
      tion from epic (a multitude of figures busy at court) to lyric mode,
      that of a single figure's perception and reaction.

110 3.361 *stinging fly:* This same image occurs toward the end of Book 1,
      describing the rage that overcomes Heracles on hearing about the
      loss of Hylas.

110 3.373 *Sudden muteness:* This careful description of the effect of erotic
      attraction on the psyche is one of several passages in Hellenistic po-
      etry (another is the second part of Theocritus' *Idyll* 2) that imitate a
      famous poem of Sappho, fr. 31 V. ("that one appears to me like the
      gods"). Sappho's poem implicated several contemporary medical im-
      ages. Hellenistic poetry, with its awareness of new interests in medi-
      cine, further enhanced Sappho's medical language and imagery.

111 3.382 *As when a workwoman:* This striking simile compares the fire
      of a lone woman doing handiwork at night to Medea's isolated reac-
      tion on seeing Jason. While Homer had used comparisons of the he-
      roic and everyday working culture, this simile takes the conceit a step
      further.

111 3.407 *my sister Circe:* Aeëtes' reference to his sister Circe conve-
      niently locates her in the Greek west, thus pinpointing one geograph-
      ical reference of the Argonauts' complex journey back home.

112 3.415 *Argus answered first:* Argus' surprisingly long speech serves as a summation of much of the past two books for the Colchian audience. Argus, though not the same Argus who designed the *Argo,* does include the building of the ship briefly in this summary, a building that Apollonius himself had consciously omitted in his opening to the whole poem.

115 3.528 *"Stranger, why should you tell":* Aeëtes, a figure within the poem itself, is in the unusual role of requesting narrative brevity, a hallmark of good poetry of this period.

117 3.587 *Jason shone:* Jason's physical beauty, and its effect on those who behold him, is an ongoing motif of the poem, as is its destructive potential.

120 3.718 *a timid dove:* This is another example of bird augury in the *Argonautica.* The dove is also associated with Aphrodite, so its landing in Jason's lap can be read as another instance of the erotic motif of this book.

121 3.741–42 *as fellow crewmen / to women:* Idas here takes the role Heracles had in Book 1 in reaction to the Argonauts' dalliance with the Lemnian women—an older heroic ethos disapproving of a newer one and its methods.

123 3.820 *She dreamed the stranger:* Medea's dream is in part an elaboration on that of Nausicaa which opens *Odyssey* 6, but here has a more complex nature, part exposition of Medea's desires, part prefiguring the future. Dreams and dream interpretation were a subject of great interest in antiquity.

124 3.848 *shameless as a bitch's:* The Greek term for "bitch" (*kyon*) marks this as an allusion to Helen's self-deprecating language in *Iliad* 6, where she laments her own actions in abandoning her homeland for a foreign love.

124 3.858 *She turned around, returned:* Apollonius' description of Medea's hesitation here finds a striking parallel in one of the most remarkable passages of Euripides' *Medea,* Medea's agonized soliloquy (lines 1019–80) on whether or not to kill her children.

124 3.867 *Think of a girl:* The simile varies a traditional epigram motif of the bride dead on the eve of her wedding, and so now the bride of Hades (Death). At the same time, it hauntingly recalls the hopeful young girls inspired by the Evening Star (the planet Venus) in Book 1.

126 3.908 *but no sound came:* The motif of speechlessness, first apparent on Medea's gazing upon Jason, continues here and will recur again as a leitmotif of the girl's internal turmoil.

126 3.925 *you must swear by Heaven and Earth:* Oaths, their preservation and their breaking, are a recurrent theme of the Medea narrative. Apollonius' audience may well recall that Jason's *not* keeping his

sworn oaths is one of Medea's primary charges against him in Euripides' play.

130 3.1054 *So she resolved:* Medea's contemplation of suicide is another of the detailed portrayals of her inner psychology that make the third book so different in tone from much of the rest of the poem. There are some lyric antecedents (Sappho fr. 94 V. is one), but the continued description of internal psychology is something quite new.

131 3.1104 *Prometheon:* Prometheus, whose torment the Argonauts sailed past toward the end of Book 2, recurs here as the source of Medea's magic drug. Prometheus will return again at lines 1402–4 as the origin of Jason's family.

132 3.1123 *Brimo:* Brimo is an aspect of Hecate as Underworld deity. The Greek word means "the one who roars."

132 3.1139 *Leto's daughter Artemis:* Apollonius here reworks Homer's comparison of Nausicaa to Artemis at *Odyssey* 6.102–9, yet there is a significant change in tone with the fear that Artemis/Medea inspires here. Virgil recasts the same simile at *Aeneid* 1.498–504, again with contextual difference (Dido, unlike Nausicaa and Medea, has been previously married, so the comparison to Diana is intentionally problematic).

134 3.1192 *Never among the men:* Hera's rendering Jason an object of striking beauty recalls Athena's doing the same to Odysseus at *Odyssey* 6.229–37. The encounter of Jason and Medea here is a close intertextual recall of that of Odysseus and Nausicaa.

134 3.1205 *Crows regularly sit:* This passage is a somewhat humorous play on bird augury (reading divine will through bird motion or birdcall). Talking crows feature in another poem of this period, Callimachus' *Hecale.*

135 3.1229 *Medea's heart:* This passage again recalls Homer's scene with Nausicaa at play with her maids in *Odyssey* 6, although here there is no ball (the ball, as it were, already figured earlier in the narrative of *Argonautica* 3, and will appear again in a simile in Book 4). Medea's anguished anticipation of Jason's arrival also recalls, a second time, Sappho fr. 31 V.

135 3.1240–41 *as the Dog Star, / Sirius:* The comparison of Jason to the notoriously destructive hottest time of the year is one of brilliance and foreboding. There is a close parallel description of Sirius in Apollonius' contemporary poet Aratus at *Phaenomena* 326–35.

136 3.1276–77 *I have come, / a suppliant:* This is another close recall, with important variations, of *Odyssey* 6.149–85, where the desperate Odysseus supplicates Nausicaa. One intriguing variation is that in the Homeric passage Odysseus concludes by noting that a well-married couple achieves the greatest reputation (line 185); here Jason

picks up the theme of reputation, but of two figures (line 1283) living apart.

136 3.1290 *Minos' maiden daughter Ariadne:* Jason's mythological choice of exemplum is full of foreboding: Theseus abandoned Ariadne, who had aided him in his quest to slay the Minotaur and then left her family and homeland with him, on the island of Naxos. Jason's version of the Ariadne story is geared to persuade and is also only partly true.

137 3.1317–18 *a miraculous / and winning fire:* This is often an image of a divinity, and appears in the iconography of some Hellenistic monarchs. Fire in this case, following on the Jason-Sirius comparison, has a dangerously ambiguous value.

138 3.1344 *to turn and look behind you:* In ancient magical practice, it is standard for the practitioner calling forth an Underworld spirit to beware of looking upon that which should not be seen.

143 3.1516–17 *Cadmus found / this serpent:* The narrative of Cadmus and the serpent's teeth links two of the great mythological cycles, that of the Theban royal house and the *Argonautica.* Like other Hellenistic poets, Apollonius has great interest in mythography.

143 3.1533 *The sun god Helius:* Helius here is both metaphor (for the sun) and a pertinent mythological presence as Aeëtes' father.

144 3.1552 *Lemnian Hypsipyle:* There are several mantles in the poem: Jason's cloak in *Argonautica* 1, which plays a role in the seduction of Hypsipyle; this gift *from* Hypsipyle, which figures here at the moment Jason carries out Medea's magical instructions; this same mantle then makes a reappearance in the luring of Absyrtus to his death in the first part of *Argonautica* 4; and then there is finally the mantle in which Dionysus embraced Ariadne, in which Jason and Medea make love in *Argonautica* 4. Each covering implicates earlier narrative or narratives into the present.

144 3.1579 *a special gift from Ares:* Aeëtes and Ares, the Greek god of war, are again equated. This parallelism begins already at the altar of Ares toward the end of the previous book.

145 3.1590 *Phaëthon was waiting:* The image of this Phaëthon holding his father's chariot cannot but evoke the image of Phaëthon the son of Helius. Like the son of Helius, this Phaëthon will prove, in his tragic end, unequal to his father.

145 3.1597 *the god Poseidon:* The simile may serve to evoke particularly Poseidon the implacable foe of Odysseus, and to heighten the sense of Jason's heroic isolation here in the face of a foe truly larger than life.

147 3.1669 *Think of a blacksmith's bull-hide bellows:* The simile recalls in part the Cyclopes on Jason's cloak in Book 1 as they fashion the thunderbolt of Zeus.

149 3.1759 *the seedlings grown:* Many editors assume a missing line between this line and the next.

150 3.1785 *The sun went down:* Again a book concludes with nightfall. Whereas the other books of the *Argonautica* cover longer periods of time, the entire action of Book 3 encompasses only a few days.

BOOK 4

151 4.1 *deathless Muse:* The poet does not name this figure. Some scholars assume this to be Erato, the Muse of the proem to *Argonautica* 3, and that this is one of several factors that bind the two books as a unit, one that centers on Medea and Jason. Other scholars point to the different, more heroic-epic direction of *Argonautica* 4, especially as outlined in the proem, and suggest that this is rather a changed Muse, the typically unnamed one of epic poetry (cf. the opening lines to Homer's *Iliad* and *Odyssey*).

151 4.4 *wondering whether:* Questions in epic, as the late Thomas Rosenmeyer observed, are generally phrased as "x or y, then y." The second option usually prevails. See "Apollonius Lyricus," *SIFC* 10 (1992): 177–78.

151 4.14 *Hera, meanwhile:* Hera will continue to play an active role in this book of the poem. The simile that follows is a typically heroic-epic one, thus confirming the direction that the poem now follows.

151 4.26 *She would have drained:* The lines capture two features of Medea in particular: her emotions as a young girl (this is the second time she contemplates suicide), a strong feature of Book 3, and her role as a sorceress, which will repeatedly come to the fore in Book 4. The choice of action here reflects, on a different level, the change of direction the poem takes now from that of the previous book.

152 4.37 *heartfelt lamentation:* The final version of Callimachus' *Aetia* closes with the young queen, Berenice II, dedicating a lock of her hair for her husband's safe return from the Third Syrian War, a lock that itself laments its being severed from its sister-locks, and that ends up in a heavenly apotheosis in the lap of Arsinoe-Aphrodite, figured in cult terms as Berenice's mother. This is one of many striking parallels between the poetry of Callimachus and Apollonius' *Argonautica*.

152 4.41–42 *"I wish . . . / before you ever reached the land of Colchis":* This is a very close echo of the opening two lines of Euripides' *Medea*. In Euripides' play these lines are spoken by the children's nurse. The difference of speaker underlines some of the conventional differences of tragedy and epic.

155 4.149–50 *sacrificed / the gilded miracle:* This image recalls the final

one on Jason's cloak in Book 1, where the golden ram appeared to be speaking to Phrixus.

156   4.172 *a pile of smoldering wood*: This simile recalls the one in *Argonautica* 3 that compared Medea's initial passion to the fire a workwoman lights at night. The lyric-heroic division again comes forward; here Medea, in heroic mode, is subduing a dragon.

156   4.182 *Jason, terrified*: Jason's heroism is once again complicated by Medea's own superhuman action.

156   4.203 *Just as a maiden*: This brilliant simile is very revealing about Jason in multiple ways. The goal of the *Argo*'s voyage is the "heroic" obtaining of a magical object, yet this is actually done by a woman, a local princess, through magic. The simile highlights Jason as object of desire, yet as a young girl; it both casts light on a new aspect of male sexuality (object of desire) and problematizes Jason as hero.

158   4.244 *"infamy of Greece"*: Hellas, "Greece," here is worth noting. The term, rare in Homer, does not appear in Homer's poetry for the conceptual space "Greece." As Thucydides famously observes (1.3), Homer does not make the distinction Greek vs. Barbarian. This marks Apollonius' poem, albeit before the Trojan War in mythological time, as a latter-day epic.

158   4.257 *as thickly as the dead leaves*: The simile is in part prophetic, as the Colchians who subsequently embark will not return to Colchis.

158   4.267 *His son Absyrtus*: With the reference to Helius a few lines earlier, we again recall the image of Phaëthon, who proves unequal to driving the chariot of his father Helius, as Absyrtus will not survive the attempt to replace Aeëtes at the head of the Colchian force that pursues Jason and Medea.

159   4.298 *Holy dread prevents me*: This is a reference to *aporreta*, elements of ritual that must be kept secret. *Aporreta* are a typical feature of initiation rituals, and also of magic and witchcraft.

159   4.307 *but what that route would be*: This is the key moment that allows for Apollonius' new return route for the Argonauts.

160   4.321 *the Apidanian Arcadians*: The Apidanians appear in the opening section of Callimachus' *Hymn to Zeus*. Callimachus' narrative of Zeus' birth in Arcadia is reflected at several moments in this passage of Apollonius.

162   4.396–97 *ever had observed / seagoing vessels*: There may be an implied reference here to one tradition about the *Argo*, that it was the first boat.

163   4.442 *"Jason, what is this plot"*: Medea's speech here appears to recall, at several points, Medea's denunciation of Jason in Euripides' *Medea* at lines 465–519 of that drama.

164 *4.469 wretch:* The Greek term *sketlios,* "wretch," is an erotic leitmotif of this book, culminating in the address to Eros at line 565.

164 *4.486 Themis:* Themis is the divinity who oversees what is morally right, such as the validity of oaths.

166 *4.533 the sacred raiment of Hypsipyle:* Once again a piece of clothing is the instrument that instigates action, and this is again a gift.

167 *4.565 Wretched Eros:* The apostrophe of Eros is the culmination of the theme, one that pervades the second half of the *Argonautica,* of love leading mortals to commit wrongful acts.

167 *4.586 as a little boy:* This simile highlights Absyrtus' vulnerability, particularly at the hands of his sorceress sister.

168 *4.605 smeared his sister's mantle:* Murder of the innocent results in *miasma,* or pollution, and the potential for revenge by the Fury that arises from the blood wrongly spilled. Here Medea's being bespattered by her brother's blood (to take part in the killing of a sibling is a particularly grievous sin) is emblematic of the process of guilt and punishment imagined in Greek religion.

168 *4.611 and spat the taint out:* A widespread belief in many cultures that licking the blood of the murdered will quiet a potentially vengeful spirit.

169 *4.640 people orphaned of a leader:* These lines are in part reminiscent of the situation in the *Iliad* upon Achilles' withdrawal from fighting. Not by chance are these lines spoken by Peleus—Achilles is his son.

170 *4.691 Heracles, you see:* Once again Heracles appears on the *Argonautica*'s periphery. The passage brings together two episodes in Heracles' life, which are perhaps best known now from two different fifth-century Athenian tragedies. One is Sophocles' *Women of Trachis,* in which Hyllus figures as an adult and wherein Deianeira, Heracles' last wife, in an attempt to recover her husband's love, is the accidental cause of his death. The other is Euripides' *Madness of Heracles,* which tells of Heracles' killing his wife, Megara, and their three children.

170 *4.707 a grazing herd of cattle:* There is a distant recollection here of one of the scenes on Jason's cloak in Book 1. All of the scenes on the cloak are recalled, in one way or another, in the course of the poem.

171 *4.708 Come, tell me, goddesses:* This new appeal at this point in the poem is a marked new beginning. Here Apollonius takes the Argonauts beyond the traditional narrative of their return ("so far abroad," line 714, is emblematic of this new narrative).

171 *4.736 queen Calypso:* Calypso in the *Odyssey* harbors Odysseus at the end of his first attempted return to Ithaca from Troy; we find him there at the opening of the poem. As the point from which he comes to the Phaeacians and begins his reintegration into mortal society, Calypso comes at the end of a series of marvelous figures, several of whom we will now encounter in *Argonautica* 4.

172 4.745 *one of the* Argo's *beams:* Although Apollonius declared at the beginning of the *Argonautica* that he would not narrate the building of the *Argo,* in fact the theme repeatedly resurfaces in the course of the poem, thus allowing for a different, more episodic than linear narration of what the poet himself claims to have been a theme already much treated by earlier poets.

172 4.765 *Phaëthon:* Phaëthon is a son of Helius, and so brother to both Aeëtes and Circe. On the one hand, the Argonauts are once again traveling by the visible remains of earlier mythology. At the same time, by evoking Phaëthon in Italy, Apollonius gives a kind of legitimacy to this part of the poem, where in fact he is traversing new terrain.

172 4.774 *the Heliades:* It is worth noting that Ovid, in the second book of his *Metamorphoses,* has Phaëthon, the Heliades, and Coronis in this sequence, although there are other figures as well.

174 4.850 *because a dream had troubled her:* Once again Apollonius makes use of the Nausicaa episode in the sixth book of the *Odyssey,* here bringing it together with the Circe episode in *Odyssey* 10. A dream is the cause of Nausicaa going to the river to wash the household clothing, and by the river she meets with Odysseus. Circe in *Odyssey* 10 lives apart in a forest, surrounded by animals into which she has transformed various mortal men. She fears Odysseus' resistance to her magic and enables his return. Here Circe is Medea's aunt, Jason has a foreign princess with him, and they are in need of ritual purification for a murder they have committed.

175 4.862–63 *some mélange / of limbs:* These are Empedoclean forms, a sort of primordial collage of parts, not entirely formed. Empedocles' influence is felt elsewhere in the poem, particularly in the ball that Aphrodite gives to Eros at the opening of *Argonautica* 3.

175 4.882 *and he alone escorted:* There is a reminiscence here of Odysseus' lone approach to Circe's house in the tenth book of the *Odyssey.*

176 4.902 *to expunge the deed's contamination:* In Greek religion, one guilty of murder must be first purified of pollution. This need for purification is separate from any subsequent judgment the guilty may encounter (compare the case of Orestes in Aeschylus' *Eumenides*).

177 4.934 *in the Colchian tongue:* Homeric epic poems do not acknowledge a plurality of languages per se (the Trojans in the *Iliad,* for example, speak the same Greek as their Greek opponents). This

reference to the "Colchian tongue" is a moment of later realism in an epic narrative, e.g., the Ptolemies ruled over many peoples, and these spoke many languages.

178 4.967 *Iris:* Iris is an anthropomorphic realization of the rainbow, and is frequently Hera's handmaid, often (though not here) to do Hera's will in a malevolent context.

178 4.974 *and summon Thetis:* Achilles summons his mother in the first book of the *Iliad.* Subsequently Thetis in *Iliad* 18 will go to Hephaestus to ask for new armor for her son. These are both recalled in this passage.

178 4.980 *Aeolus, who regulates the gales:* Aeolus, the keeper of the winds, is a figure from the tenth book of the *Odyssey:* he gives Odysseus a bag in which the winds are sealed, and on the approach to Ithaca Odysseus falls asleep, his men open the bag, and the winds are released, thus preventing them from reaching their homeland. In this passage Apollonius juxtaposes two figures from the two Homeric poems.

179 4.1011 *Scylla and Charybdis':* Two monstrous dangers from the twelfth book of the *Odyssey,* where Odysseus must choose between facing one or the other. Scylla and Charybdis represent the fearful dangers of the sea, in contrast with the Naiads, who are benevolent.

179 4.1013 *I myself have nursed:* Hera in the *Argonautica* has a rather different characterization from that of the *Iliad,* not to mention the wrathful figure of Virgil's *Aeneid* and Ovid's *Metamorphoses.* Apollonius sketches a side of the goddess from the beginning of the poem that is protective and nurturing. Even in the various references to Heracles her malevolent role is much played down.

179 4.1032 *a heartfelt wedding:* This wedding is in fact the origin of the Trojan War. The goddess Eris ("Strife"), not invited to the wedding, casts a golden apple among the gods with the epigraph "to the fairest," which results in the judgment of Paris, which in turn leads to the abduction of Helen, and so on. But in the time frame of the *Argonautica,* where Achilles is still an infant, the Trojan War is yet to come, and the poet can decorously omit direct reference to the strife over the golden apple, though the opening of Book 3 is an elaborate allusion to this contest.

180 4.1042 *that he wed Medea:* This reference to the future, after-death marriage of Achilles and Medea, cannot but surprise the poem's audience, given that the second half of the *Argonautica* follows the love and early adventures of Jason and Medea. There is certainly an ominous note on the future of the relationship of the latter couple.

182 4.1121 *and raised a frightening cry:* The narrative of Thetis' attempt to make Achilles immortal closely follows the parallel scene in the

Homeric *Hymn to Demeter,* where Demeter, disguised as an old woman, is surprised by Metaneira as she attempts to make the latter's baby immortal through fire. Apollonius' reconfiguration of this scene emphasizes the different natures of Thetis and Peleus.

183 **4.1141** *the clear-voiced Sirens:* The Sirens figure in the twelfth book of the *Odyssey.* Apollonius' use of many of the figures from Odysseus' wanderings draws the attention of his audience to the Odyssean quality of this part of the *Argonautica,* which features a journey into the unknown.

183 **4.1148–49** *while she was still / unmarried:* A second reference, this time to the opening of the Homeric *Hymn to Demeter,* to Persephone as a virgin.

183 **4.1157** *if Orpheus of Thrace:* In contrast to the *Odyssey*'s narrative of the Sirens, where Odysseus, bound by his men, listens to the Sirens' song, Apollonius has Orpheus compete with the Sirens, and Orpheus' song overpowers theirs.

184 **4.1190** *had retired from the forge:* There is almost a partial ring composition here. We first hear of Hephaestus at his forge in the opening scene of the third book of the *Argonautica,* when Hera and Athena come upon Aphrodite alone. Indeed, one section of the fourth book, the voyage among the figures of Odysseus' voyage, is about to end, as did Odysseus', with the arrival among the Phaeacians.

184 **4.1196** *As dolphins during tranquil weather rise:* The collection of Homeric hymns that Apollonius' contemporaries would have known began with the *Hymn to Dionysus* (now fragmentary), which features a famous metamorphosis of pirates into dolphins. It is unclear whether, and to what extent, that poem may be in play here as a model, but this passage, coming so soon after allusions to the Homeric *Hymn to Demeter,* is of particular interest in that regard, among others.

185 **4.1216** *pick up a ball:* Another allusion to the Nausicaa episode in *Odyssey* 6, an episode that Apollonius plays upon again and again in the course of the second half of the *Argonautica.* As the Argonauts are shortly to arrive at the home of Alcinoös and Arete, the parents of Nausicaa (who has not been born at this time), the allusion is particularly appropriate.

185 **4.1223** *Mighty Hephaestus stood:* Unlike the *Iliad,* which is replete with scenes of the Olympians watching the battlefield below, scenes like this in the *Argonautica* are rare. Here their presence marks this superhuman effort as truly extraordinary.

185 **4.1234** *where Helius' cattle graze:* In a masterful stroke, Apollonius has the Argonauts pass by the cattle of Helius, the final, disastrous episode in Odysseus' wanderings before the shipwreck that brings him to the island of Calypso. His men's assault on Helius' cattle is the

last episode that Odysseus narrates to the Phaeacian court, where Jason and Medea are now to find themselves.

186 4.1257 *Muses, forgive me:* The gesture is a particularly Pindaric one, when a poet alludes to, or briefly narrates, a myth involving unsuitable behavior among the gods. The passage is especially striking as a brief self-referential reference to the poet in the "act" of composition, and of the modern scholar-poet laying out two ancient explanations.

186 4.1265 *nursemaid of the Phaeacians:* Apollonius' own take on the history of the Phaeacians that Athena (in disguise) provides to Odysseus at the opening of *Odyssey* 7. Throughout the following episode, the audience is repeatedly reminded of the earlier version of reception among the Phaeacians and so of Apollonius' own recasting of this in his *Argonautica*.

186 4.1270 *Alcinoös and all his people:* In *Odyssey* 7, Odysseus, with Athena's aid, approaches the palace of Alcinoös in concealment, in part to avoid any maltreatment by the Phaeacians along the way. The arrival of the Argonauts is rather an occasion for initial public rejoicing, until this is interrupted by the arrival of the armed Colchians.

187 4.1290 *Alcinoös' wife Arete:* Odysseus, on arrival at Alcinoös' palace, first must supplicate the queen, Arete (her name means "virtue" or "excellence" in Greek). Her role in Odysseus' salvation remains fascinating and in part enigmatic and is the subject of a large scholarship. Here Medea, a young woman, supplicates an older female figure. While this is appropriate, there remains a certain paradox, as Medea is repeatedly likened, by allusion, in the second part of the *Argonautica* to Nausicaa.

187 4.1308–9 *a perfect / life:* Medea's prayer for Alcinoös and Arete thematically, though not verbally, echoes Odysseus' prayer for Nausicaa at the conclusion of his supplication of her in *Odyssey* 6, which includes, at line 154, a reference to the blessed state of Alcinoös and Arete, Nausicaa's parents, whom Odysseus does not yet know.

188 4.1351–52 *a poor, / hardworking woman:* This simile recalls two similes in Book 3, that of Medea's initial erotic arousal compared to the fire a workwoman keeps at night, and the description of sleep coming to all, even to a mother who has lost her children. The reworking of the earlier similes into this one keeps alive the image of Medea's erotic suffering, now turned into true epic fear.

190 4.1389 *Antiope:* Antiope was the daughter (in one of several ancient mythical versions of her story) of the Theban king Nycteus. Beloved by Zeus, she bore him two sons, Amphion and Zethus, who were brought up by herdsmen. Persecuted by her father's wife, she flees to

the house of two herdsmen, who turn out to be Amphion and Ze-
thus. The story is the subject of Euripides' fragmentary drama *An-
tiope.*

190 **4.1390** *Danaë:* Daughter of Acrisius. Zeus came to her as a shower of
golden rain in the prison where her father confined her. Her father
then placed Danaë, and her son Perseus, in a chest that he had cast
into the sea. The story was narrated in lyric poetry by Simonides (fr.
543 *PMG*) and by Aeschylus in his fragmentary *Dictoulkoi* ("Net
Drawers").

190 **4.1393** *Echetus:* Echetus is a savage king of Epirus, father of Merope.
The extant sources for this tale are fairly late. Arete here combines
the catalog (an epic tradition) with a Hellenistic scholar's eye for con-
tested narrative versions and/or unusual detail.

190 **4.1406** *war down on Hellas:* As noted earlier, *Hellas* is not a term
used of the Greek world in Homeric epic; rather, it is a coinage that
comes to define Greek vs. Barbarian. A "war" on "Hellas" evokes
the Persian Wars, and indeed Aeëtes, coming from the far east of the
known world and associated with the Sun, can easily be aligned with
the one-time Persian kings.

191 **4.1450** *Zeus' Nysaean son:* This is Dionysus, a god with whom the
Ptolemies claimed close association. For a recent, somewhat novel
and very accessible study of the spread of the Dionysus cult in the
Hellenistic and Roman periods, see Hunter 2006 ch. 2.

191 **4.1458** *glinting golden fleece:* The fleece has been a leitmotif through-
out the poem, and we have seen it in several settings: as a living thing
on Jason's cloak and as the guarded object that Medea and Jason
take from its dreadful guardian. At its beginning the golden ram
bears Phrixus and Helle away from their stepmother Ino, at its end
here it serves as the bedding for Jason and Medea, the latter also flee-
ing a cruel parental figure.

192 **4.1469** *The nymphs had come:* The setting of this wedding serves in
turn as the model for that of Aeneas and Dido in *Aeneid* 4, where at
lines 165–68 the woodland nymphs sing the wedding song, and Juno
serves as the *pronuba* (matron attending upon the bride).

192 **4.1483** *sang the wedding hymn:* A wedding hymn was a genre of lyric
song, known as an *epithalamium* (the song sung "before the cham-
ber"). There are several references in Apollonius' poem to other types
of song, which may reflect the interest of his period in categorization
of earlier poetry.

192 **4.1485** *was not the place:* The passage leaves open a certain ambigu-
ity about the wedding, and about whether it in fact constitutes a true
wedding, leaving open, and unresolved, a very important issue for
the future of both principals.

192 4.1491–92 *we / the members:* An unusual philosophical comment on the ephemeral nature of human happiness that, coming so closely upon the wedding, casts a pall on the whole scene.

193 4.1500 *Dawn had returned:* This is Apollonius' version of, and elaboration on, an image fairly common in Homer, but not in the *Argonautica*. The lines here may be meant especially to recall the opening of *Odyssey* 8 and Alcinoös summoning the Phaeacian leading men to take counsel on the future of Odysseus.

194 4.1533–34 *dancing / a cyclic dance:* Another evocation of actual cult practice, and the type of song that accompanies it.

194 4.1555 *and settled on the island opposite:* Apollonius' poem includes a number of references to settlements and their future histories, a way of weaving history into an epic narrative. Callimachus does something very similar in his narrative of Acontius and Cydippe, in the third book of his *Aetia.*

195 4.1579–80 *the land / of Pelops had arisen into view:* This passage reworks Odysseus' first approach to Ithaca (*Odyssey* 10.29), when his ship is then blown off course by his followers' illicitly opening the bag of winds given to Odysseus by King Aeolus. The "dismal gust of wind" that blows the Argonauts off course is a recollection of the Homeric passage.

197 4.1645 *odd omens have been witnessed:* Ancient historical narrative often includes both natural and supernatural phenomena as testimony of difficult times. Here Apollonius is evoking that tradition.

197 4.1655 *fall in the sand, and die:* This is the second time that the heroes of the *Argo* have given up hope, and prepare to die. The scene, particularly with the shrouding of their heads, may recall the end of *Odyssey* 5, where Odysseus, exhausted and shipwrecked, buries himself, more like an animal than a human, to await a very uncertain future.

197 4.1665 *swans release their dying proclamations:* The idea that swans sing most beautifully before dying is a belief that recurs in a number of Greek authors, particularly Plato's *Phaedo,* which the poet may be in part recalling here.

197 4.1676 *the guardians of Libya:* These divinities are the daughters of Poseidon and Libya, thus their fitting role in bringing the Argonauts from Libya to the sea. The same group of female maidens (called "ladies, heroines of Libya") feature in an elegiac fragment of the poet Callimachus (fr. 602 Pf.) with their mother, here probably Cyrene. As is the case with Odysseus, the Argonauts are often helped in their return by female figures.

200 4.1770 *I sing at the Pierides' command:* The poet's recourse to the Muses' authority here marks both a debt to the epic tradition (an ap-

peal to the Muses to give veracity to a more than human account (the Catalog of Ships in the second book of the *Iliad,* for example) and the extraordinary nature of the story. Bearing a ship to the sea has strong parallels in Egyptian religious belief and practice.

201 4.1796 *Heracles had already shot:* Once again the Argonauts are preceded by Heracles, whose peregrination just precedes their own. The description of Heracles from one of his victims at lines 1837ff. is an especially vivid one.

202 4.1833 *they emerged out of the trees:* There are several types of nymphs associated with trees in Greek belief. Apollonius is evoking something of that image here.

204 4.1912 *Then, O Canthus:* The deaths of Canthus and Mopsus continue a trend in the poem of significant deaths of heroes in pairs. As with the frequent paired arrivals at the poem's opening, this is particularly appropriate to a heroic narrative involving a ship and oarmates.

205 4.1941 *the lethal sort of asp:* Snakebite was a constant danger in North Africa, particularly from the asp. In some accounts of her death, Cleopatra VII commits suicide by holding an asp against her breast—this is the version popularized by Shakespeare. The poet Nicander (probably second century BCE) wrote a poem in hexameters, the *Theriaca,* on various creeping animals. The poem survives in its entirety; it includes a long section on snakes.

205 4.1956 *the Gorgon's freshly severed head:* The narrative of Perseus and the Medusa is known to us from several ancient sources—the most familiar one is in the fourth book of Ovid's *Metamorphoses*— but the myth is much older. Here Apollonius uses a traditional Greek myth to emphasize the earlier presence of North Africa in Greek mythology, a gesture very common in Hellenistic poetry.

205 4.1967 *Slumber the Loosener of Limbs:* Sleep and Death have a long tradition as partners, both in poetry and in art. Apollonius' description of the death of Mopsus is influenced both by earlier artistic tradition and also by medical descriptions of the effects of poison (the death of Socrates in Plato's *Phaedo* is a famous example of the latter).

206 4.1981 *and mourned the man:* The description refers in part to a *threnos,* or song of lament. An interesting feature of the *Argonautica* is the variety of song forms that this heroic epic evokes. A famous *threnos* in epic hexameter is the conclusion of *Iliad* 24.

206 4.1989 *As when a serpent:* This simile may evoke the Egyptian belief that the arc of the sun passes from west to east at night, while a serpent threatens its nightly voyage. On the presence of Egyptian culture and beliefs in the *Argonautica,* see esp. Stephens 2003 ch. 4; on this particular passage, see Mori 2008 Introduction.

208   4.2070 *As when a trainer:* The simile encapsulates the previous events
      (a stallion's emergence from the sea at lines 1749–55; now for a sec-
      ond time salvation comes from the sea.

211   4.2158 *Father Zeus, profound astonishment:* One of the great inter-
      ests of poets of this period was paradoxography, the study of strange
      and unexpected phenomena.

212   4.2216 *Epiphany:* This episode of Apollo at *Anaphe* ("radiance"),
      which occurs here toward the end of the *Argonautica,* is one of the
      earliest episodes of Callimachus' *Aetia,* again suggesting a close
      knowledge of both poets of each other's work.

213   4.2230 *because of all this humor:* Laughter and the ludicrous have a
      place in many Greek rituals, including, perhaps most famously, the
      initiations at the cult of the goddess Demeter at Eleusis.

213   4.2237–38 *Euphemus happened to recall / a dream:* Euphemus'
      dream looks to the future, when Thera will in return become the
      source of the great cities of Cyrene. There is a longer narrative of the
      clod of earth at the opening of Pindar's longest ode, *Pythian* 4, which
      Apollonius places, significantly, toward the end of his own *Argonau-
      tica* narrative. The Hellenistic era took great interest in dreams and
      dream interpretation.

214   4.2289–90 *To this day / the Myrmidons:* The final *aetion* of Apollo-
      nius' poem. Like Callimachus' four-book *Aetia,* Apollonius' *Argo-
      nautica* is replete with *aetia,* and the two poems have many other
      shared features in common. Callimachus' elegiac poem, though, is
      not a linear narrative in the same way as Apollonius' *Argonautica.*

214   4.2293 *O heroes, offspring of the blessed gods:* The ending of the
      poem, like the opening line of the first book, is markedly hymnic.
      Here the poet addresses his heroes as figures of the distant past, and
      addresses them as objects of prayer themselves. It is they, the heroes,
      rather than the traditional Muses, whom the poet calls upon to watch
      over his song and its life in the future. In the ancient world heroes,
      such as Heracles or Jason, were themselves the objects of cult ritual
      as figures more than mere mortals but less than gods.

THE STORY OF PENGUIN CLASSICS

Before 1946 . . . "Classics" are mainly the domain of academics and students; readable editions for everyone else are almost unheard of. This all changes when a little-known classicist, E. V. Rieu, presents Penguin founder Allen Lane with the translation of Homer's *Odyssey* that he has been working on in his spare time.

1946 Penguin Classics debuts with *The Odyssey*, which promptly sells three million copies. Suddenly, classics are no longer for the privileged few.

1950s Rieu, now series editor, turns to professional writers for the best modern, readable translations, including Dorothy L. Sayers's *Inferno* and Robert Graves's unexpurgated *Twelve Caesars*.

1960s The Classics are given the distinctive black covers that have remained a constant throughout the life of the series. Rieu retires in 1964, hailing the Penguin Classics list as "the greatest educative force of the twentieth century."

1970s A new generation of translators swells the Penguin Classics ranks, introducing readers of English to classics of world literature from more than twenty languages. The list grows to encompass more history, philosophy, science, religion, and politics.

1980s The Penguin American Library launches with titles such as *Uncle Tom's Cabin* and joins forces with Penguin Classics to provide the most comprehensive library of world literature available from any paperback publisher.

1990s The launch of Penguin Audiobooks brings the classics to a listening audience for the first time, and in 1999 the worldwide launch of the Penguin Classics Web site extends their reach to the global online community.

The 21st Century Penguin Classics are completely redesigned for the first time in nearly twenty years. This world-famous series now consists of more than 1,300 titles, making the widest range of the best books ever written available to millions—and constantly redefining what makes a "classic."

The Odyssey continues . . .

The best books ever written

PENGUIN (🐧) CLASSICS

SINCE 1946

Find out more at www.penguinclassics.com

CLICK ON A CLASSIC
www.penguinclassics.com

The world's greatest literature at your fingertips

Constantly updated information on more than a thousand titles,
from Icelandic sagas to ancient Indian epics, Russian drama to
Italian romance, American greats to African masterpieces

•

The latest news on recent additions to the list, updated
editions, and specially commissioned translations

•

Original essays by leading writers

•

A wealth of background material, including biographies
of every classic author from Aristotle to Zamyatin, plot
synopses, readers' and teachers' guides, useful Web links

•

Online desk and examination copy assistance for academics

•

Trivia quizzes, competitions, giveaways, news on
forthcoming screen adaptations